MASONIC RENEGADE

Max Sargent Corporate Espionage Mystery Thriller 4

BEN COLT

Max Sargent Corporate Espionage Mystery Thrillers
available in the series by the author BEN COLT
can be read in any order

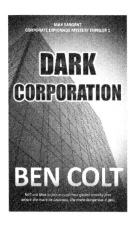

"You swore the sacred oath. You know the deal, once you join, no one leaves! It's for the protection of everyone."

David Durham moved to a corner of the VIP suite overlooking the prestigious football match. The home team Chelsea was playing against visiting titans Manchester United. The Stamford Bridge stadium was, as always, at its forty-one thousand crowd capacity and with Chelsea 1-0 up, the crowd noise was deafening as the home side were urged on to score again. The blue shirts, scarfs and hats bristled across the crowd's mass, surrounding the pristine green floodlit pitch.

"I can't carry on, it's just too risky," David pleaded.

The voice on the other end of the line softened. "David, you've already managed to sway things without any problems. You're the CEO of one of the UK's largest energy firms, you can do what you want. You know our method is fool-proof."

"That was a while ago, things have tightened up since then. Governance at my firm has improved, as CEO I was the one that brought in more controls. I can't risk being suspected of favouring the firm again," David tried to reason.

The voice on the line didn't pause to reply. It was measured, clear, the hint of welcome empathy heavily masked with determination.

"You knew what you were signing up to when you joined. You have been extremely well rewarded for both your own efforts and the contributions of your brethren. The risks of you *not* doing this are greater than worrying about one of your employees questioning your decision!"

"What do you mean?" David asked nervously.

The other voice gave a brief but audible sigh. "You know exactly what I mean. I will not allow anyone to threaten our order. Everything we do is based on secrecy and conviction."

The Chief Executive thought for a moment. His eyes were facing the pitch beyond his suit-clad guests, who were just outside the VIP room in their private seating area. Manchester United almost scored an equaliser, but he didn't see anything. His gaze was a trance as he weighed up his options.

"Hmm, I'm really not comfortable with all this…"

"I'll be over to you in a couple of days, in London. Let's meet up then and talk it through? Just don't do anything rash until then alright?"

David frowned, he was right on the cusp between throwing in the towel by whistleblowing or battling on with what was expected of him.

His silence was punctuated by the other man saying, "I won't ask you again!"

It was this comment that jolted him to a decision. The sect's leader sounded threatening now. David reminded himself that he was the Chief Executive of a huge company and not used to being threatened, by anyone.

Some of his guests were looking around at him as the football game neared the final whistle. Their host was missing the most exciting last few minutes, as Chelsea fought to defend Manchester United's attacks and hold onto their single goal victory.

David regained his authority with the caller. "No. I'm sorry. I will not continue with this ongoing burden placed on me. I'm not having it! I'll likely lose my job, but at least my integrity will be saved. Best I come clean with the authorities and explain everything." Pleased with his decision, David was about to hang up, but the caller had a closing remark which sent a chill through the senior executive.

"I can't let that happen!" The tone was earnest. "I'm sorry

too."

David was now flustered. "What do you mean by that? You can't stop me!" Then almost shouting into his mobile, "You know what, I'm going straight to the police after this game. That's right, and there's nothing you can do about it!"

He removed the iPhone from his ear and abruptly hit the 'call end' icon on the screen. His heart was racing from the exchange and the decision he'd come to. A lot of people would be affected by his choice to leave the organisation he'd willingly signed up to.

He'd always known it had been a big risk, but with risks, came rewards. Perhaps he was being too hasty? This was an enormous thing to do, it would change his life, his career, his family. He might have to pay fines, return the money? Crikey, could he receive a prison sentence?

As David made his way out onto the VIP balcony to re-join his concerned guests, he contemplated everything he'd been through to get to this juncture of his career and life. Flashes of memories went through his mind, past jobs, board meetings, corporate struggles, joining the Freemasons, his family and lifestyle, and being appointed CEO of Gaslec. And now all this. He had been rewarded as they'd promised, well rewarded.

He reminded himself how dangerous it could be to cross swords with the Grand Master. Perhaps he should wait until they met in a few days. He would give him the reassurances he now so desperately needed, maybe offer him an extra bonus to smooth things over?

The other man on the call with David Durham, the Grand Master, gritted his teeth as he sent a brief text, then shook his head to himself.

Down the long corridor behind the many private boxes and sponsors suites, a phone vibrated signalling a new message had arrived.

The mobile's owner didn't belong with any of the hospitality suites. He didn't have any invitation from one of the box host's, but had gained access to the VIP floor and a gallery room overlooking one end of the pitch. He'd had to hastily buy the VIP access pass from a ticket tout outside for two-hundred pounds cash.

He peered at the text, it read simply, 'Mustn't leave the stadium'! A nervous excitement jolted inside him. He permanently deleted the message and patted his pocket to check he had what he needed inside. The reassuring shape was there. As he left the gallery he collected one of the free blue Chelsea banners which he draped around his neck and a home team cap which he put on and adjusted the peak low over his forehead. He came out into the long corridor which offered a view of the full length of the stadium's VIP box doorways.

In the closing minute, the Red Devils were frantically pressing at the Blues' goalmouth. Again and again, their attempts at scoring were defended by the home team. A corner was given with fifteen seconds left, it would be their last chance. The excitement throughout the stadium was electric. The ball swooped and curled into the foray of players in front of the Chelsea goal and one of the Manchester United star players rose above the others to head the ball.

Thousands of fans gasped and then as the ball flew just over the crossbar, the home fans exploded in celebration as the final whistle went.

David Durham's guests shared the excitement of a great match between two of the UK's top teams. The hospitality suite had been such an amazing evening for them. With the game over, guests and fans departed quickly, pouring out of suites and all of the stadium exits. Within minutes most of David's suppliers, business associates and friends had said their thank you's and farewells and left.

He made his way out of the suite leaving the catering staff to tidy up. The long corridor of the Millennium suites in the West Stand bustled with club staff, organisers, the rich and famous, guests and officials. Some leaving, some chatting, staff trying to get back into suites to clear up the extravagant evening's aftermath.

David felt happier having decided not to go to the police. If he wanted to sway the tender process towards a favoured firm, he damn well could, he was the Chief Exec for crying out loud. And more rewards and pay-outs would be welcome. He had his eye on an old AC Cobra sports car, time to treat himself.

He made his way to one of the lifts and seeing the call button had already been pressed, waited patiently. Within moments a handful of other people leaving had flocked around him, some in suits, some casual, mostly chatting, celebrating, and drunk.

'Ping'. The lift doors parted and the intoxicated group eagerly barged into the small space until it was full. Nine people in all closely pressed together. The doors closed.

The free-flowing and limitless alcohol in the suites had dispensed with the usual British lift courtesies of not moving or speaking once inside. Football and executive revellers in the lift continued to freely enthuse about the match, argue about what the professionals should have done and bump into one another as the lift descended on its short journey.

The fan with banner and cap had perfectly blended into the throng, mirroring the other occupant's jovial body language and movements. However, he was careful to ensure his face was masked from the small CCTV dome in the lift's top corner, by the peak of his cap.

With the jostling movements around him, it was easy to withdraw the knife handle from his pocket and move it closer to the target. Concealing what he held within his hand and weaving his forearm between squashed bodies like a stalking serpent, it got closer to David Durham.

In the confined space there wouldn't be any room to thrust the weapon. But that was fine. This assassin didn't need to take a jab to strike effectively. The knife he held was unique, specially made for his father in Italy.

It was a large stiletto switchblade. He only needed to

position the handle tip next to the target and press the button. The powerful custom spring inside would shoot out the uncompromising six-inch steel blade from the end, with enough force to effortlessly penetrate garments, muscle and even bone.

David Durham stood quietly amongst the rabble, smiling politely at the others, sharing their excitement. Just as he caught the eye of the fan two people away from him, he felt a sharp, very precise pain in the side of his chest. So subtle that for a moment he put it down to a mere muscle twinge.

The blade had passed straight through his jacket and shirt, then up into his left-side oblique muscles, between two of the lower ribs, through his left lung and into the bottom of his heart.

As the button was instantly pressed again, the blade retreated back into its handle just as fast as it had darted out. The meticulous assassin would dissemble it later and clean off any blood particles from the blade now back inside.

The lift gently softened its descent and 'pinged' once more as the doors opened. David Durham felt his legs start to give way as his heart struggled to maintain its rhythm, with blood seeping out of the precious pumping cavity. He felt feint but continued to be propped up by the other bodies squashed around him. Until they started to exit the lift.

The assassin adeptly manoeuvred himself past several of his jovial lift companions and was third out through the doorway. He immediately mingled into the throng of departing fans passing the lift and made his way out onto the large concourse beneath the towering stadium. The crowd's flow took him to the Britannia Gate out onto Fulham Road, and he was gone.

As the lift occupants filed out, David Durham held a hand against the pain at his side and managed to look down to see blood staining his fingers and shirt. Bewildered and now in shock, his brain fought through the descending dimness with the realisation he'd been stabbed. But how? When? Who?

Why?

In disbelief he swayed and reached out for the last fan leaving the lift. Without the people around him anymore his legs gave way and he grabbed at the younger man's jacket as he collapsed to the floor.

The man had watched the game in one of the other hospitality boxes and although he'd been one of the quieter men inside the lift, he'd still had his fair share of alcohol that evening. He instinctively tried to catch the older suited executive and knelt to stop him crashing down hard onto the lift floor.

"You okay mate?" he offered pathetically, "had a bit too much booze eh!"

David looked at his blood-stained hand and held it towards the man.

"Good God, what have you done pal?" Even with a few drinks in him, he could see that the poor man lying before him appeared to have been stabbed. "Bloody hell!" He looked out through the doorway and started shouting to passing fans. "Help! Help me, this guy's been hurt! Call an ambulance! Tell the officials, now!"

Some of the people passing by just continued on, either not believing him or just wanting to get home without getting tangled up in some thuggery incident. A few people began gathering around the lift entrance, offering help and concern. Someone rushed off to find the nearest stadium employee, another called for the ambulance and police.

David Durham knew he had moments to live. He had just enough consciousness remaining to connect being stabbed, with his conversation with the Grand Master ten minutes earlier. Those words flashed into his dwindling thoughts, 'once you join, no one leaves!'.

With the last of his energy, he turned to the man now cradling him on the lift's floor. David loved his wife more than anything and the most natural last thought of a dying man would have been to say, 'tell my wife I love her'. But instead, just seconds before he drifted into death's embrace, David Durham whispered the only thing that mattered to him, that he simply had to impart.

"It's all… in the book… of souls!" Then, with his last breath, which was cut short as his heart stopped, "B…"

Later that same day on Long Island east of New York, somewhere in the Hamptons, there was a gathering. A gathering unlike any other.

Dusk had been overtaken by the night's gloomy darkness. A cool breeze from the Atlantic Ocean danced across the large private and secluded estate.

A handful of interspersed men ambled around the perimeter, their dark attire blending into the green and grey vista. Each of them carried a gun, as they casually surveyed the landscape for any trespassers. They were guarding something, or someone, where secrecy was of the utmost importance.

Two sides of the huge property edged onto one of the large Hamptons bays, with several water inlets creeping into the land like persistent cracks in a wall. Most of the grounds were left to nature's embrace, with overgrown fields and woods dotted around. These lush areas were interjected with well-maintained pathways, sun terraces, lawns and ornamental gardens, accentuated in their wild surroundings.

All of this framed the large subtly lit mansion in the centre of the estate, barely visible from any point of the perimeter. It was hidden away from the world and any prying eyes or passers-by.

A little way from the house at the end of a long, sweeping lawn, a group of cloaked figures stood gathered around one of the water inlets. They were spaced out a little, as if not wanting to get too close to any of the other attendees. No one spoke.

Dim, low-level lighting along the paths and water's edge,

cast shadows amongst them. But none of their faces were visible. Each wore a black cloak with hoods pulled down over their foreheads, shrouding the faces underneath. Yet even these were further obscured with dark veils of light fabric, which only allowed the eyes of each person an unobscured view of the proceedings.

In the centre of the gathering, set back from the water's edge by a wooden jetty, stood the leader of this group. Only his steely, uncompromising eyes were visible under the black hood and face covering. Unlike the others who tilted their heads down in secrecy and deference, he looked straight ahead. Occasionally, without moving his head, his eyes searched to each side to check his gathered brethren. Some were confident, relishing the ceremony. Others were nervous, uncomfortable, longing to get back to their expensive cars and the normal world beyond the estate.

The small motif stitched onto the chest of his black cloak was a lighter golden colour to those everyone else had. A subtle delineation, but one with powerful differences which all those attending knew, observed and in some cases, feared. He was the Grand Master of the sect.

He waited behind an old wooden lectern, his bare hands placed confidently on either side of the top, upon which lay open a very old looking book. The pages twitched gently in the breeze, but their weight kept them from turning over.

His demeanour and body language were different to most of the other cloaked figures around him. He was still, commanding, in control, at ease with the unusual and somewhat bizarre ritual they were carrying out.

It was absolutely necessary though. The subtle intricacies of the event had been carefully thought out. A handshake, signed contract or verbal arrangement simply wouldn't reflect the gravity of what was being entered into here. No, those who wanted to offer themselves up and be accepted into this particular order needed a memorable physical and visual experience. They had to be reminded that what they were agreeing to was an unbreakable pact. They had to appreciate that others were also contributing for the greater good and were heavily committed as well. This wasn't an optional membership club one could simply leave with a quick chat or an email. They each needed a stark reminder of the lifelong expectations of the sect they would benefit from, as long as the rules were adhered to.

There was movement on the far bank across a hundred feet of the inlet's calm water. Everyone there raised their heads an inch to focus on the light of the lantern being lit up and placed at the front of a small wooden boat alongside another small jetty.

Two dark figures got into the boat as one appeared to hand something to the other. Both were wearing the obligatory black hooded cloaks. The first sat near the front, facing forwards, looking towards the group across the water with the large mansion gently lit far in the background. The other person stood at the rear where a single oar was attached to the side of the boat near the back, like a gondola. He started manoeuvring the long stick using it efficiently as both a paddle and rudder. They moved away from the bank and proceeded slowly and gracefully across the water, ripples softly lapping onto the side of the hull.

All eyes were on the men in the boat. Thoughts concentrated on the significance of the two figures' parts in this play, being almost opposite roles.

The man seated in the ancient-looking ferryboat took several deep breathes under his hooded veil. This was a nerve-wracking experience he'd never forget. The man paddling behind him noticed his passenger's shoulders heave up and down taking in the cool, fresh air and trying to settle his nerves.

He smiled under his hooded veil and thought to himself, 'Just like all the others, the ceremony always gets to them. You just do the right thing and serve the Grand Master, tow the line and you'll be fine. If not, then I'll be right there behind you, just like I am now!'.

The short trip across the water felt like it took ages for the passenger. He could now clearly see each of the dark figures ominously lining the water's edge around the approaching wooden jetty.

'Jesus this is freaking me out', he thought. The night's procedure had only been briefly explained to him, leaving a lot to the imagination, deliberately. And not being entirely sure what to expect, his mind started to entertain the notion of surprises, and fear of what could await him!

'Come on, I've worked hard to get here, think of the benefits, this is a real coup being invited to join. Pull yourself together!'. He forced a smile in readiness to be greeted, then felt stupid remembering his mask hid the gesture from the others.

The traditionally designed boat approached the platform jutting out over the water and slowed to a halt, bringing them alongside.

The man behind him gave a forced, slight bow and offered something over to him to take. He took it. He was then beckoned to exit the boat and go to the lead man standing behind the small lectern, who now raised his arms a little by way of greeting him.

He carefully placed the small item he'd just received onto the book and then stood back a pace.

The Grand Master then spoke in well-rehearsed, strong words and was now in full flow of the ceremony being undertaken by them all. He looked straight into the eyes of the man in front of him, always checking how the soul behind them was reacting to the oaths and responses.

The man being indoctrinated remembered his cues and lines, and delivered them perfectly, despite his dry throat.

The small item was presented back to him with more words, rules and values.

At the end of the ritual, the Grand Master wrote something onto the first available blank page inside the old book. Then closing it, brought the proceedings to an end, congratulating the new inductee.

The dark figures now finally broke their sombre silence and started clapping the new brother that had joined their elite cause. For the first time in days, the man at the centre of the ritual began to relax. 'He was in!'

Most of the people there came over to him and shook his hand with welcoming but brief words of congratulations and encouragement. But everyone continued to wear their protective disguise and most of them had no idea of the identities of any of the others. Except for the Grand Master and the ferryman.

The gathering started to break up and they all made their way back towards the mansion and large driveway. There were a couple of inconspicuous, dull cars, deliberately so. But most of the vehicles parked around the forecourt were expensive luxury cars including a Rolls-Royce, Bentley and Maybach. A few supercars were also parked up with the latest models of McLaren, Ferrari and Lamborghini each represented.

As they strolled through the ornate gardens and across the large lawn, the ferryman caught up with one of the figures and whispered for him to go into the house before he left, to see the Grand Master.

It was like being told the headmaster wanted to see you and he'd be holding his cane, ready to beat someone. The man receiving the quiet summons instantly felt sick and almost wet himself, but quickly managed to pull himself together and continue walking as if it was of no consequence.

"Sure," he replied feebly.

'Maybe it was good news?' he feebly thought to himself.

The rest of the attendees peeled off to the side of the house and made their way towards the courtyard. The Grand Master entered the patio doors of the large study, with the ferryman cajoling the other man towards the same doorway. Only the cloaked figure of the sect's latest recruit remained a little way behind, strolling towards the building, being the last one to leave the waterside.

The summonsed man entered the study, which he'd been in just once before when being congratulated on one of his past contributions to the cause. This felt different though.

The large office looked like it may have once been a dining room. The big rectangular space had its walls clad in dark oak panelling with intricate patterns painstakingly crafted into the wood. The original, highly polished wooden floor was covered in lush, elaborate rugs. An eclectic mix of paintings and artwork adorned the walls and ornate lights and fixings looked like they were a hundred years old.

The Grand Master sat behind a solid desk, his hands laid out on the dark red leather top. The old book sat to one side of the desktop. He had lowered the hood of his cloak which now rested around his shoulders and taken off his veil mask.

"You may remove your coverings brother, you're quite safe here," said the ferryman now standing behind the man, which made him jump.

"Yes of course." He pulled back his veil and hood in one go. Then filling the awkward silence, "Is everything alright?"

"You tell me?" replied the man behind the desk, leaning back into his chair.

Now the man was worried and nervously looked at the Grand Master and the ferryman still behind him. This felt bad.

"You were pleased with the work I managed to get assigned to the sect weren't you?" He only got a slight nod, so felt he had to continue. "I'm sure there will be more big contracts coming up, in fact, there's going to be a big marketing push at the bank I run. I'll make sure we get that. It'll be worth tens of millions…"

Zap, crackle!

The acute electrical buzz of the stun gun thrust into his back cut through his words instantly. The single second of fifty-thousand volts passing through his cloak and shirt into his body, caused internal havoc and crippling pain.

He dropped to the floor contorting his body, arms and hands, as the voltage disrupted the brain's messages to his voluntary muscles. This caused him to lose his balance, muscle control, with confusion and disorientation. And it hurt like hell! He almost passed out, which would have been a momentary reprieve from the pain, but unfortunately, he stayed conscious.

As his body started to recover itself from the literal shock, he could see the ferryman standing over him, holding the small black two-pronged device.

The newly indoctrinated brother still outside had heard the awful crackle of the hand taser and the clenched cry of the hapless victim in the study. He instinctively ducked down, hoping he wouldn't be seen, his dark cloak blending into the night's gloom. Realising what had happened inside the study, his heart raced. 'What the hell's going on in there!' he thought to himself, panting lightly.

After a few moments, the floored man inside slowly gathered himself and knelt up.

"Jesus Christ! What the hell was that for?" holding up a hand in submission.

The ferryman continued to stand over him ominously as if waiting to be given the nod for another jab with the stun-gun.

The man outside retreated carefully back down the lawn. He was due to see the Grand Master after his initiation, but there was no way he was going to gate crash what was going on in the study right now. He'd pretend he was further away and walk up again when it was all clear.

"It's come to my attention that you may be having doubts about your lifelong tenure with us?"

"Who me? No. What on earth gave you that idea?"

"You recently met another brother and I'm told, spoke of leaving the sect?" The Grand Master leant forward across the desktop, accentuating the question.

The man kneeling struggled to his feet to gain some comfort from raising himself above the level of the leader. He wracked his brains searching for any plausible reason why someone else might say this of him.

"You know that once you join, there can be no possibility of leaving," pushed on the Grand Master. "Secrecy and loyalty are paramount here, for everyone!"

Then it clicked into place. "Oh, you mean John, when we bumped into one another at a business function," remembering the chance encounter with another brother. "But I didn't say anything about leaving," he pleaded.

His interrogator lowered his head slightly with dissatisfaction.

"Didn't you say that you 'wondered if anyone ever gets to leave'?"

The phrase now clicked into place and matched his memory of the light-hearted chat he'd had with another member of this exclusive sect. His face fell indicating his recollection and guilt.

"Well, yes, I did say that, kind of." Thinking quickly. "I didn't say that *I* was thinking of leaving, I just wondered if anyone else had ever left, that was all. Not me!"

The Grand Master looked up with a hint of acceptance with what could be the truth of the matter. The ferryman picked up on this and reluctantly stepped back in resignation that he wouldn't be required to inflict another stun.

"You're not wanting to leave then?" he checked.

"No! Absolutely not. I'm committed. Let me prove it to you, just you see what I can do in the next few months, that'll show you!"

"You understand your comment somewhat perturbed John and that he had no choice but to come to me about it," said the leader, relaxing back into his chair.

Elated that the trouble was now likely over, the man heartily agreed. "Yes, of course, it was a stupid thing for me to say, I can see how it could be interpreted," checking both of the other men's demeanours, "wrongly though," he added.

"Alright then, let's draw a line under this and move on

shall we?" offered the leader, producing a captivating smile of conclusion and the end of the meeting.

"Indeed," agreed the man, moving towards the door leading towards the large hallway. His eyes were now focused on his exit route out as fast as he could politely muster. "I'll be in touch regarding that big job we'll have very soon," he parted.

The man outside, now further back down the lawn, began strolling up the soft incline towards the study. The ferryman appeared at the patio doors and although noting the approaching brother was a little way off and likely wouldn't have heard anything, still eyed him suspiciously as he drew closer.

"Is he waiting for me?" asked the inductee innocently, hoping he'd got away with his doubling back.

The ferryman nodded, then went inside to tell the Grand Master and placed a single chair in front of the desk. He then took up position to the side of the room on a small seat.

The newly joined man came in cautiously and removed his hood and veil, then lowered himself into the waiting chair.

"Relax Brandon," said the Grand Master beaming at him. "No need to be nervous now, you're one of us!"

Having just witnessed how the last person was treated, Brandon thought 'that's exactly why I *am* nervous!'. He returned the smile nonetheless.

"Let's drink to your new journey," said the Grand Master patting the old book on the desk, "before we just spend a little time for me to go through the rules and expectations, and of course some of the, shall we say, admin. You've set up an offshore account?"

Brandon nodded.

The ferryman had risen on cue and brought the two of them a stiff drink, abstaining himself.

"Cheers!" said Brandon, downing the Louis XIII cognac. He could tell it was very expensive.

"I'm fascinated to see where this will lead us, my friend,"

said the leader. "With your particular background, I feel we're starting a new era of opportunity for the sect, one which will be hugely profitable for all of us!"

The smooth cognac quickly made its way through Brandon's body, warming him as he wondered what on earth he'd gotten himself into.

Brandon Cuffney had just joined a dark, sinister and secret old sect. A business advancement and profit-sharing club that was now crossing the line from harmless, to dangerous.

The irony was that he was already part of another far-reaching and indomitable organisation. One that would test both him and the Grand Master.

Brandon was an agent, in the Central Intelligence Agency!

2

Max Sargent felt himself starting to glaze over as he stared into the CCTV monitor's screen. The picture was unmoving, a lifeless still of the living room inside the apartment they were watching. He stirred himself away from the boring picture and shuffled his chair over to the high-powered binoculars for a better look. They sat on top of one of two tripod stands next to each other, the second stand held the video camera. His partner Greg listened to his headphones, motionless, bored.

A woman passed through Max's view making her way to answer the door it seemed. The movement and signs of life were a welcome boost to what had been a thoroughly dull and long stakeout. Three days of being holed up waiting for something revealing to take place, had felt like three months. Snatched takeaways, restless sleep shifts and conversation topics exhausted, had worn down the two men's enthusiasm.

Max had recently finished an assignment that couldn't have been more opposite to this uneventful stakeout. There'd been corporate undercover investigations, high profile robberies, people dying, all ending in an international chase against the clock to save the nation's pride.

Afterwards, his superiors had thought he needed a rest and something easy, so he'd agreed to a quiet observation job on a corporate suspect looking to scam a fortune off the stock market.

"Greg," Max glanced round to his fellow MI5 agent, "recording and sound all okay?"

The other man stirred and checked that the digital recorder was operational, capturing everything in the apartment. He re-tuned the highly sensitive directional microphone also aimed through the slightly opened balcony door. Permission to eavesdrop had been swiftly granted by one of the judges assigned to MI5's 'quick request' cases. Only a week ago a staff member of the target had whistle-blown their suspicions to police. They in turn passed the information onto MI5 Cyber, being a potential corporate crime yet to be committed.

"Yup, all recording fine and I can hear her answering the door right now." He pressed a button to patch the sound feed through the small speaker sat on the table between them.

They listened to the door being opened. "Hi darling," said a female voice, "glad you decided to pop in after all, it'll be worth your while."

Greg gave Max a knowing look.

MI5 had requisitioned the empty apartment the two men had been in for several days. It wasn't due to be released for sale for another week and unusually had been completed just ahead of schedule by the builders.

They were at the new Battersea Power Station living complex, comprising of a number of large buildings full of apartments. The site had shops, walkways, gardens and luxury living accommodation, sprawled around the old four-chimney power station on the edge of the River Thames. Developers had turned a rundown desolate and derelict area, into one of the most sought-after new property complexes in London. And being on the edge of the river, the new apartments were getting snapped up in tranches as they got released.

Max and Greg were in one of the three hundred flats of the two buildings called Prospect Place, just to the south of the power station and river. They had a clear view of the apartment in question, several floors below them in the building directly opposite, just seventy feet away.

They listened as the conversation continued in the target's apartment.

"Well, I have to admit I nearly didn't pop over," said a man's voice.

"Oh. Come in then," offered the female, "I'm sure we can

sort out any final concerns you have."

Max watched as the elegant woman, late thirties, led the man across the lounge and sat him down next to her on a large leather sofa. She moved closer. He looked nervous in her presence. Greg moved nearer to the speaker as the man continued.

"What if this whole thing gets out? We'll be for the high jump, the London Stock Exchange will throw the book at us and have us charged. I'm not going to prison for this, it's insider dealing for God's sake!"

The woman moved even closer and put her hand on his shoulder. Max could see he wasn't happy about her advances, even though she appeared to cut an attractive figure.

"Now come along, we've been through everything, it's fool-proof," she said. "We both buy up a load of shares from each of our online gaming companies using our offshore ghost accounts. Then we announce jointly that we're planning a merger, which will make us the second-largest online betting firm in the UK. The share prices for our companies go through the roof, we both sell making a bundle, before then encountering merger issues and calling the whole thing off," she coaxed, leaning over to kiss him.

He gently ducked away from the advance. "Stop it! We've done all that, it was great, but no more. I know it was all part of getting me to commit to this scheme," he said. "Suspicions might have been aroused with our earlier meetings."

She continued to slide a leg over his, her skirt riding up as she did so, revealing the top of her stockings. He was starting to relent to the overwhelming urge to take her once more.

"So we met a few times, that's what two company bosses do when they're discussing a merger." She now straddled him and started to undo his clothes. "Come on, let's seal the deal one last time, then tomorrow we buy and next week sell. We'll make millions!"

The man began to succumb to her writhing body as she pulled her dress straps from her shoulders and edged the top down to her waist. But then he remembered why he'd wanted to visit her. It was not for sex. He had to tell her to her face the whole thing was off.

"No! No! Get off me," he shouted, "I'm not going to jail for seven years, not for millions and not for this!"

Greg tapped Max on the shoulder. "That's it Max, we've got everything we need for a conviction. We should pay them a visit now and make the arrests."

Max continued looking through the binoculars. "Shouldn't we let them have their fun first?" he said smiling.

They were then startled with the next exchange over the speaker as Max watched on through the binoculars, Greg viewing the CCTV monitor.

The man tried to get up but she stopped him, pressing him back into the sofa. Her hand seemed to go behind one of the cushions and as she pulled it out, they were both horrified to see she was holding a small ladies Derringer pistol. She raised it to the man's chest.

"We're going to do this right now and seal the deal," she snarled. "No one turns me down for sex, nor a money-making deal like this! Promise me, now!"

The shocked and now frightened man held his hands up. "Jesus, what the hell are you doing, you've got a gun, just calm down, let's talk about this?" he pleaded.

Max and Greg were already up and moving to the door, leaving the recording devices continuing to capture what was transpiring in the other apartment across the way. Unknowingly Greg knocked against the CCTV camera jolting its aim away from the other apartment.

As they bolted towards the lifts Greg was on his radio to MI5 Thames House HQ and asking for police backup to be sent to the other flat. "Better get the firearms unit and an ambulance as well!" he added.

The lift down five floors seemed to take forever and they darted through the opening doors, through reception and across to the other building. Staff inside looked quite perturbed as the two men ran in brandishing their MI5 badges and demanding to be let through. Without waiting for an answer they'd already jumped the low retractable barrier and were furiously pushing the buttons for a lift.

They pushed past a couple exiting the lift and stood there in awkward silence as they rose to the third floor.

Greg grabbed Max's arm as the doors opened once more.

"Mate, we're not armed, they have a gun in there, we should wait for the others?"

Max paused for a moment. "I think we should get in there and talk her out of it, we can't just shy away."

As they looked at one another trying to decide, there was a muffled 'BANG!' just two doors down the corridor. They froze for an instant.

"Come on!" said Max as he raced to the apartment. Max got to the closed door then backed up as Greg reached him and lunged at the door with all his might, front kicking the middle just above the electronic lock. The door mechanism splintered through its light wooden frame and burst open.

The two men now moved through more cautiously, not knowing what to expect inside. They couldn't possibly have guessed what they'd find.

As they moved through the small hallway towards the lounge, they could see the legs of the man, and then the woman's, splayed out on the floor from the sofa. They guessed that the woman had shot him and collapsed on top of his body in distress or exhaustion.

Max entered the room and was surprised at the sight in front of him.

The woman was indeed lying on top of the dead man's body. He'd been shot through the head by her. Fresh blood seeped from the small bullet hole by his temple.

Max could see there'd been a struggle and that the small gun was being held by both the woman and the man.

It was now that he realised the woman's body lay limp and lifeless on top of his. Her head lay on his shoulder, next to where the bullet had exited the other side of his head. Max then saw the small puncture hole on the side of her head as well, but no exit wound.

Greg had also taken in the scene and spoke first.

"Oh my God! They've both committed suicide?"

Max gathered his thoughts. "No. This was no suicide pact. It looks as though they fought over the gun, maybe he got the upper hand on her and started to aim it at her, but look," he pointed to their heads, "a single shot killed them both!"

The small round had passed through his head with enough velocity to exit and then go into her head as well.

"How come?"

"I reckon they both fought for control of the gun and when it was pointing at them both, one of them decided they'd rather both die than be the one to get shot, so squeezed the trigger!"

Sirens sounded outside as the police, firearms van and an ambulance arrived.

They looked down at the two fraudster lovers and shook their heads.

Max spoke. "Sex, money and greed, a lethal combination."

Greg patted his shoulder. "Not such a dull stakeout after all, eh Max?"

Back at Thames House, MI5's headquarters by Lambeth Bridge on the River Thames, Max was at his desk finishing off his report for the stakeout. His department boss Si Lawson, Head of MI5 Cyber, came out of his office and waved him in.

"Got your report done from the stakeout Max?" Si asked as they sat down at his desk.

"Just finishing it now."

"Bit of a shock for you and Greg I imagine?"

Max drew breath, "Yeah, to be honest, it was. One second we're getting the scoop about their plan to falsely elevate their share prices, the next all hell breaks loose!"

"I'm probably stating the obvious, but always assume

something's going to happen when you do a stakeout, they rarely end up with absolutely no drama," said Si knowingly. "They're like fishing, just sit back, relax, but be ready to strike when the moment comes."

"Fair comment boss. What's the latest view on what happened from the police? I'm sorry the CCTV camera got knocked when we were running out of our flat," said Max.

"It happens. Seems they'd both had a few meetups, formally at their respective offices and as we now know, less formally to 'seal the deal' as she put it! They had their own offshore accounts loaded up with money ready to buy up tranches of shares." Si leant back in his chair. "Any announcement from these two betting firms to merge would have tripled their share prices. They'd both have made tens of millions by selling, once the markets reacted to their trumped-up claim of an intended merger. But I guess that's less relevant now they're both dead. When the facts come out I reckon their firms will take a big hit on their valuations, confidence will be lost, it'll hurt the staff and shareholders pretty bad."

"Do they know who shot who, or might they actually have agreed a suicide pact, like Greg thought?" asked Max.

"My guess is we'll never know who shot who or whether they agreed, or perhaps it was an accident through struggling for the gun. Probably be given as 'death by misadventure' by the coroner."

Si pushed his reclining seat back upright. "Anyway Max, moving on. Got something up your street to do some digging on. No idea what's behind it but you might come up with something."

"Okay, what's happened now?" said Max looking interested.

"Heard of Gaslec?"

"Of course," replied Max, "one of the UK's biggest utility firms, use them myself at home for my gas and electricity. Why?"

"A few days ago their Chief Exec died, a David Durham."

"Heart attack from too many posh dinners?" guessed Max.

Si frowned at the quip. "Well, his heart was certainly attacked, with a long sharp-tipped knife!"

Max gave an apologetic grimace.

Si explained. "He'd just finished entertaining a bunch of VIP's at his firm's Chelsea Stamford Bridge hospitality box and without any provocation, someone stabbed him in the lift as he was leaving."

"What!"

"We're pretty sure it wasn't some thug, no robbery involved and with the expert placement of the blade, police are convinced it was an assassination. That's why they've passed it onto us here, we need to rule out any possible foreign or terrorist connection, given as you say, it's one of the country's largest utility providers."

"Didn't anyone see this assassin? CCTV? Others in the lift?" asked Max.

"Police are trying to trace the other people in that lift from the poor-quality CCTV, some faces are visible, a couple aren't, where they wore caps hiding their faces. But we do have one witness, the man in whose arms David Durham died."

"What did he say?"

"Unfortunately, he didn't see anything or anyone suspicious in the lift, but before Durham died he said just one thing.

"What?"

'It's all in the book of souls'!"

"The book of souls?" repeated Max. "Was that it?"

"Yup, oh, apart from starting to repeat presumably 'book of souls' again. All he got out was 'B'," said Si shrugging his shoulders.

Max thought. "Could have been something else starting with 'B…'?" suggested Max.

"Maybe?"

"And this long knife, what about that? How come no one

saw anything inside a lift?"

Si picked up a piece of paper. "According to the autopsy done yesterday, they believe the single stab wound and path to be consistent with an approximate six-inch length, slim, sharp-tipped blade, expertly aimed just once from a difficult angle to puncture the heart."

Max screwed up his face. "Surely someone would have seen the killer wielding such a large blade to get in a stab at Durham?"

Si gestured, "In a crowded lift you can't really see much below shoulder height, can you? Maybe it was a fold-out knife or one of those butterfly knives where the blade folds out of two parts of its handle." He scanned the autopsy document further down. "Ah! Seems the police asked the same question and were told that possibly a stiletto could have been used, powerful enough not to require a jabbing motion to inflict its damage!"

"Wow," exclaimed Max, "not heard of one of those being used before, but bloody effective when you think about it. Blade in and out, job done!"

"Yes, if you know what you're doing," added Si. "I suggest you get off to Gaslec and start your inquiries there. I've squared it off with the Met, given your previous history working alongside them, you can now work independently of having them with you, just keep me posted," Si said standing up signalling the chat was over. "Oh yes, just one other thing, a little odd," he pushed a piece of paper over the desk. "They found this old coin in his wallet."

Max looked at the pictures of a small, very old looking coin, front and back and took a picture of it with his phone.

"Just an old coin that got mixed up in his loose change?"

"You'd think so, but the police had it checked out, look at the unusual markings, a stag and palm tree on one side and a bee on the other," said Si pointing at the pictures. "Apparently it's a Greek obolus, or danake coin, used around 300BC."

"Is it real?"

"Yup, worth a few grand to a collector, no idea why Durham had it though, just keep it in mind."

Max got back to his desk and typed a search into the Google box, knowing the police would have doubtless done the same. He wanted to see what got thrown up with the query 'book of souls'! Hoping to find some famous Egyptian book kept in a museum somewhere that may shed some light on this mysterious assassination, he was disappointed.

The first few pages of results were dominated by web pages for the English heavy metal band Iron Maiden, who released their sixteenth album in 2015 called 'Book of Souls'! It was the sixth song, over ten minutes long, written by a couple of the band members. Max spent the next half hour reading everything he could find out about the album and the song, including the lyrics. The words were littered with references to wealth and riches, the underworld and afterlife, all recurring themes in the band's songs.

Max struggled to make any connection with the Iron Maiden song and Durham's demise. Frustrated, he gave up and consoled himself with maybe finding something at the huge corporation Durham ran, Gaslec.

He went through the company's website, annual report and after looking at the board's executive biographies, wondered who their lead procurement person was, his old profession. Max opened up the 'management team' page on their site and scanned the faces peering off the screen.

He saw the title 'Chief Procurement Officer' and looked at the picture above. His expression dropped. Recognition of the man's face caused Max to say out loud, "Oh my God, not him!"

3

The A4 Bath Road going West out of Slough, had seemingly attracted many large companies to base themselves on its long stretch of road. Surrounded by industrial estates, there was an eclectic mix of telephony, software, retail, service and utility corporations dominating the area, with an equally diverse landscape of building designs.

Perhaps the lower rents and property prices had attracted them, with fast road and train access into London. More likely though, it was the surrounding executive belt including prestigious Windsor, Eton, Stoke Poges, Henley-on-Thames and Marlow, that attracted Chief Executives wanting to move out of the City and be nearer their plush country mansions. A brief commute in their chauffeured luxury cars, beat a tedious ride on the public trains and underground.

The Gaslec site had its large five-story offices partly encircling its front courtyard and entrance roundabout. The firm had been there long before David Durham took over and housed some six thousand staff covering most departments except its field operations. The enormous parking area behind the building was now struggling to accommodate the increase in staff and they tried to encourage using a company bus and 'share a car' schemes with little success.

Gaslec's turnover was twelve billion and with a profit of almost one billion, it was a force to be reckoned with. It had a lot of power, over consumers, shareholders, staff and suppliers. And that power had culminated at the top, with David Durham their Chief Exec.

Max knew from his own experience, that strong characters in such leading roles in these big companies, could within reason, pretty much do what they wanted. Max had also seen how this power, when unchallenged, could put a lot of temptations in front of these corporate kings and queens. It wasn't a long jump to start thinking that David Durham's murder could have something to do with what was going on here.

He drove into the car park at the rear and slotted his inconspicuous VW Golf into one of the few empty visitors bays, thankful he didn't have to start cruising round the hundreds of cars in search of a free spot.

He entered through the rear doors, passing security guards, which led him into the large, open reception. The long desk of busy receptionists was set to the side so it could handle people coming in from the rear car park and also the front, main entrance.

Max gave his name, asked to see the Chief Finance Officer and was given an ID badge to wear.

Minutes later a middle-aged woman appeared through the lift doors.

"Mr Sargent, good morning, I'm Monica, Ms Collins' personal assistant. Would you like to follow me and I'll take you to see her in her office?"

As Max watched her press the fifth-floor button, the top floor, he smiled at the un-inclusive, outdated view that the top executives still hid themselves away from their workers at the top of the castle. No doubt one of the floors below held the hundreds, maybe thousands of staff working in finance, all for their lady boss who didn't want to sit with them.

They went up to the fifth floor and the PA walked ahead of Max down a long corridor, past a row of director's offices, secretary's receptions and suites. They passed an open door with the nameplate on it showing 'Chief Executive Officer'.

David Durham's expansive office lay deserted, showing some signs the police had done a superficial search through cupboards and files. Max also noted the lavish setup with mahogany furniture, a matching mini boardroom table for meetings, the latest TV, projector and Apple computer, none of which were standard employee issue. This seemed like the office of a leader who liked the trappings of the big role he filled.

They turned into the office labelled 'Chief Finance Officer' on the door and as Max entered, the woman sitting behind a large desk covered with piles of paperwork, got up to greet him.

"Miranda Collins, CFO." She welcomed him with a firm handshake as the PA left shutting the door. "Please have a seat," as she returned to her chair.

She was younger than Max had expected, probably late thirties, with a plain visual attractiveness not lost on him. The short dark hair was cut in a sharp high bob and the black-rimmed spectacles gave an interesting frame for her brown eyes. An accountant by trade, stints with two of the top global consulting firms and a meteoric rise through the ranks, had put her into this highly coveted CFO role. As she sat down she seemed to comically disappear behind the desk and piles of documents laid out across its expanse. Max had to refrain from wanting to tell her to raise her seat higher.

She was busy and came straight to the point. "So, Mr Sargent, what can I do for you? We've already told the police everything we can, which wasn't much I'm afraid. I'm a little surprised the big MI5 have got involved?"

"I appreciate your time today Ms Collins…"

"Miranda is fine," she interjected.

Max nodded. "The apparent murder of such a high profile executive in charge of one of our biggest utility companies could imply a potential National, even terrorist risk. We simply have to check these things out you understand."

Miranda accepted the superficial explanation.

"How would you describe David Durham?"

The somewhat obvious question appeared to surprise her.

"Oh, well, he was a superb Chief Exec, hard worker, expected loyalty, got the results, tough but fair as they say."

The answer fell flat, standard stuff thought Max. He

pressed on.

"Did he get on with people, was he easily persuaded, perhaps status-conscious?"

"Mr Sargent, what is it you're pressing for, just cut skirting around, I'm busy?"

Max viewed her carefully at the touchy response, looking into those brown eyes, searching for some hint of her off-beat reaction. She confidently met his gaze.

"Ms Collins, Miranda, I'm trying to establish why someone would have your Chief Exec killed, after all, that's what appears to have happened," explained Max. "He held a powerful position, with influence over utility pricing to consumers, staff and suppliers. Maybe he'd gotten himself into something over his head. Any ideas would be helpful, please."

She warmed slightly to the more direct, honest approach from Max and sat back in her chair to consider what he'd said. After a few moments, she leant forward again.

"Off the record as it's a subjective, personal view," she waited for Max to acknowledge her, "he was a little power-hungry, always wanting more. Liked his perks shall we say. But you should probably have a chat with his wife Angela Durham if you want more about the man behind his work façade. I think they may have been having marriage problems so you'll either get nothing, or maybe a lot!"

Max felt he was starting to break through the standard line of answers so pushed on.

"Potentially corruptible? Any staff he favoured or hired in? Suppliers he'd rehire or award big contracts to?" he probed.

She spoke more quietly. "Potentially, yes maybe he could be swayed if it benefitted the company, or himself. Interesting you mention suppliers?"

"I used to be in procurement in a previous life," said Max.

"Ah, okay, our procurement head did work with him before, and they do sometimes go for suppliers that don't necessarily get everyone's vote."

"Any particular suppliers?"

"You'd need to ask our procurement chap, he'd have all the info. Joe Patterson."

Max feigned surprise. "Really?"

"You know him?"

"A while back I had a Joe Patterson work for me as one of my managers when I was a CPO. Can you introduce us again, but I'd appreciate you stressing that his cooperation is really important?"

"Do I detect a history between you?" she inquired as they both got up.

"Let's just say we didn't always see eye to eye," said Max with a wry smile.

Miranda took Max down a floor which from the signs over the doorway, he could see had departments including Human Resources, Corporate Services, Legal and Procurement.

Row after row of staff they passed looked up or stole a glance at the person their CFO was escorting through the offices. At the end of the huge open plan floor, Max could see Joe sitting in his small glass partitioned office amongst his purchasing team of about twenty staff. They were responsible for handling the processes, tenders, governance and policies, determining how the firm's money was spent and with which suppliers.

Their eyes met as Joe looked up to see who Miranda was bringing towards him. He did a double-take, froze for a second, then had a face on him like thunder. Max mused that perhaps Joe was scared that Miranda was replacing him, with his old boss. Joe remained seated up to the point they entered his office.

He was medium height, slightly overweight with thinning hair already showing signs of grey at the sides. His dull coloured but intense eyes, almost maniacal eyes when angry, were set deep in a rounded face. His gold Cartier watch gleamed in contrast with his smart dark blue suit.

"Miranda? What's all this about then?" he asked

cautiously, staying behind his desk. The offish body language was obvious and made him look childish.

"Sorry to disturb you Joe, but I have someone who needs to speak with you about David Durham's murder. I'd like you to assist in any way you can."

Sensing the strain between the two men, she took her leave and closed the door as she went, parting with, "I gather you know him. Max Sargent! He's with MI5!"

About ten years ago when Max was already a Chief Procurement Officer, he inherited a buying department when starting a new role. Joe was one of his mid-level managers with his own team of two female buyers and two young male junior buyers. He was good at getting results through his negotiations and was known to be tough on suppliers, but also on his staff. Joe reported into one of Max's procurement directors, who had mentioned he was having management issues with Joe, but that he'd handle it and Max didn't need to get involved.

Joe was a hard task master in his little team, but more so with the girls. His alpha male urge kicked in to dominate them all by pressing home his seniority, with constant demands, many unrealistic, picking at faults and laying on the pressure.

The demeanour of his four staff began to visibly crumble and stress, anxiety and the beginnings of closing down kicked in. Max queried this with Joe's director who got denials from him when it was discussed, embarrassed he wasn't handling the situation.

Then the two female buyers, followed in quick succession by the two juniors, made appointments to see Max. They'd all had enough. Breaking down in his office and thoroughly demoralised, they each made formal complaints against Joe for bullying and intimidation.

Max had to send Joe home, not a good discussion, whilst a formal investigation was conducted by himself and HR. After interviewing Joe's four staff, the director and other members of the department, it was clear to Max that he had enough evidence to fire Joe for gross misconduct.

Joe was summoned in to see Max and HR to be dismissed after the evidence had been discussed, but Joe fought the accusations every step of the way. Before Max could fire him, he'd walked out threatening to involve an employment lawyer and fight through a tribunal.

Max had the evidence but didn't want to put the four staff through yet more regurgitation of the awful circumstances and intimidation, with Joe shouting at them across a hearing. He now just wanted to end the matter, so was forced to guide HR to negotiate a compromise agreement with Joe, knowing he was guilty.

Joe Patterson left the company with a written reference, his CV intact and a small payoff, to go about the rest of his career unscathed. Neither party could speak of the incident with the mutual Non-Disclosure Agreement, effectively a gagging order. With Joe unwilling to hold out his hand for a courtesy handshake, the injustice of a bully getting away with it came flooding back to Max.

He looked around, "So you've managed to do well for yourself after all Joe?"

"I have," he said with relish, "and who'd have thought you'd make the jump from CPO to MI5, I'd love to know how that happened?" asked Joe with seething contempt.

"Let's put aside the past shall we," Max offered, "I'm here to find out more about David Durham. Tell me about your relationship with him?"

The answer was brief. "He was my boss."

"Did he get involved in your procurement work, supplier selections?"

"No, why would he?"

"Did he hire you?"

"Yes, so, I was clearly the best at the interviews."

"Was there anything you felt suspicious about him?"

"Nope."

"Can you think of any reason why someone would want to

kill him?"

"No!" exclaimed Joe raising his tone angrily. "What's with all these questions?" Some of the staff outside glanced round nervously.

Max had had enough. He leant across Joe's desk, "Now listen to me, I'm getting the feeling you're obstructing a murder inquiry, a serious offence! I've let you have your little tantrum, time now to stop sulking and press the reset button my friend. Let me remind you once and for all, I could have taken you to the cleaners ten years ago, fired you and your career would have been ruined. If nothing else, you owe me. So, we can do this here, or I can call in officers to take you to the police station, your choice, but you need to start impressing the hell outa me right now! Don't view me as your old procurement boss, I'm with the government's Military Intelligence Services now, so don't in any way confuse the two!"

Joe retreated back into his seat, floored by Max's onslaught. He now looked worried, the macho façade crumbled as Max stared into him.

"Jesus Max, okay, okay, I'm sorry alright," he pleaded. "I'll tell you what I know, everything, just don't embarrass me in front of my staff out there for crying out loud, I don't want to go to any bloody police station okay!"

Max thought, 'the bully has shown his true colours, a pathetic cowardly bluffer' and allowed himself a final observation, "I sincerely hope you're treating those staff out there with respect?"

Joe ignored the question.

"Let me tell you what I can to help, have a seat, Max." He cleared his throat and gathered his thoughts.

"Well, go on then, everything?" Max pressed his advantage.

"I worked with David Durham at our previous company, I was his Procurement Head. We got on well, but he did expect me to follow his instructions when he felt he knew best on supplier selections. That's fair enough, we all have our views and he was the boss after all. So when he came here to run the place, he brought me in also, knowing I'd support him, get his tickets to the Cup Final, Wimbledon, the Grand Prix and make sure any perks offered by suppliers went his way."

Max raised an eyebrow questioningly.

"All above board Max I swear."

"Any particular favourite suppliers of his?"

Joe pondered. "No, not really, nothing untoward, just his occasional opinion on shortlisted suppliers."

"Do you have any big tenders in progress or happening soon, big contracts coming up?"

Joe thought for a moment. "We've just awarded the clothing deal to a Chinese manufacturer for all the engineer's uniforms, worth millions though he didn't get involved in that. We do have a big consulting contract currently at the shortlist stage, worth over forty million. It's a top to bottom review of the whole firm that David Durham and the board wanted."

"Who's on the shortlist?" asked Max.

"The usual lot, Ernst and Young, Boston Consulting, McKinsey and another big firm."

"Who?"

"Brookshaws. They're pretty big now, kinda the new kid on the block, really giving the others a run for their money, big money!" joked Joe. Max didn't laugh.

"Who did Durham and you use at your previous firm out of those firms?"

"He'd used McKinsey before, but having said that they'd already been appointed when he arrived. Oh yes, and Brookshaws. They were offering more than the others, for slightly less cost. It was close, but David had wanted them over McKinsey, he thought they'd be keener to impress us. We're talking tens of millions, God, we should have been consultants Max!"

"And had Durham expressed any preference on who should win this consulting contract here at Gaslec?"

"No not yet, we've just got to the shortlist stage, but Brookshaws are the favourite."

"Whose favourite?" asked Max.

Joe looked surprised. "The process of course Max. You'd always tell us, let the process decide!"

'Touché' thought Max. "Nice," he said with a hint of sarcasm to Joe. "I think that'll be all for now, but if I think of anything else I'll be in touch."

Joe rose as Max turned to leave. "Oh Max, I guess as full disclosure, I should mention that I may not be here much longer."

Max turned back. "What do you mean?"

"I'm just concluding the terms negotiation for a new job somewhere else, looks like it's in the bag. They'll want me to start immediately."

"But won't you need to work your notice out here at Gaslec?"

"Not really. You see David Durham gave me written permission before he sadly died, to leave immediately if I got the job!"

Max had to hide his surprise and disdain at this revelation, but asked casually as he opened the door, "Where's the new job then?"

"Sorry Max, can't say, had to sign a Non-Disclosure Agreement when I interviewed. You know how it is, some of these organisations like to keep the top roles under wraps until it's all tied up!" The relish in Joe's tone had returned, which Max didn't like one bit.

Max was on his way to David Durham's home to meet his wife Angela. He took the M4 motorway west out of London from his Clapham home, past Heathrow, Slough where Gaslec was, then off into the Oxfordshire countryside at Maidenhead.

The picturesque town of Henley-on-Thames nestled on the river and centred around the one small bridge built in 1786 crossing the waterway, next to St Mary's church and the town hall. The area provided beautiful homes either hidden away in the countryside or for those with many more millions to spend, scenic, sought after locations alongside the famous part of the river.

The Henley Reach stretch of the river just up from the town and bridge, provided the main setting for the salubrious annual Royal Henley Regatta, since 1851. This was one of the 'must go to' British summer sporting events and would attract the rich and famous from all around, partly to watch the rowers battling up and down the river, mostly to drink, eat and be seen.

Max turned off at the bridge and headed north towards the Henley Business School and soon came upon a long-walled estate by the road, sporting large, high wooden gates. They opened once he pressed the buzzer and as he drove in, the spectacular hidden grounds, driveway and mansion were revealed, all on the edge of the river.

He couldn't help feel that the twenty-million or so property was beyond even a Gaslec Chief Exec's pay grade. Perhaps the wife was the one with family inheritance and money?

Angela Durham was already waiting to greet him at the front porch towering around the entrance doorway. A tall, slim middle-aged woman, with immaculate makeup, jewellery and dress sense managing to enhance her plain looks. The strain of being the younger wife of a high-flying executive who spent most of their time at work, had taken its toll over the years. Mutual discussions about separation and divorce had taken place between them, heated at first, recently they'd been more cordial as they both realised it was over.

She led Max through the hall and into a large lounge overlooking the river at the back of the massive house. Coffee and biscuits were already on a table and she chatted away to Max whilst pouring. She seemed to like the company Max felt.

"I'm so sorry about your husband," offered Max.

"Thank you, quite awful. I can't imagine what on earth he'd gone and done to deserve such treatment. Poor man," she said.

"You have a lovely home here, was it with one of your families before?" probed Max.

"Oh goodness no, neither of us came into the marriage with much other than David's rising career," she replied. "He's done so well, it's all down to him."

Max was surprised. "Did he ever share with you details about his earnings?"

She looked puzzled for a moment. "Why on earth would he do that? No, that's quite personal isn't it." Max was starting to see they had an 'at arm's length' type of relationship. "He obviously did well, top roles, lots of bonuses and the like, the money came in thick and fast these last number of years."

"Can I ask why you say that Mrs Durham," ventured Max carefully. "About lots of bonuses? They're usually only paid once a year?"

Angela sat down. "I've really no idea about all that, but David seemed to have regular windfalls. He'd said to me before he died, that we could almost have anything we wanted now. I'm waiting for our accountant to tell me exactly what money there is, I honestly couldn't tell you at the moment."

"Did your husband ever talk to you about anything he was concerned about or unhappy with?"

She shrugged her shoulders. "Not really. Maybe people at work, the difficult ones, but he'd always sort them out."

"Anything else, at all?" Max felt he was getting nowhere, she barely seemed to know anything about her own husband.

"Well, the only times I saw him perhaps a little pensive, were the odd board meeting, or was it maybe the shareholder's meetings, I don't know which is which. And sometimes when he had duties to perform at the club."

"The club?" repeated Max.

"That's what he called it anyway. The Freemasons, Mr Sargent. David was high up in the Masons, surely you knew that, or the police should have. He was quite important I gather, often going off to their strange ceremonies, meetings and dinners. No women allowed you see, so I never really got involved in all that. Would have been nice to have gone to some of their bashes, quite posh from all accounts."

"Interesting," said Max not meaning to say it out loud. "I mean I don't know much about the Masons, an ancient secretive cult aren't they?" he joked.

Fortunately, Angela smiled in agreement. "They may well be for all the information David ever told me about them. Been with them for years and I still don't know anything about what he got up to! With his funny tunics and codes. A lad's club. He once said it was the 'boy scouts for men'."

They looked at one another and had the same thought, thankfully for Max, she said it first.

"Oh my, you don't think the club had anything to do with his death, I mean he was murdered after all?"

"I'd like to think not," assured Max, "but of course we'll follow up all leads Mrs Durham. "Just one last thing, did your husband collect coins at all?"

Max got his phone out and showed Angela the picture of the Greek coin sides that Si Lawson had let him see.

She screwed up her face. "What an odd-looking coin, looks foreign and very old. No, he had no interest in coins. Why?"

"It was found in his wallet, probably just got mixed up in change," said Max dismissing the matter.

"David didn't carry cash, let alone change, used his cards for everything, as we all do these days," she said.

They both gave a frown in unison. "You've been most helpful," thanked Max as he left.

As Max drove out down the driveway, he realised how little he knew about this club, the Freemasons, which seemed quite bizarre. Everyone had heard of them, they were there in plain sight, with their clubs, or rather lodges as they were called, in most areas and big towns all over the modern world.

Surely an organisation so large and far-reaching couldn't be involved in any kind of criminality? He reminded himself that it was often the big, powerful and wealthy organisations, where problems and potential corruption would tempt even those with the utmost integrity.

Max wanted to find out more about this unusual club. He wondered if the Freemasons could somehow be involved in Durham's assassination?

4

Max updated Si Lawson back at MI5 Thames House and having come up with nothing on a 'book of souls', did some more research on Durham, Joe Patterson and the mysterious obolus coin. Nothing of real interest came up other than he managed to get hold of bank records for Durham, at least those that were accessible.

They'd bought their Henley estate a few years ago for seventeen million cash, no mortgage. But the funds to cover this were only transferred into the account of the solicitor's handling the purchase the day before, from an offshore account.

Nothing unusual about top execs having an offshore account to hide their true wealth and avoid tax. But it was clear David Durham had much more money than his UK accounts showed. Max felt there was no point asking his wife Angela, she had no idea of her husband's financial details. He put it down to savvy investments, share dealings and the like. These top directors were often in the know about such opportunities, he thought to himself.

Max quickly looked up this fast-growing consulting firm Brookshaw's, that Joe Patterson had mentioned. He was surprised to find that despite its size and scope, it was still a privately owned company. Usually, such large firms have gone public, sold out or raised cash from shareholder investors and therefore have transparent accounts. After some more digging, he discovered the firm was run by Gillian Brookshaw in the UK and her brother Brett in the US.

There was little information about turnover and profit, though he concluded they could have revenues of a half to one billion given the amount of consulting contracts they were winning. But on the face of it they appeared to be as Joe had said, the up and coming, exciting, professional new management consulting firm, taking on the big guys.

Si Lawson walked over to Max.

"You wanted to find out more about the Masons. I put a call into one of their senior exec's, Sir Philip Edwards, I think he's now their Communications Director or something. Been a Mason for ages, he's an ex-Met colleague from way back so you can trust him. He'll see you today at his office in the Freemasons' Hall.

"They have their own building?"

"Of course," replied Si, "you really don't know much about them, do you? Huge place between Holborn and Covent Garden, it's the HQ for the United Grand Lodge of England."

Max caught a black London cab outside Thames House which took him on the short fifteen-minute trip past the Houses of Parliament, Westminster Abbey and Big Ben.

"Are you one of them guv?" asked the taxi driver.

"One of what?"

"A mason?"

"No, just visiting."

"They're a funny lot aren't they guv, with their secret handshakes and world domination stuff!"

Max busied himself with his notes on questions to ask. "I don't think it's like that at all."

"You just be careful going in there guv, you never know what happens inside that big building, with their weird ceremonies and such like!"

Max kept his head down careful not to catch the driver's eye in the mirror again. They drove up Parliament Street to Trafalgar Square, up The Strand then Drury Lane.

The taxi dropped him off at the juncture of Great Queen Street and Wild Street. Max stood back and gazed upon the corner entrance of Freemason's Hall. It was a subtle but huge building. Two large houses and gardens were originally bought by the Masons in 1775 and expanded over the centuries, when its current form took shape in 1933, covering over two acres of prime London real estate.

The somewhat dull four-storey limestone sides of the building looked plain but mysterious, as if attempting to blend into its surroundings and not draw attention to itself, or maybe hide what lay behind its walls. Max walked up the four shallow steps to the tall front doors between two large stone columns. Above the entrance, the carved dates 1717 and 1967 straddled a small clock, over which sat a high square tower with smaller columns around it.

He went inside and entered a different world, of art deco ornaments and styling, highly polished marble floors, walls covered with smooth wooden cladding, interjected with signs, symbols and images of importance to the Freemasons. It was like stepping back in time and was truly magnificent.

"Max Sargent?" greeted a distinguished, smartly turned-out older gentleman in the large entrance hall. "With Si Lawson's bunch at Box 500 eh?" referring to MI5's old wartime PO Box number.

"Yes, Sir Philip, thank you for seeing me so quickly," said Max shaking his hand.

"Let's go up to my office, one of the perks of being on the Executive here, and when we're done I can give you a quick tour. Quite a place isn't it."

Once they were settled in Sir Philip's small but well-appointed office, they quickly dispensed with the idol chat over a tea.

"So what you brought you to this job from the Met?" asked Max.

"I did a stint in the army, military police. Loved the police part but not the confines of the army, so left and joined the Met. After thirty years with them ending up with the Deputy Commissioner job, which got me my knighthood, I didn't want to fully retire. I wanted some sort of role so I could at least be doing something. Can't be at home all day annoying the wife eh?" he joked.

Max smiled sympathetically.

"I'd been with the Freemasons for over twenty years, quite high up, and they kindly offered me the role of Director of Communications, what with my police PR experience." He leant forward, "To be honest I have a couple of wonderful ladies who do most of the day-to-day work, brilliant they are."

He sat back again. "We have about a hundred staff running everything for the three-hundred-thousand or so members across forty-eight premises. Though worldwide there are about six million Masons. We've been around for some three-hundred and thirty years you know!"

"Are you like a company, is there much money involved?" asked Max innocently, trying to gain anything which might relate back to Durham's murder.

"Good grief no my boy," Sir Philip pretending to be shocked. "We're here to make money only for all our charitable causes, we raise about forty million each year for them. Our only income comes from the annual dues, about seven million, half a million from investments and same again for hiring out the hall. Total income is only about eleven million, so you see it's not about money at all my dear fellow."

Max cleared his throat and ventured, "So what is it all about, if I may ask, Sir Philip?"

"Of course my dear chap, Si said to give you the full story. It's believed that as far back as medieval times, stone masons were starting to get together to better themselves, agree on standards and be recognised as the skilled craftsmen they were, for when turning up at new building sites looking for work. The secret words created were to prove they were, shall we say, qualified stone masons, to get hired. They'd gather in huts, or lodges, hence the term still used now for local gatherings of masons."

"I didn't realise masonry went so far back," admitted Max.

"The first known London lodge was recorded back in 1691 and on 24th June 1717, four lodges met at the Goose and Gridiron ale house just up the road here and established the first premier grand lodge," Sir Philip held out his arms, "which became what we are today, the United Grand Lodge of England. Then over the years the masons began to accept honorary or gentlemen masons into the fold. As you can see Max, I'm no bricklayer," he joked.

"So the masons are all about charity?" checked Max.

"Good grief no, it's so much more than that," corrected Sir Philip. "The four cornerstones of the masons are integrity, friendship, respect and then we have charity. Everything about our existence is for the betterment of us as people, helping others, through our own education, charity and knowledge, in a safe benevolent brotherhood environment."

"How does a mason progress through the ranks so to say, I've heard quite a few masonic names used?"

"We are all brethren or brothers, and progress from apprentice through stages such as steward, deacon, warden to worshipful master and grand master levels. We do this by the quality of our actions and our understanding of masonic standards, rituals and long-standing traditions. Each stage is denoted with more impressive apron attire, chains and in recognition of the older ways of masons, different signs, words and handshakes are known to the varying levels of craftsmen, or ranks as you put it."

"Can anyone join?" asked Max.

"Absolutely," said Sir Philip proudly. "They go through an interview and have to be proposed of course, but anyone of good character can join. Hardly a secret cult, eh my boy! Some past masons include presidents, Roosevelt and Washington, prime ministers like Churchill, royalty like George VI, and all sorts of other people such as Sir Christopher Wren, Henry Ford, even John Wayne and Clark Gable!"

Max was beginning to understand that the masons were an entirely legitimate and upstanding bunch and didn't deserve all the speculation surrounding them.

"I noticed a lot of symbols as we walked through the hall,

your main one being the compass and set square?"

Sir Philip was relishing imparting a better understanding of freemasonry to his younger visitor. "Like any organisation with centuries of history, symbols were adopted as being easier to portray meanings than the lesser-used written word. The compass and square are two of the main tools of the architect or mason. The compass symbolises keeping within boundaries, being measured. The square represents square conduct or giving a square deal, acting with integrity."

"I saw some pictures with the letter 'G' in the middle, what does that stand for?"

"That's open to interpretation, but usually it signifies the importance of geometry to a mason, but it can also stand for God, being the grand architect of everything. To be a mason you must believe in a supreme being, its form though can be of your choosing. We all have different ideas about what God could be, so we accommodate that. Interestingly we don't allow members to talk about religion at meetings, too contentious, along with the other topic frowned on, politics!"

"I can see Sir Philip that the freemasons don't deserve all the silly views they've attracted over the centuries," noted Max, acknowledging the lesson he'd been given which had completely changed his mind of this legitimate organisation of brotherhood and charity.

"You honestly couldn't find a more upstanding bunch trying to do good for their communities," agreed Sir Philip. "As I've mentioned we're open to anyone, men only still I'm afraid. We've nothing to hide, for heaven's sake we're open to the public here with tours and a museum. There's no talk of favoured business deals and stupid myths, like the all-seeing eye above the pyramid on the back of dollar bills, has nothing to do with masonry. Neither did we exist in King Solomon's times, the Knights Templar or by decree of the Pope!"

Max chuckled.

Sir Philip admitted, "This whole transparency and view of masonry is one of the things we know we need to improve and we're working on it all the time now. So now to you Max, what's prompted this interest from you and Si, some murder inquiry he mentioned?"

"Yes. The Chief Exec of Gaslec was assassinated we believe and we're trying to chase down what few leads we have. When he died he mentioned a book of souls, does that ring any bells for you in relation to masonry?" asked Max.

"Book of souls," repeated Sir Philip, "I'll be darned if I've ever heard that term, sorry." Then perking up, "There is a book on constitutions, that's the masonic rules as laid down since 1723, but not book of souls?"

Max shook his head and next showed Sir Philip the picture of the coin on his mobile. "Do you recognise this coin?"

Sir Philip stared at the picture, "Oh dear my boy, not much help am I, no idea what that coin is at all, looks old?"

"Okay thank you, not to worry. Lastly, the man murdered was a mason, I wondered if you knew him or how I might find out more about what he did within the freemasons, a David Durham?"

"Oh crikey," tutted Sir Philip, "I know a lot of masons, but that name doesn't sound familiar. Not to worry, we can check the archives on your way out. Follow me and I'll show you the Grand Hall, it's quite something."

They left the office and went back downstairs again. Sir Philip took Max over to a stained-glass window depicting an angel holding a model of Freemasons' Hall. He showed Max the framed paper below.

"This whole building is in commemoration of the three-thousand three-hundred and twenty-three masons who fell in the Great War. Their names are recorded here with the four figures of the armed services at the corners."

"Who are these below," asked Max pointing to four larger golden statues below the casing."

"That's King Solomon, Moses, Joshua and St George. Now over here we have the solid bronze doors to the Grand Hall, each weigh's over a ton. The pictures carved onto the doors show masons building King Solomon's temple."

Sir Philip lightly pushed the perfectly hung heavy doors and led tMax into the impressive Grand Hall. It was a stunning art deco blend of amphitheatre and church, with large golden organ pipes behind the main dais. Rows of floor and elevated or floating seating surrounded the central space, on which a large black and white chequered carpet lay, with a golden throne-like chair at its head. Everything was immaculately polished, cleaned and pristine.

"Have a look at this," offered Sir Philip proudly, leading them to the centre and looking up. "Isn't that coving magnificent. Thirty thousand mosaic pieces placed by hand."

The central recess in the ceiling showed several depictions at its sides and corners.

"What are the pictures of?" asked Max.

"The figures in the corners represent the four cardinal virtues, prudence, temperance, fortitude and justice. Then at the points of the compass, we have Helios the sun God, the Duke of Connaught's crest, he was the Grand Master at the time of the Hall's building, with St George and the dragon. Also, a serpent eating its own tail encircling the moon, for wisdom and eternity and finally Jacob's ladder, on which are the cross, anchor and flaming heart. These represent faith, hope and charity."

"Wow, what a lot of messages all on one ceiling," joked Max, looking around and taking in the vast room's splendour.

They then walked through some corridors and up a flight of stairs into a large archive room resembling a cluttered library, with rows of shelving, some computers and an old microfiche machine, used to magnify records minimised and packed onto transparencies.

The attendant was absent, so Sir Philip sat at the computer desk.

"Right, let's give this a go, what was this deceased chap's name again?"

"David Durham."

"We should have all members on here at least going back a hundred years. They're still inputting all the names before that from other records we keep." Sir Philip peered into the screen scanning the contents. Durham, Durham, ah yes, here we are, David Durham, a member of the Thames Valley group at the grand lodge of Berkshire."

"So he is, or rather was a mason," confirmed Max, "up to his recent demise."

Sir Philip looked surprised. "Was, being the operative word."

"What do you mean?"

"He certainly *was* a mason, but he resigned from us about three years ago! Very unusual for anyone to leave. No reason given, he just left us?"

Max was shocked by this revelation. "That's a surprise, his wife thought he was attending masonic events all these past years. Begs the question where he was going. You said it's unusual for members to leave the masons?"

"Absolutely, joining's a big commitment and whilst of course some leave, it is pretty rare. Back in the early years of masonic history, there were a few tussles over the values of the freemasons and a couple of opposing organisations were formed."

"How do you mean Sir Philip? Do you have many members leaving like that?"

"Just after the masons were set up in the seventeen-hundreds, some Duke of Wharton was expelled and they established an anti-masonic sect called the Gormogons, to ridicule masonry. Then some London lodges disagreed with the masonic values and started another organisation confusingly called the Grand Lodge of the Ancients, with the Grand Master being the third Duke of Atholl. But after the fuss died down they reunited with the masons in 1813."

"Any other leavers displaying contempt for what the masons stood for?" asked Max.

Sir Philip pondered. "There was one other prominent

expulsion. A Thomas Appleby. After all the nonsense with the Duke of Atholl, I'm guessing he was one of his supporters, he tried to continue rallying support for a breakaway grand lodge of sorts. He was a devoted businessman, a power-hungry trader who felt the masons should be all about favouring and helping one another make money through its connections, specifically making more money off non-masons. He was caught soliciting members for their own selfish advancement and profiteering. So the freemasons expelled him. Quite a kerfuffle by all accounts."

"What happened to him?" queried Max.

"He went to one of the big havens for trader's of that time, to continue his somewhat dodgy business club's dealings. Went underground with his associates, likely other ex-masons, then over the years probably dissipated. Don't know anything more about them."

"Kind of a masonic renegade eh!" noted Max. "Where exactly is this trader's haven?"

"Venice, dear boy, Venice!"

5

"I told you the freemasons were legit," smiled Si Lawson knowingly. "They wouldn't allow anything dodgy."

"Not got much to go on here have we," admitted Max. "A top exec with more money than can be accounted for, not so odd these days! An old coin and a so-called book of souls, neither of which we have any clue about and a killer wandering about with a long sharp knife!"

"What about this dubious masonic renegade you mentioned from two-hundred years ago setting up in Venice!"

"What about it?" shrugged Max.

"Well, it's a lead isn't it?" said Si holding his hands out. "There's little more you can do on the book or the coin. May come to nothing, but find out more about this Thomas Appleby character. Go to Venice if you have to, it's all we've got!"

"What would I do in Venice? As you say, all this happened two-hundred years ago."

"Surely they have property records of some kind, start with finding out where he lived out there!"

Max got back to his desk. He needed to get some kind of lead on this Thomas Appleby person who fled London to Venice sometime around 1813. After several hours of googling, inquiring at land registry's and ancestry information portals, he came up with what appeared to be his London address, showing that Thomas Appleby lived in Richmond, south-west London from 1810 up to 1835.

He couldn't find anything relating to a move to Venice, Italy though. Max's inquiries led him to start researching the Italian land registry held for each area of the country, the Registro Catastale. He found there was a separate deeds register, the banco dati ipotecaria, which held information on property ownership. However, it seemed that records going back a hundred years were sketchy at best. He sat back in his seat frustrated.

Si Lawson's deputy Vince, came over. "Everything alright Max, you look a bit fed up?"

"Italians! Not the best at record keeping are they!"

"Good God no, you'll be lucky," agreed Vince, "what you after then?"

"I'm trying to find out where a Brit lived in Venice around 1835. All I have is a name."

Max took Vince through what he knew about Thomas Appleby and the masons.

"Why do you think he moved to Venice in 1839," asked Vince.

"That's when he seems to have sold his Richmond house."

"But you said he fell out with the masons in 1813'ish, so surely that's when he'd have gone to Venice? He probably held onto his London home to return to maybe?" Vince suggested.

"Good point, thanks, right I need to get onto the Venice land registry," said Max buoyed up again.

"That'll be hit and miss, but you could always put in an RIU with our oppos in the Italian Secret Service."

"What's an RIU?"

"Richiesta informazioni urgente. An urgent information request," explained Vince. "Send it off to the Agenzia Informazioni e Sicurezza Interna, the homeland information part of their services and just say you're following up a lead on a personal ancestor or something," suggested Vince. "They love all that family stuff out there, maybe you'll get lucky, cover 1813 to 1840 to be sure."

Max looked up the information request procedure on the MI5 intranet portal and emailed off his urgent request under the cover of wanting to find out more about a potential ancestor.

The request was picked up by a keen junior researcher, Tommaso, inside the huge square government intelligence building on Piazza Dante in Rome. His job was to decide who to pass foreign agency requests onto across the Italian Intelligence Services.

The ambitious clerk took the view that if he could assist as many staff as possible whilst doing his job, then one day it would rub off on him. It would undoubtedly help his career advancement and provide a bountiful network of contacts owing him favours, always useful in the intelligence business.

When the email came through the urgent information request portal, he immediately noticed the majestic MI5 crest on the top. It showed a golden-winged lion with fishes tail surrounded by green petals, red roses and three portcullis', with 'Regnum Defende' underneath, meaning 'defender of the realm'. This got him excited and he was eager to add such a prestigious contact to his growing network.

Seeing that it was a more personal request regarding the British operative's family, Tommaso took it upon himself to immediately contact the Venice land registry himself. Leveraging his position with the Rome Intelligence Services, perhaps a little too much, he had staff at the Venice office rushing about, looking through old paper record files for anything resembling the name of Thomas Appleby between 1813 and 1840.

Two-hundred-year-old property records across Italy were dubious and inconsistent at best, but fortunately, because of the precious land grabbing by the waters of Venice's trading city, records for that region were in pretty good order.

By the end of the day, Tommaso proudly replied to Max, with the Venice address of a Thomas Appleby which he owned from 1814 to 1835. He also advised, 'that the property is currently registered to an overseas company called Venetian Properties based in St Kitts and Nevis'.

Tommaso cheekily ended his reply with, 'Glad I could help you with your family quest, hoping you'll be able to return the favour one day'!

Max flew into the Marco Polo Venezia airport and avoiding the half-hour bus or cab trip into the main city's island waterways, took the more expensive but glamourous water taxi.

Venice is located in the northeast of Italy and is the capital of the Veneto region. Its name is derived from the ancient Veneti people who inhabited the area by the tenth century BC and is now known as the City of water, of bridges, canals and masks. Built on a group of one-hundred and eighteen islands, settlers drained areas of the lagoon shoring up banks and drove thousands of closely spaced alder tree trunks into the mud and sand until they reached the harder clay below. Alder trees were known to have water-resistant properties, allowing large wooden and then limestone foundation plates to be laid on top of the piles.

Also known as the sinking city it is believed to be sinking at a millimetre a year and high tides and heavy rainfall often cause flooding in many of the squares and walkways.

Huge cruise ships sail close by using the port of Venice through the Giudecca Canal, bringing tourists to this famous, beautiful and unique city on the water.

The sleek speed boat with its highly polished and varnished wooden slats, sped across the smooth turquoise water of the stunning lagoon. Max looked out over the roof of the small boat's cabin and could see the rooftops and towers of Venice ahead of them. They passed by the smaller land mass in the water that was Murano and the tiny, deserted Isola Campalto jutting out of nowhere like the top of a rogue iceberg. They approached Venice and passed under the Via Della Liberto bridge which accommodated the SR11 road and railway lines into the city on the water.

The water taxi driver chose to go right through Venice using the Grand Canal, which wound its way right through the centre of the mass of buildings, squares, narrow walkways and canals. It was more interesting for his passengers as well as himself and would usually provide a better tip at the end, having taken the fascinating waterway through this famous city. He'd lived in Venice all his life and never tired of the constant waterways bustling and activities to be seen every day.

They passed under the impressive Rialto bridge with its central archway and six further arches on either side. The most photographed bridge in Venice was first built as a pontoon in 1173 and has been rebuilt from wood to stone many times over the centuries, collapsing twice, accommodating shops and markets. In 1591 the stone bridge we see there today remains.

As they emerged from the Grand Canal into the Bacino San Marco lagoon they passed the Basilica Santa Maria to their right, and beyond across the water the two large islands of Giudecca and San Giorgio Maggiore. The boat veered off to the left and slowed right down to negotiate a narrow waterway into the buildings. They pulled up after fifty feet and the taxi-man pointed to Max's hotel, the Baglioni Luna, whose entrance was just yards in front of them.

Max obliged with a healthy tip as a porter from the hotel eagerly grabbed his single case, smiling at the thought of securing an equally generous tip, albeit for carrying Max's luggage ten yards into the hotel lobby!

Max settled into his hotel and ventured out into St Mark's square to have a look around and grab dinner. He would find Thomas Appleby's house in the morning. He grabbed a coffee and cake at the Café Florin in the centre of the famous piazza, sitting outside people-watching. He then walked past the Campanile di San Marco tower to the ornate St Mark's Basilica, with its high domes and four prancing horses above the entrance arches.

Turning right towards the lagoon on the Plaza San Marco, he passed the Doge's Palace and came to the water's edge, standing between the two famous granite columns. On the tops were the city's two patrons, the winged lion, the symbol of St Mark the evangelist, and San Todaro the city's first protector.

Rows of gondolas lined up along the water's edge, their gondoliers touting for the evening's business targeting naïve couples too embarrassed to complain about the high fares.

Max found a small bustling backstreet café noticeably favoured by locals, always a good sign the food was going to be good. He ordered a platter of thinly cut prosciutto ham, cheeses and soft mozzarella with a bottle of chilled white wine and thought about how to approach the house he would visit in the morning. He had one shot at finding out as much as he could about someone who lived there almost two hundred years ago. It was a long shot.

The next morning Max had breakfast in the hotel then using his phone's map, started to make his way to the address Tommaso had given him, which was about three hundred metres walk west of the hotel, at Calle Drio la Chiesa Street.

He zig-zagged through the maze of interconnecting narrow walkways, with buildings towering high above the confined alleys. Almost every other shop seemed to be selling either glassware or fancy masks, two of Venice's top tourist souvenirs.

Reaching the street his map pinpointed, the house number was right by the bridge over the Rio Di San Moise canal. Max noticed that the building had several windows overlooking the small adjacent canal, with some very old looking, rotting doors just above the waterline, leading into some kind of loading bay or boat house under the home.

The house was larger than its neighbouring properties, rising three floors upwards over the narrow access alley. The innocuous entrance doors looked unremarkable.

He gathered himself before pressing the buzzer, wondering who if anyone would answer and thinking to himself, 'so this was where Thomas Appleby lived almost two-hundred years ago after fleeing the London masons'. He had to get inside.

Max heard the buzzer ring somewhere deep inside the house and after a short while the door opened revealing an untidy looking man in his fifties. He had thick dark hair with matching beard, fit-looking, probably ex-military from the tattoos, but now a little overweight.

He nodded questioningly but said nothing.

Max mustered his basic Italian. "Mi scusi, parla inglese?"

"Si, I speak English," replied the bulky man in good English with an Italian flavouring.

"Ah, good," said Max. "Do you live in this house?"

"Yes, me and my wife, why?"

On seeing this man, Max had made a wild assumption that this dishevelled chap was not the owner or director of the property owners. Nor did he appear to have the sort of money needed to be setting up offshore property accounts.

"Erm," Max pretended to have forgotten, "your name again?"

Stunned by the confident question the man surprisingly obliged. "Claudio. Claudio Marcato."

"Yes, of course, Claudio, that's right," said Max. "Did you get the message from the office?"

"What message?" Claudio was starting to look bewildered.

"The St Kitts office of course. Oh no, they said they'd advise you I'd be dropping in to do a random check for the owner," bluffed Max. He tutted, "I'm so sorry, how embarrassing for both of us. I would have you call them right this instant, but it'll be three in the morning there, they'll all be asleep. Damn it!"

Claudio fell for it. "What was it you needed to do here anyway?", conscious not to let down the owner.

Max pretended to look appreciative. "Oh that would be so good of you, all I need to do is have a quick look round, just make sure everything's in order, then I can report back all is okay and we're both in the clear eh!"

Claudio frowned as he pondered, so Max helped his

decision along.

"Only take ten minutes then I'll be gone?"

"I probably should check, can you come back later?"

"Sorry, I leave Venice after this visit. It should have been communicated to you after all, might you have missed their call or email?"

Claudio relented and opened the door. "Come on then, let's get this over with."

They went into the cool building and immediately ascended a stairway up to the main living floor, above the boathouse Max assumed. The inside was in stark contrast to the old building façade portrayed outside. The interior had undergone many renovations over the years and now looked modern, with clean walls and furnishings. Too clean to be this man's taste thought Max.

"How long have you been here Claudio?" asked Max pretending to check out the room and nodding in satisfaction.

"Five years maybe."

"Caretaking?" ventured Max with bated breath.

"Of course, I couldn't afford somewhere like this. But the money is pretty good to look after it. Me and the wife just move out whenever one of the owners wants to stay here. Only a couple of times a year for a long weekend."

"Met them? The owners that is? I'm probably like you, just the hired help, I've no idea who owns the place, I just work for the property company they've registered it under." Max knew he was pushing his luck but this Claudio seemed malleable enough.

"No not met them. I'm told when to have the place all tidied up ready for their visits," said Claudio. "My wife does all that anyway."

They went up to the next floor which comprised four large bedrooms and several bathrooms. Then up again to the charming roof terrace overlooking the rooftops and out across the lagoon beyond.

"Do you know any of the history of the previous owners

of this house," asked Max, hopeful.

"Only that it's had socialites, businessmen and going way back, traders. But everyone in Venice was trading something in those days."

"Well everything seems to be in good order thank you Claudio, I'll make my report that you're looking after the place."

They went back downstairs and as they reached the hallway, Max noticed another door underneath the steps.

"Just need to look inside there, then I'm gone," he ventured.

Claudio's demeanour changed a little, for the worse.

"Didn't the office tell you? No one goes in there, only the owners have the keys. I can't let you in there, I'll lose my job. This is our home, I can't upset the owners at all, they'll fire me!"

Max had touched a nerve. "What's in there then?" He immediately regretted asking.

"I don't know and don't want to know," snapped Claudio, his tone and volume raising. "What did you say your name was again?"

Max knew his time was up and made for the door quickly. As he exited he turned to Claudio, "Thank you so much, the name's Smith!" With that he left the stunned Italian in the hallway, starting to realise he'd probably been made a fool of. He was seething. Claudio lunged out of the door and looked both ways at the bridge then the alleyway, but 'Mr Smith' had gone!

Max took a longer route back to his hotel, just in case Claudio had tried to follow or find him. He wanted to know what was in the boathouse, that was so secret even the caretaker wasn't allowed in there. He decided to lose himself on a long ferry restaurant tour which would keep him away from the area for the rest of the day. He would return to the property tonight, much later. He had an idea about seeing inside this mystery boathouse.

Claudio got angrier and angrier, especially when his wife returned from the Rialto market and he relayed what had happened. She was furious that he might have done anything to jeopardise their cushy accommodation and caretaker income for house-sitting a luxury Venetian property. She demanded he called the property owners and told them everything, and told him to hope they'd be allowed to stay on, or else she was off.

Late afternoon Claudio called the number he had for Venetian Properties in St Kitts and Nevis. He explained everything to one of the office staff. They in turn made a call to one of the owners. Twenty minutes later, Claudio's phone rang.

"Claudio?" said the male voice calling. "I own the house you are caretaking, we've not met. The office told me you had a visitor today wanting to look round, a Mr Smith of all names?" The voice was strong, assured. Claudio immediately felt uncomfortable. This was his boss after all.

"I'm sorry, we take care of the house like it's our own Sir," he bumbled, "the man seemed so genuine, I really…"

"Did you show him the basement or tell him anything about that private room?" cut in the voice. "You know that's out of bounds don't you?"

"Yes sir, I mean yes I know, but no I didn't let him anywhere near the basement, threw him out when he asked about it I did Sir," reported Claudio trying to win back his superior with the inflated account. "He won't be coming back that's for sure Sir!"

"Let me be clear. If you and your dear lady wish to remain the caretakers of my house, you make sure anyone showing any interest in my private room," the voice paused, "is severely dealt with!" Another pause. "Do you understand Claudio? Severely!"

At this point, with his home, marriage and life on the line, Claudio would do anything for this mysterious owner, even hurt someone, badly, if that's what it took.

"I understand," he agreed. "But I'm sure that's the last of it, Sir."

"It had better be for your sake!" The tone lightened. "Nice talking to you at last Claudio, look after my house please!" With that the caller rang off, leaving a stunned, chastised, but determined Italian staring blankly at his phone.

After his boat tour, Max had bought a couple of short but sturdy screwdrivers from a local shop. He waited until two AM that night, then quietly slipped out of his hotel to return to the property. He passed only several other people near St Mark's square. Once he disappeared into the back alleyways, everywhere was completely deserted and quiet, just the occasional bedroom light on or the flickering of someone's TV.

Reaching the small bridge by the house, he waited a few moments checking each way down the long walkway on both sides of him. All still. He climbed over the metal railing of the bridge next to the house and carefully lowered himself onto the narrow brick ledge that ran along most of the building's waterline.

He took out the two strong screwdrivers and placed the first into one of the small eyelet hooks he'd seen earlier in the wall, likely an old fixing for an ornament or something. He let go of the bridge rail and holding himself onto the ledge with the screwdriver anchor, he shuffled along to the next eyelet and did the same.

Just as he put his foot down and shifted his weight forward, the old brickwork gave way, crumbling into the canal's water and lurching him down. He fought to keep his balance, putting most of his weight back onto the screwdriver's grip in the eyelet.

Then to make matters worse, he heard footsteps approaching from the alleyway beyond the house entrance. He regained his foothold on a different brick, pressed himself tightly up against the wall and froze.

The footsteps neared, came level with his and climbed up

the few steps of the small bridge, then continued down and back along the far walkway. Had the passing late-night worker glanced down the canal, they would have seen Max clinging to the side of the building above the canal.

Max breathed out and was now next to the rotting doors of the boathouse. He retrieved the first screwdriver and gently placed it behind the padlocked clasp holding the two doors shut. He thought he heard a movement from within the house and froze again to check. Nothing. He slowly but firmly levered the metal shaft down and broke the rusty clasp screws away from the crusty wooden doors. The latch swung aside and he quietly pushed one of the doors inwards.

A large dark cavern was revealed through the gloom of the night, covering the entire basement area under the house above. He tested his weight on the door. The hinge fittings were still sound and he swung himself onto a narrow walkway running into the space. He pushed the door back out again. Max turned round and activated the torch light on his phone.

The basement lit up revealing itself. To Max's surprise, the space consisted of two areas, a boat dock and what looked like a very old prayer room or chapel. The canal water came under the house about halfway, enough for a mid-sized boat to dock and was then held by a thick retaining wall. Steps down from the walkway he was on, led into the chapel room which was just below the canal's waterline but remained dry and dusty.

Max presumed the water access was usual centuries ago for a trader to bring in and store their goods. But he was intrigued by the storage space which had been converted into a good-sized meeting room of some kind.

He held up his light and started to take in the faded depictions around the cavern's walls. Much of the ancient plaster was crumbling or flaking off, but had been untouched since it was decorated centuries ago. Why would someone want to preserve this room so carefully, having done so much renovation above throughout the house? Max felt like he was viewing some sort of hallowed temple.

The murals now started to become apparent to him, and as he took them in, he began to get an ominous feeling. Could these pictures date back to when Thomas Appleby lived here? They certainly looked old enough.

Down one side of the wall, like a gothic storyboard, depictions began with Venetian boats and stern looking traders talking, buying and selling at markets. Then there were modest amounts of goods, food, bags of coins and yarns of silk laying about. Lastly, the traders were shown fighting with hooded figures, maybe skeletons many apparitions of Death with their scythes, and being slaughtered, their bloody bodies abound.

Max turned and lit up the wall opposite. This time the traders were shown laughing, eating and drinking while they bought and sold their goods. The piles of riches were larger, more treasures, coins, gold and jewels, food, metals and shiny weapons, swords and spears. From this, the traders were pictured travelling to a dark lake and paying a ferryman, another hooded figure, to cross the expanse of misty water. As they reached the far shore, a scribe appeared to be writing their names into an old book, before they ran towards the picture on the last wall.

Max now turned the light onto this far wall which both murals led onto. He winced, taking in the inglorious image. A God-like bearded man stood on top of a huge pile of wealth and riches, larger than he'd seen on the other walls, of all kinds of wealth known to man.

The God figure wore an ancient helmet and held a long bident, a two-pronged staff. Beside him sat a three-headed, dark dog and further behind were depicted a crowd of wispy, ghostly figures holding out their arms or bowing down in deference.

Max was no mythological expert, but even he recognised the pictured scenes as embodying the God of wealth, Pluto, also known as Hades, God of the underworld!

Crash!

The door in the corner of the room burst open splintering the lock. Claudio stormed in, glaring with rage. He held a large kitchen knife in his hand.

"You again!" he sneered, starting down the steps at his returning intruder.

Max was taken by surprise as Claudio was already coming at him. All he could do was deliver a sharp kick to his knee hoping to incapacitate him. His foot blow glanced off Claudio's thickly set leg above his kneecap, sending him down onto the floor, but only for a moment.

As Claudio cursed and began to rise, Max turned and ran up the steps to the walkway alongside the boat dock. Seeing he'd closed the door he realised he was trapped. He couldn't dive under the doors as they both had metal bars protruding down under the waterline. As Max turned round, Claudio came up the steps to face him. He was more alert this time, as he edged towards Max menacingly, waving the knife.

In such a tight space Max knew he had little chance of avoiding the gleaming blade. He did the only thing left to him, and jumped into the cool water at the base of the entrance doors, gambling that Claudio wouldn't follow him in.

The big man on the dockside ledge watched Max in astonishment but didn't follow. Max opened the loose gate and swam out into the small canal. There were a couple of boats to his left, but he made for the bridge. Managing to get a grip hold on the wall, he hauled himself up and was about to climb over the railing, as Claudio appeared above him! The knife blade slash just missed Max's arm, as he pulled back, falling into the canal again. Claudio growled, but stood firm, waiting to see what Max would do now.

Max looked back to the boats and made his way to them. He dragged himself into the first boat which just had a single paddle inside. Jumping across to the next boat he was luckier, it had a small outboard motor on the back with a simple pull cord starter. The tiny engine fired up on Max's first tug on the cord. He untied the rope and slowly pulled out, making his way along the narrow waterway. He turned back to see Claudio disappear from the bridge.

Max passed under another bridge then took the next right turn in the canal into Rio Fuseri, hoping to have now left Claudio behind. The small boat approached the next bridge Pont de le Colonne. Max passed under the small bridge and as the front of the boat emerged, a large dark figure came thudding into the small craft almost toppling it over in the water!

Claudio had guessed Max would take the first offshoot and knowing the lanes like the back of his hand, had run to the bridge to intercept him.

Claudio steadied himself and raised the knife up, but Max had already grabbed the only item in the boat, being a short-handled wooden paddle. As the knife lunged down towards Max's shoulder, he dived aside slamming against the boat edge, but managed to take a hefty swipe with the paddle, at Claudio's head.

The paddle blade caught him on the temple and momentarily stunning Claudio, sending him flying across to the opposite lip of the boat, his head and torso draped precariously over the water. As Claudio came round, Max gave him an almighty shove and pushed him out into the canal.

Max grabbed the outboard's steering bar and throttled up. The tiny motor worked hard to gather speed, but simply wasn't fast enough to avoid Claudio's grip on the back corner of the boat! As he dragged behind Max through the water, he waved his knife furiously at him. Realising he wasn't going to be able to haul himself up into the boat whilst it was moving, Claudio started fumbling with the motor's mechanism. He found the small fuel pipe connecting the engine to the small tank on top, and pulled at it!

The outboard spluttered, then stopped, as the boat slowed down. Max could see Claudio was readying himself to climb aboard, so stepped over to him and delivered a firm stamping of his foot onto Claudio's forehead, knocking him from the boat and back into the water.

Max quickly examined the detached fuel line, replaced it, pulled the cord and slowly but surely throttled away from Claudio, left cursing in the canal!

"You don't know who you're messing with Smith!" shouted Claudio, shaking his fist, still believing that to be his real name.

Max passed under another bridge then turned right again into Rio Orseolo o del Coval, which led to a small Bacino docking area just by a corner of St Mark's square. He'd accidentally done a complete loop through the canals. Max retreated to his hotel and would fly back to London first thing in the morning to try to figure out the strange basement discovery in Thomas Appleby's old house.

Claudio was left dejected. As he hauled himself out of the canal, he began to worry about the prospects of facing up to the threats and anger of the mysterious, stern house owner. He then realised he had more immediate explaining to do, with more immediate potential consequences, to his wife!

6

"Ed, we have another person that may become an issue," said the strong voice on the phone. "I won't know how I need you to proceed for a couple of days though. It'll be a tricky one, he has a bodyguard that sticks with him in public. Except that is, for one particular location. I'll send you the details and temporary VIP membership."

Ed Davies preferred using his shortened name whilst in the UK, but defaulted back to his full name, Eduardo, when in Sicily. His wealthy English father married his mother, a beautiful Italian girl. With property businesses in both home countries, he spent his youthful years between their Ficarazzi beachside home east of Palermo and their Sussex country house on Ashdown Forest. He spoke both languages fluently and cut a dashing figure with the best looks that both nations' breeding could offer. Dark hair and eyes, strong chiselled face, tanned skin and a slim, sporty physique.

Ed had taken up a career in management consulting and after several stints with some of the top London firms, he found a reason to give his loyalty to a new, fast-rising consulting firm. He'd fallen for the company's boss and with his good looks and charm, eventually won over this powerful, single woman and they became lovers. Neither was looking to get married, but maybe one day this was on the cards for them. They remained discreet and professional at work, but a few of the senior staff knew they were together.

His mother's maiden family name was Lamfilata, which originated from two names of their ancestors, Lama Affilata, meaning sharp blade. Included on their family crest were two stiletto daggers. Ed's grandfather had an impressive collection of many historic and rare knives from over the centuries, owned and apparently used by their family.

Stilettoes were originally fixed bladed, long pointed daggers. Over the years they were refined to include sprung-loaded blades that flicked out of the handle side, flick-knives, and also the more modern, deadly straight-out switchblades. Ed had adopted his grandfather's interest in knives and eventually, the temptation of wanting to use these beautiful weapons became too much to resist. He now relished the occasional challenge to perform with his stiletto for the woman he loved, or rather her brother.

Rob Malony had done well. He was a corporate raider and had made hundreds of millions with hostile takeovers, buy-outs and boardroom manoeuvres. He had an eye for seeing through company accounts and director's spin and was able to spot how companies could be tweaked, stripped and repackaged, to make money. A lot of money.

Part of his success had been the consulting firm he'd always used to help with his nefarious corporate schemes. He would utilise their skilled management workforce to swoop in and do his bidding, stripping, firing, rebranding and selling off assets.

He'd been happy to use company money which could be offset against tax, to pay the premium consulting rates this firm charged, knowing he would get a separate bonus share at a later date by involving them.

But Rob now felt he was putting too much business this firm's way and not getting enough of a reward in return. He'd spoken to their boss, but in some way, this man was also *his* boss. For many years ago Rob had joined this other man's particular organisation and promised his loyalty for consulting contracts in return for bonuses generated by others like him doing the same.

The conversation hadn't gone well as Rob had been reminded of how he'd been helped to become so successful and the deal they struck years ago. Rob's ego was bigger now and he was too used to getting his way in business.

They'd fallen out, maybe only temporarily, but the other man had given Rob a couple of days to come to his senses. Rob wasn't feeling inclined to bow down and knew he should make the call to insist on greater rewards.

His chauffeur slowed the gleaming black Mercedes-Maybach and pulled up at 89 Pall Mall. Rob finished a business call and stepped out from the luxury of the back of the prestigious two-hundred-thousand-pound limo. His bodyguard Jones had already got out of the front passenger seat and was on the pavement waiting for him.

Years of unpopular business deals, arguments and firing senior directors had built up quite a list of influential businessmen lining up to see his decline, or even demise. He'd never actually been attacked, but he could easily afford someone like Jones to protect him, besides it looked good having a bodyguard.

They went into the private member's establishment, the Royal Automobile Club, this being their London building, along with another country estate at Woodcote Park Epsom.

The club was founded back in 1897 and has become a prestigious organisation open to most people to be proposed and seconded to join. Events centre around automobiles, racing, sports, golf and entertaining. The Pall Mall site offers members accommodation, a gym, squash, snooker, Turkish baths, pool and restaurants including the Great Gallery with its iconic classical interior.

Most days Rob held a meeting here at one PM over lunch and so would arrive at about twelve-thirty to have his regular pre-lunch swim. This helped to clear his mind of the fast-paced and often contentious morning and reset for the afternoon's dealings. It was a ritual.

Rob dialled the other man he wanted more from as he walked through the hall onto the spa area. The line picked up.

"Listen, I've been considering everything and how much

business I'm bringing to the organisation," said Rob hiding his nerves behind the pretence of rushing somewhere. "I know I'm contributing more than others, so I must ask you to give me a bigger share in return?" The line remained silent. "Hello, are you there?"

The strong voice spoke calmly. "Yes, I heard you, though I'm not liking what you're suggesting. We take account of what each brother contributes to the greater cause and bonuses are apportioned accordingly. That is why you get more than others, it's entirely fair."

"Well not for me, I want more," insisted Rob, getting carried away with his forced bravado. "I'm going to have to look at using another consulting firm if that's the case."

"That's not what you and I agreed, you know we can't allow that. I'm not one of your business deals where you think it's acceptable to renegotiate terms or renege on an agreement!"

"Well I won't be pushed around either, That's it, we'll draw a line under our arrangement and have nothing more to do with one another, fine by me!" snapped Rob.

Just before Rob hung up, he caught the other man parting with, "As you wish, we'll draw a line under this."

"No one holds me to ransom," fretted Rob to his bodyguard. Jones nodded back obligingly as they entered the pool area.

Moments later Eduardo's mobile buzzed. He picked it up with a tinge of excitement and read the text that said simply, 'You're on'!

Eduardo already had his swimming shorts on so made his way out to the large twenty-six-metre long, six-lane wide swimming pool, heated to a comfortable twenty-eight degrees. Situated just below the ground floor of the huge RAC building, the pool was lined with Grecian features and pillars, with an impressively high ceiling.

Eduardo had been swimming at this pool for the last few days, at precisely twelve forty, to coincide with Rob Malony's regular visits. Both Rob and Jones the bodyguard had already become accustomed to this other member, swimming his lengths at the same time, then doing their final length underwater back to the changing rooms.

For the visits to the RAC, Eduardo had been adorning himself with a false thick beard and bluish contact lenses for an eye colour change, along with dull, unremarkable dark-grey swimming shorts. His equally false temporary membership pass and lack of CCTV cameras at the private club, would all make identifying him later near impossible.

Rob came out to the pool and dived in straight away to start doing lengths, watched by Jones who stood on the far side of the pool midway, watching his boss less acutely. After all, no one could get near him while he was in the large pool. He could see just three other swimmers, including the chap that always seemed to be here at this time.

After ten minutes of swimming lengths, Rob had a final part of his calm-down routine that he always did. He waved at Jones, who grabbed the inflatable lilo beside him and threw it into the pool by his boss. Rob always ended his pool session with five minutes of meditation on his lilo in the centre of the pool, a bizarre ritual that other members had to ignore and swim around.

There was now only Eduardo and one other swimmer, along with Rob in the middle. Eduardo finished his penultimate length and started to take deep breaths at the far end to get the air into his lungs and bloodstream. Jones looked over to him, but was used to this man's procedure, thinking, 'God why do they all have to stick with the same routine every day!'.

Rob was floating in the centre with his eyes shut and the other swimmer started another length from the opposite end of the pool, in the lane between Jones and his boss. The disturbance in the water would prevent Jones from seeing into the pool below his boss.

Eduardo took in a deep breath and went under, pushing off

strongly from the end. Keeping his eyes open he hugged the bottom of the pool, his chest brushing the mosaic tiles as he went.

He ascended slightly as he approached the underneath of the lilo floating above him. He now grasped the handle of his stiletto concealed in a crotch pocket between his legs. He adjusted himself under water, to keep up his forward momentum, so the bodyguard would see him continuing past the lilo.

Then as he came directly under the long float, he positioned the stiletto's handle between two of the pillows of air and pressed the button.

The long blade shot up through the plastic beading seal between the pockets of air without piercing either of them. Eduardo's aim had been precise, the blade tip speared Rob's heart instantly killing him. The blade retracted back into its handle as Eduardo swam on, beyond the underneath of the lilo.

Jones watched momentarily as the other member swam under his boss as he always did, constantly moving along beneath the undulating water's surface, as the other swimmer passed by. He thought he noticed Rob give a minuscule flinch, but it was nothing, perhaps he'd just dropped off and was having a dream. Rob appeared to remain quietly at ease with the world, his eyes shut.

Eduardo reached the other end, exited the pool and within three minutes had left the building.

After another three minutes, Jones was wondering if he should wake his moody boss to remind him of the one PM lunch meeting. 'Nah, he's still got time to change, I'll leave it a while longer' he thought, putting off disturbing the man.

At five-to-one Jones softly and but firmly called to Rob. "Boss? Boss!"

Rob didn't move a muscle. Jones strained his gaze at Rob's chest just to check he was indeed still breathing, then realised he couldn't see any movement. He now felt vindicated in waking him and shouted this time. "Boss, Rob, Sir!"

Jones felt sick. Had something happened? He jumped into the pool, swam to the lilo and shook Rob. He noticed blood trickling into the pool off the end of the lilo.

Pandemonium ensued, shouting, dashing around, hauling him out, blood everywhere, waiting, police and ambulance arriving. It was chaos.

An unidentified RAC member had apparently stabbed Rob Malony, but would never be found. The pool had to undergo a full chlorine shock and cleansing procedure, at the insistence of the board of directors and for a while, a full-time lifeguard was employed at the pool to appease members. A metal detector was installed in the entrance, but soon removed again after complaints from the club's old guard that it infringed their privacy. The RAC's PR machine barely blinked, no mention of the crime appeared in any newsletters and within a few weeks, the scandalous murder was brushed over and forgotten at the famous club.

The Met police added the case to their growing list of unsolved, open murder inquiries. With it involving the death of a seemingly run-of-the-mill asset-stripping businessman, no one ever thought to share the suspect case with MI5.

When Max returned to MI5's Thames House he told Si Lawson all about his trip to Venice and the home of Thomas Appleby, with its mysteriously preserved basement room, loyally protected by the caretaker.

Si immediately asked Vince his deputy to do more digging on Thomas Appleby and what happened to him in Venice and after he left that house in 1835

"There's definitely something going on here, but I can't quite make the connection yet, other than Durham and Appleby both left the masons," said Si. "What do you have on the strange murals on the cavern walls?"

"Unfortunately, I didn't take any pictures as I was

interrupted by this Claudio fellow," replied Max, "but I've sketched them out." He showed Si his drawing. "After a bit of research, I'm clear about what it's portraying, at least most of it anyway."

"Fire away then?" said Si eagerly.

"The ancient civilisations like the Romans worshipped many Gods, and one of them was Pluto, God of wealth. In Greece, he was also known as Hades, God of the underworld, where at the time most things of value came from. Precious metals, stones and the like, all came from the ground," explained Max. "They would even bang on the ground when kneeling and praying to Hades, believed to be living beneath them, to attract his attention."

"So the figure on the end wall was Hades?" checked Si pointing to the sketch.

"Right. The unseen God, God of wealth. Eldest son of the Titans, Cronus and Rhea. Hades over-threw his father with his brothers Zeus and Poseidon, then divided up the world between them, earth, sky and sea respectively. Hades ruled the underworld with his wife Persephone, with the help of his three-headed dog Cerberus."

"So this is them standing on all their riches, in the picture?" observed Si.

"Indeed. And Hades has with him two other symbols of power from the Gods, his helmet of invisibility, or helm of darkness and also his bident, the two-pronged spear."

"And the trident went to his brother Poseidon," chimed in Si proudly. Pointing to the picture again, "So this part of the mural must be the boatman part?"

"You've got it," confirmed Max, "this is the River Styx which separates Hades' underworld with that of the living. Not to be confused with beliefs about Hell, dead souls..."

They both looked at one another at the mention of the word 'souls'. Max went on.

"Dead souls would have to pay Charon the ferryman for Hades, to cross the Styx and reside with Hades and untold riches forevermore."

Si clenched his fist. "Souls! This book of souls that Durham mentioned. It's gotta be related hasn't it!"

Max was also keen to add, "And that coin Durham had, wasn't that an obolus, a really old Greek coin, something to pay the ferryman perhaps, or at least a symbol for it?"

They knew they were onto something now.

"And the other wall, what's that about then?"

"Not sure yet," said Max. "It looks like it's portraying an alternative path to the route to Hades, with less riches and death at the end for those who don't worship him and do his bidding, like a warning. Don't know?"

Vince came rushing over, looking very pleased with himself.

"Hey guys, I think I've come up with a couple more pieces to your jigsaw puzzle. Boss, you asked me to check more on Thomas Appleby." Si nodded. "Well, he owned both his Richmond London house, and the house in Venice, until 1835, so I tried to find out what he did then. He dropped off the radar until I checked who he sold his London home to that year."

"Well?" said Max eagerly.

Vince continued. "He didn't disappear. It seems in 1835 Thomas Appleby returned to London, but he didn't sell his house on, he simply changed the name on his house deeds, to his own new name. For some reason or other, at the same time, he'd changed his surname."

"What to?"

"He became… Thomas Brookshaw!"

The penny immediately dropped. "Oh my God, it can't be. Brookshaw Consulting! That's the same firm the Gaslec procurement chap said he and Durham had used before."

Si was quickly on the same page. "So maybe this Brookshaw firm is a legacy of Thomas Appleby, or rather Thomas Brookshaw?"

"But how does that tie in with Hades and Durham's murder?" asked Vince.

"I'm not sure yet," pondered Si, then looking to Max, "but we need to have a look into this consulting firm, maybe pay them a visit, see if they're legit."

"Agreed!"

Across the office Alan, their technology geek was politely waving to get Vince's attention. Vince nodded back, then turned to Max.

"By the way Max, Alan's come up with a new upgrade for your mobile, it's on test so not yet officially approved, but we thought you might like to try it, you never know when these little techie gizmos will come in handy." Vince waved Alan over. "Alan, explain to Max will you?"

"I'll need your mobile for twenty minutes Max, got a new app for you I know you'll like," said Alan, waiting for Max to reciprocate his enthusiasm, which Max did willingly. Alan had helped him before on several cases, with his homemade gadgets and apps.

"So what does this one do?"

"Oh, it's brilliant Max. I call it HDC!" Alan then waited for the obvious question, revelling in the moment.

"And what the hell is that?"

"Hard drive copier!" Alan enthused. "It's amazing! You can copy the entire hard drive files off someone's PC!"

"How?"

"As long as they're logged into their system, you know the name of their PC's wifi network and you're within say twenty feet, my app infiltrates their system, then does an instant copy dump of everything on their hard drive, files only not programs. I'll have to increase your phone's memory. I've tried it out, actually works!" Alan explained excitedly, almost jumping for joy.

"You could make a fortune with that couldn't you?" joked Vince.

Si cut in. "Not something that will ever be commercially available I'm afraid Alan, too many copyrights, privacy and data protection laws, not to mention outright theft. No, this is just for us, on trial, but as Vince said, might be useful."

Max handed Alan his phone. "Sounds interesting, put it on!"

Max wanted to follow up on a hunch and see if the ownership of the Brookshaw Consulting firm might have any tie in with the Masons. He sat back at his desk and after a few select searches, found the details of the owners of Brookshaw Consulting. His heart sank when he saw that the UK Chief executive was a woman, listed as Gillian Brookshaw. Knowing that the Mason's only took in men, that put the notion that this led back to the famous society to rest. Reading on, Max found out that Brookshaw Consulting was founded by Gillian's father, Simon Brookshaw.

He could also see that Brookshaw Consulting was still privately owned and that it had a holding company called Headshell. This over-arching company was conveniently registered in St Kitts and Nevis, the Caribbean offshore tax haven, affording the owners extra layers of privacy and non-disclosure of accounts.

There was little information available on Headshell, but by trawling through google images, often a good way to lead to relevant articles less likely to be found, Max discovered that Headshell was headed up by one Brett Brookshaw!

Max put in a call to the Freemasons and asked to speak to his high-level contact there. Sir Philip came on the line.

"Max my boy, how's it going then?"

"Good thank you, Sir Philip. I wondered if I could impose on you once more, to look up a couple of other names in your register? Firstly a Simon Brookshaw, then a Brett Brookshaw?"

"Brothers eh? I'm actually near the archives room as it happens, let me pop along there and ask them, they'll find it much faster than me," offered Sir Philip setting off.

"Actually, Simon is the father, Brett the son," corrected Max.

"Right, hang on then." A few moments later Sir Philip

could be heard politely asking the girl in archives to look up the first name on her system.

"Well I never," exclaimed Sir Philip.

"What?" asked Max eagerly.

"Says here, Simon Brookshaw was a mason for some thirty years, up to his death five years ago. Poor chap was suspected to have committed suicide. But there's a flag in our notes against him."

"A flag for what?"

"Oh nothing much, we just keep file notes on anything out of the ordinary on all brethren, just observations and the like. It says, 'Simon tends to frequently raise the topic of mutual business opportunities, verbal reports indicate that some brothers have found such discussions uncomfortable, no formal complaints made. Simon has been building up his new consulting business. No action taken'."

"Interesting," noted Max.

"Well in defence, you're bound to be talking to your brothers about a new business venture, though to be clear the masons do not allow any kind of commercial favouritism or business dealing to be discussed at our meetings."

Max wondered to himself 'it's what happened outside of mason's meetings I'm more concerned about'.

"As you say, no action taken," allowed Max, "I'm sure it was all above board. Could you also look up his son, a Brett Brookshaw please?"

He heard Sir Philip prompt the girl at the archive's computer.

"Ah yes, here we are, Brett Brookshaw, yes he was a mason here for about ten years, then it looks like he went to America and joined the Grand Lodge of New York." Max heard Sir Philip talking to the girl at the desk. "What's that tab for young lady?"

The girl replied, "We've started sharing notes on brothers with international lodges Sir Philip. Someone else must have added something, let's have a look." She opened the hidden tab revealing a flag and notes entered by the Grand Lodge of New York.

Sir Philip read it out to Max. "Dated a few years back, it says, 'Following receipt of two anonymous complaints from GLNY brothers, citing being subjected to threatening business coercion offers, Brett Brookshaw has been suspended pending investigation and a disciplinary hearing by the Committee of Inquiry'!"

"Wow," commented Max, "that sounds pretty heavy?"

"It is," agreed Sir Philip, slightly perturbed, "a mason is then usually given the choice of a hearing, or they can resign."

Max picked up on a particular word. "You say 'usually' Sir Philip?"

"I've not seen this before," muttered the knight looking quizzically at the archive girl. "There's no mention of any board of inquiry being held, nor investigation, simply an update to the notes made six months ago."

"What does that say then?"

"Suspension lifted!"

7

Brett Brookshaw leaned back in his large armchair and looked out at the nearby Empire State Building, then across Lower Manhattan, where he had a modest apartment, to the World Trade Centre beyond. His offices on the fifty-seventh and fifty-eighth floors of the art deco Chrysler Building afforded him magnificent views of New York, which only true wealth could buy.

The decision was an easy one, but he made them wait, holding their attention, relishing the powerful grip he controlled over them.

Those in the room behind him remained silent, waiting for him to close the meeting with a final judgement, on the last agenda item they'd discussed. There were six of them, four men and two women. They sat on each side of the long dark wooden, highly polished meeting table, with their boss at the head.

"Alright, let's increase staffing by up to twenty per cent across Brookshaws' US and UK consulting divisions. Perry and Gillian, go ahead with the recruitment drives," instructed Brett. "Thank you all," he said, closing the meeting without turning his chair round.

"Brett, I'll call you back shortly," said the voice of his sister Gillian from the speakerphone.

Those in the room got up to leave and as Brett now swung round to usher them out with an engaging nod and smile, their faces lit up once more as their emotions danced to his behest.

He exuded unwavering confidence and determination. He was a man others found easy to follow, or be persuaded by. Brett had always had the gift to lead and convince people. With the combination of sharpness of mind and intellect, impeccable grasp of the English language and vocabulary, and the looks of a hardened warrior, he was someone you'd follow into battle no matter what.

He was six foot tall with a strong, robust physique that filled out his black, tailored suit and crisp white, open shirt. His skin appeared slightly weathered and rugged for someone who hadn't hit fifty. Wavy, brown hair with a matching tightly trimmed beard, framed dark eyes capable of portraying the full spectrum of emotions and control he used every day. Some had said his gaze was truly mesmerising, that it held you until he was ready to let you go again.

Brett's office held an eclectic mix of artefacts and pictures, amongst which was an ornate sword resting on a display stand within a casing. Once owned by a ronin Samurai whose master was killed. His expert swordsmanship came to the attention of the one-hundredth Emperor of Japan, Go-Komatsu, who ruled from 1382 to 1392. The Samurai then became the Emperor's top assassin and bodyguard. Brett won the sword at a Sotheby's auction for half a million dollars. It was just something he was drawn to having to own.

Pictures and prints surrounded the boardroom table and his desk at one end, among which included a smaller framed painting in one corner, barely noticeable. Painted in 1550 by an Italian artist, it depicted a man half-swathed in linen, sitting on a marble seat. He's grasping a two-pronged staff and has a small helmet crown on his head. The other arm is held out as if beckoning towards something out of frame, likely his wife Persephone and behind him in the dark background, feint figures are depicted of people kneeling and lying down in worship to him.

A passer-by would guess the understated picture to be a photographic reproduction, possibly of some mythical deity, and certainly not the three-million-dollar original masterpiece it truly was, of the God Hades.

Brett grew up with his younger sister Gillian and had a privileged childhood, but one with constant opposing forces. His mother was a doting, loving and carefree woman, wanting to spoil her children and give them praise for anything half worthy of adulation. Whilst Simon his father was a strict disciplinarian, with any resemblance of praise being metered out with only the best, winning performances, for both physical and academic achievements.

Whilst his parents loved one another, their polar opposite views had a deep effect on the young Brett, who struggled to adjust to their differing barometers of life, reward and expectations. It was this that brought out Brett's resolve to create his own success and control those who might judge him.

During his teens, Brett attended Tonbridge School in Kent, an expensive choice which his father believed provided the very best of starts for his son. It did, but the boys boarding college gave Brett more of a proving ground to start honing his manipulation skills. Whilst he was handy at both sports and academics, he was not the top sportsman, an accolade that usually went hand in hand with being the most popular boy as well. But where Brett may have just fallen short in sports, he made up for with his consuming personality, gathering followers across the school as pupils became indoctrinated with his confidence and persuasion.

After college Brett attended Exeter University studying Business and Psychology, for him a powerful combination that would further enhance his valuable skillset. He spent a year on exchange at the University of California Los Angeles, which sparked his love of America, vowing one day to take full advantage of 'the land of opportunity'!

Brett then followed his father into both the Freemasons and the management consulting world. Although Simon was establishing his own consulting firm, he urged his son to gain experience with another big provider, so Brett joined one of the top global consulting firms where he learnt about the workings of such a business, from within.

He learnt very quickly that whether at college or work, most people by nature just want to be told what to do. They seek an inspiring, confident, strong leader they can follow and benefit from their reflected glory and status. But even those few alpha-types Brett found he could usually persuade to join him, or just occasionally when required, help push in the right direction.

He'd use promises of future promotion to rise above any doubters. Sayings were used like 'you're either in the boat, my boat, or you're sinking in the sea, which is it?'. And for one particularly troublesome combatant who simply wouldn't relent to Brett's efforts and was starting to cause problems, decisive treatment was required.

By chance one day Brett found himself with access to this colleague's laptop, unbeknown to anyone else. It took him just thirty seconds to draft a time-tagged email to the whole department from him saying simply 'This company treats us like crap!' Once Brett had left the area and the delayed email got sent, his nemesis was believed to have communicated this awful message to over sixty staff including his managers. The damage was done and despite strenuous, bewildered denials, the man was dismissed for gross misconduct and bringing the firm into disrepute.

The huge international consulting firm provided a networking paradise for Brett, who greedily added contacts, favours and prestige to his personal portfolio, calling in markers at strategic moments. His influence started to extend across their client base and when Brett found he was beginning to push business awards and contracts for consulting his way, he was further spurred on.

Equally his venture into the seemingly clandestine world of the Freemasons provided an equally attractive networking opportunity for Brett. Once he realised that he wasn't having to compete with other power-hungry stars and that the masons were indeed an upstanding organisation, he felt it was open hunting season. He saw the rules of 'no talking business', 'no favouritism in dealings' and 'no personal financial betterment' as mere challenges and tantalising temptations. The bountiful, wide-reaching and often prestigious crop of people within the masons, pillars of society and business, was simply too much to be wasted.

Brett had on too many occasions painfully watched his father Simon awkwardly suppressing his desire to use his masonic contacts for his advantage. He once challenged him on this after witnessing him miss another business deal that would have helped his Brookshaw Consulting company.

"Dad, that guy was ready to be nudged the right way and give you a consulting contract, it just needed a little push and a deal could've been closed with him?" suggested Brett.

His father looked embarrassed at being scolded by his son in business matters. "How dare you! You're in no position to give me advice, that's not the way things are done here in the masons." Then he uttered a challenge that would change everything. "If you think you can do any better, then go ahead smartass!"

Later that evening Brett had a long, calm chat with his father and agreed now was the time to leave his consulting firm and join the family business, Brookshaw Consulting!

Brett persuaded his father that a little business discussion was only natural at such masonic meetings, and that surely if all things are equal when awarding deals, it must be better to favour a fellow mason and 'keep it withing the family' so to say!

Slowly but surely, Simon Brookshaw began using his position within the masons, to at least explore business dealings, when such opportunities presented themselves. He never overstepped the mark though and whilst a couple of high integrity masons mentioned it to their Grand Master and a file note was made, nothing overtly untoward was ever proven.

Brett, however, was bolder in exploring opportunities with

anyone, be they masons or not. Now firmly ensconced within the consulting firm carrying his name, he also started to harvest the bountiful contacts with influence within his masonic circles.

As always, people were charmed by his captivating gravitas, which lent itself nicely to him progressing through the freemasons ranks quickly. If a mason that he was grooming backed off, Brett had the social skills to cover it over and befuddle the other man into thinking he was just imagining it and that Brett would never dishonour the masonic core principles.

Then Simon succumbed to one of those TV ads enticing you to go online and find out more about your ancestry and where you came from. He bought an initial report which the ancestry company generated mainly using their computer's algorithmic searches of many databases of genealogy, births, deaths and marriages.

Simon was intrigued to discover that he was the great-great-grandson of their family tree's first recorded ancestor, a Thomas Brookshaw, from 1836. He eagerly relayed all this to his son Brett, who was curious as to why they could only go back a hundred and eighty-odd years. He then took it upon himself to dig some more. He wanted to surprise his father with more historical information about their ancestry, so paid the online firm to perform a premium search for more information, which was handled personally by one of their in-house experts.

After a few weeks, Brett was rewarded with a new report, part of which had identified that Thomas Brookshaw was, in fact, the newly changed name of a certain Thomas Appleby. It also mentioned that this person lived in London, was known to be a 'business trader' and spent some years in Venice, before returning to London where he died.

The mention of 'trader' and 'Venice' hooked Brett into wanting to find out more, but the online ancestry firm said they had exhausted their research capabilities and glibly suggested that Brett employ a specialist private investigator. So that's what Brett did.

It took them much longer than it took the influential MI5, but after seven months of digging, researching, emailing and calling, the investigator finally discovered where Thomas Appleby lived in Venice.

Brett travelled to the iconic 'City on the Water' and upon enquiring at the house of his ancestor, was welcomed in by an elderly widow, to have a look around. It was then that he cast eyes on the walls of the shrine cavern and dock in the basement.

They were only in the neglected boathouse for a minute, but as luck would have it, that was all that was needed for Brett to notice one tiny inscription on the wall. Almost hidden in one corner of the pictures in front of them, in painted writing, were the words, 'Piero Jilani per Tommaso 1819'!

Brett later found out that Piero was the artist of the murals, but immediately knew that 'per Tommaso' was Italian, meaning 'for Thomas'. With the date coinciding with the time he knew his ancestor lived here, he struggled to hide his excitement from the old woman.

Revisiting her the following day before departing, he poured praise onto her home and said that having fallen in love with the house, offered to buy it off her at a premium, with the agreement that she would have the money now and be free to live there until her passing.

The old lady willingly took Brett's money and divided it up amongst her five surprised but incredibly grateful children. Not only did they get their inheritance early, whilst their dear mother was still alive to see them enjoy it, but also an instant sale of the property well above market price.

Brookshaw Consulting was storming across the UK consulting world snapping up contracts, not only through natural expansion and hard work, but also helped by Brett's sister Gillian joining the firm, bringing yet more business experience. But also in no small part due to Brett's influence and a plethora of willing contacts lining up to impress and favour him and his company over the bigger names competing for most contracts.

Simon Brookshaw eventually retired after his wife passed away and Brett took over the firm. His plan was to pass leadership of the well-established UK business over to Gillian, leaving him free to mirror their company's exploits and development across the pond in America.

After the Venetian widow died passing the house onto Brett, he escorted his elderly father on what would be their last overseas trip together, to Venice. Simon was getting old and frail, so Brett asked Gillian to come as well and between them, they could chaperone their father for this final excursion.

They spent a day taking Simon around the famous landmarks of Venice, along with a boat tour and gondola ride. Then Brett took his father and sister to the empty house at Calle Drio la Chiesa Street. After a walkaround, during which his visitors were growing increasingly suspicious about why they'd been brought there, Brett took them down to the basement.

As Simon and Gillian gazed upon the dusty old murals on the wall of the cavern, Brett enthusiastically told them more about their ancestor Thomas Appleby and that this was where he lived while trading away from London, in the merchant's city on the water.

"He would have used this boathouse to receive shipments of the goods he was trading," said Brett. "But I also think this waterway was used for indoctrinating his followers. It was his version of the River Styx, where fellow traders would come to be sworn into his organisation."

Simon and Gillian looked at one another as they tried to make sense of Brett's imaginary deductions, but he was convincing, given the evidence.

"Look here," enthused Brett pointing at the murals' signature. "The artist has signed it 'for Thomas' and dated it when our ancestor lived here. One wall depicts those traders who are true and proper in their dealings, but with only small wealth and trappings, forsaking the alternative way."

Gillian then pointed to the other wall, "This way here?"

"Yes, these traders are using their connections to gain more wealth and more deals. They are following the path set out by Thomas Appleby and what I believe to be the secret business organisation he set up!"

"In worship of this character here," noted his father looking upon the figure shown on the end wall.

"Pluto, the Roman God of wealth and riches," announced Brett proudly. "Also known to the Greeks as Hades, God of the underworld. See here, this is Charon the ferryman, taking souls, in this case, Thomas' followers, across the River Styx to the kingdom of Hades, where they have untold riches!"

"So this is why you've brought us here is it?" asked his father.

"Yes Dad, isn't it incredible, this was our ancestor's house, where he ran his wealth creation organisation. A secret business cult perhaps. I've always told you to use your contacts more. Thomas Appleby was doing just that almost two hundred years ago Dad. I thought you'd be pleased about me finding all this out for you. I've bought this house for us, it's ours now, it's back in the family!"

Simon sighed. "I think you're letting your imagination run amok, son."

Gillian however was more inclined to appreciate what Brett had said. "It does kinda make sense Dad. It may well be that Thomas Brookshaw, Appleby whatever, was signing up his business connections with influence, with this basement shrine to perform some little induction ceremony, using the Hades legend to build the order around. A memorable focus for them. You've always told us how important 'the brand' is in business."

Simon shook his head, made for the steps and left the room, leaving a dejected Brett staring at the walls with his sister.

"I get it," consoled Gillian, "don't mind Dad, that was all a lot for him to take in, leave it for now eh? Great holiday house we can use."

Back home in England, Brett formed his intentions over the next six months and was determined to win over his father and impress him. He wanted one last nod of appreciation from the old man.

Visiting him one evening, they sat by the fire after dinner and Brett pitched his plans to follow in the footsteps of their ancestor Thomas Appleby. He was going to set up a secret business sect. One where favouritism and financial gain were underpinned by the symbols of Hades.

The God's helmet of invisibility would stand for the absolute secrecy his organisation and members must adhere to. Hades' bident spear would signify unwavering determination and force of the sect. Cerberus, Hades' three-headed guard dog, would symbolise the need for guarding and protecting the Hades organisation from threats, both internal or external.

Brett took some of the rituals and use of symbols from his experience in the Freemasons. For example, they also have so-called guards at the doors of meetings, to protect members and ensure no one eavesdrops, called Tylers.

Where the masons had their trademark symbol of the set square and compass, Brett would use the invisibility helmet and bident, for his group of followers. He was also thinking of a symbolic object or token, a sign denoting membership. For this, he planned to buy at auction a hoard of ancient Greek coins recently discovered in the Thesprotia region where Hades was known to have been worshipped.

These obolus coins dated back to around 350BC, when it was believed people, or their souls, would use them to pay Charon the ferryman to get to Hades. There, they could live for eternity amongst his riches and avoid the lower underworld Tartarus, where the Gods imprisoned their enemies in a version of what is now referred to as 'hell'.

His father was horrified at Brett's revelations. He huffed and puffed his exasperation at the devious ideas his son was talking about.

"This is outrageous! You can't just set up some illegal, insider dealing business network, for self-gain!" he gushed, fighting back coughs and shortness of breath. "This has all gone too far, Brett! First the Venice house, now all this. I won't allow it, I won't allow you to ruin yourself and everything I've worked for. I can't have you running my company if this is how you intend to work! And the mason's need to know as well, this is against everything they stand for, it's an abuse of trust, power and the people you know!"

Brett was shocked at his father's outburst but quickly fought back.

"I don't understand? I just want you to be proud of me, you never have been, not really. Don't you see, by doing this I can catapult Brookshaw Consulting to become one of the top global management firms. We'll never do that just by natural growth, I want it faster Dad!"

"Not while I'm still breathing," argued Simon. "No, I'm still on the board of my company and you haven't got my shares yet. I must tell the others about this, raise a vote of no-confidence in you, you'll have to resign, and you won't be getting my shares, I'll change my will!"

The heated exchange paused for a moment, as both men bristled over what had been said.

"Get me another brandy," instructed Simon to his son, waving his empty glass at him.

As Brett took his glass and walked behind his father to the drink's cabinet, he noticed the packet of medication his father was on for his heart and other ailments. Suddenly he knew what had to be done. He simply couldn't allow his father to take everything away from him, it was all rightfully his now, the company, the chance to make something of it and unleash his uncanny powers of persuasion and influence.

The eight small tablets crumbled into a fine powder between his fingers and with a swirl of the brandy in the glass, dissolved and were gone.

As Brett handed the glass to his father, his mind was racing to gather together his thoughts on what would happen next. 'Keep it simple, keep it as near to the truth as possible' he told himself.

He had no idea what effect so many tablets would have on his father and as he sat there in silence with the old man, starting to wonder if anything would happen at all. He didn't have to wait long. After ten minutes his father became drowsy, mumbling, swaying in his chair. Then to Brett's horror, but also some relief, Simon slumped back and appeared to pass out. Brett waited a while and then got up to see if the old man was still breathing. He wasn't.

The onslaught of the controlled medication had been too much for Simon's body and heart to assimilate. It had caused him to drift into unconsciousness, then die of a heart attack.

Brett called Gillian who was highly distressed, jumped in her car and drove straight over. He also rang for an ambulance and in such circumstances the emergency services operator also summoned the police to attend the scene. When they all arrived, Simon Brookshaw was pronounced dead and one of the paramedics found the empty packet of medication on the table by the drinks unit. When asked what had happened, Brett put on an Oscar-worthy performance, which none of them had any reason to question.

"Oh my God, this is terrible! I shouldn't have left him. We'd fallen out over how the business should be expanded, and both got angry. I left the room to go to the loo, just as he said he needed another drink and had got up. When I came back in minutes later, I found him slumped in the chair!"

The medic held up the packet. "I'm sorry sir, it looks like your father took an overdose of his meds in his drink, probably caused him to have a heart attack!"

8

Brett's phone rang, it was Gillian calling back after the board meeting. She'd been biting her tongue during the call with the others and he knew she wasn't happy.

"Finally, I've got you to myself," she huffed. "What the hell are you doing giving Eduardo instructions to..." she paused wanting to choose her words carefully, "...cancel two of my memberships here in the UK?" referring to David Durham and Rob Malony's murders.

"Calm down, I know what I'm doing," said Brett assertively. "If you'll allow me to explain."

"This I must hear! You've gone too far Brett, it's crossing the line, what if it comes back to you, to us!"

"It won't, Eduardo as you know better than anyone, is completely reliable and dedicated to you, so therefore to me as well. He assures me they were entirely clean jobs, no come-back."

"That's not fair, you're using him like you always use people!" Gillian immediately regretted saying that.

"You, I will allow making that remark," replied Brett quietly.

Gillian knew only too well that her brother lowered his voice when he was actually getting angry at something.

"Sorry!"

"Both of those members were threatening to leave the organisation and renege on one of our most sacrosanct vows, that of absolute secrecy. They could have jeopardised everything we have. With us in charge, this firm has enormous potential, huge, and will be *the* most powerful consulting firm in the world within a decade. Our network of influential people continues to grow each month."

"But surely they could have been talked round, persuaded, you're good at that!"

"I'd suggested meeting up to both of them, but misplaced bravado had taken hold of them. We can't have members breaking the rules, examples had to be set, for others!"

Gillian sighed in resignation. She never had the energy to argue with her older brother for too long, so always ended up deferring to his will.

Brett changed the subject.

"How are you getting on with that potential new recruit, the young chap that worked with David Durham?"

"Ah yes, by chance I've got one of my best girls on the case, Lisa Ely. They met before when Brookshaw's consulted for them and have had a few dates already."

"And is he still heading for that key job we spoke about?"

"Yup, in fact, I gather it's all done and dusted, he'll probably be starting next week."

"Excellent, I like the sound of him, bit of a shifty character, slippery, but will come in handy. Are you confident he'll join us? Probably needs to be sooner rather than later."

"I'll have a word with Lisa to get on and bring him into the fold," agreed Gillian.

"Great."

Brett's office glass side door opened cautiously and his assistant Sarah looked round the door to check she could interrupt. Brett waved her in whilst ending the call with Gillian, "Gotta go, keep me updated, bye."

"Brett, I've got a Brandon Cuffney in reception, ten minutes early, shall I ask him to wait?"

Brett stood up, "No, I'm free now, ask him to come through thank you, Sarah, ask if he wants a coffee, I'll have one of my protein drinks."

She disappeared, then moments later returned with his visitor and the drinks on a tray. Brett was always amazed at how fast she made the beverage orders, whether it was for just himself or an entire room full.

Brett greeted him, "Brandon, let's sit over here in the comfy chairs."

Brandon was your typical American college quarterback jock, sporty, a bit of a lad, one of the boys. The teenage buzzcut had long since been brushed down with a side-parting in an attempt to look more professional and serious. He wore a grey suit that was slightly too small for his frame and whilst accentuating some of his bulges, also looked a bit silly, with the bottom hems of his trouser legs half an inch too high.

"I was surprised to get your call, so soon after our little ceremony the other night. I don't usually encourage too much face-to-face interaction where possible."

"Understood, but this is something I had to meet you personally about," said Brandon nervously.

"So you said on the phone, I'm intrigued?"

Brandon looked around to check that the office door was fully closed and took a deep breath.

"Gosh, where do I start. Firstly apologies for surprising you like this, but just let me explain, please hear me out okay?"

"Jesus Brandon, you're starting to worry me, what on earth's this about for crying out loud?" Brett put down his drink and now gave Brandon's twitching eyes his full attention.

"I appreciate being inducted into the organisation, that's all good and I want to do more for you."

Brett added, "You've already helped us secure that massive consulting contract using your influence in the US Department of Agriculture. So?"

"Well, I haven't been entirely open with you Brett. I do indeed work for the US Government, but not with Agriculture. I'm afraid that was a cover, painstakingly constructed to satisfy all your checks on me."

"What! So who do you work for?" asked Brett, his tone more serious.

Now it was Brandon who with a hint of confidence belying

what he was about to impart, looked straight back into Brett's commanding eyes.

"I work for the CIA!"

Brett was speechless. Completely floored. His face changed as he gritted his teeth, and his eyes became even more piercing. Brandon feared what he might do next so quickly explained.

"Listen, Brett, just listen, it's all okay. Right at the beginning of this assignment, the intention was to infiltrate your, shall we say, cult, and find out what you were up to. We'd had rumblings that some business networking sect was operating and influencing big consulting deals, favouring Brookshaw's. No evidence, so no big team, just me and my Director in the know."

Brett maintained his laser-like stare at Brandon. "Go on! This had better put my mind at ease!"

"Now that I'm part of your club, and having gone through your indoctrination ceremony, well, I've had a long talk with my boss, and we want to work with you, not against you."

Brett's demeanour relaxed just enough for Brandon to notice he had perhaps turned the corner and was beginning to reassure his Grand Master.

"You have done an impressive job building up an enviable following of strong contacts across business, government, industry and the like. It seems a waste for us to come in, make a load of arrests, disband the sect and your company. So much potential would be lost," pitched Brandon, building up to the big offer.

"What does the mighty and dare I say somewhat dubious CIA want then?"

Brandon felt the door had just been opened. At least Brett wanted to hear him out. But there again, he'd probably already worked out that he didn't have much choice.

"Whilst we won't be able to give you any more contracts, the Agriculture deal was a one-off, in return for not throwing the book at you, we're interested to learn more about your more senior members with influence, those who are in one particular operational sphere."

Brett knew the pitch well, set the ground rules, drop in a threat, then make the ask.

"What sphere?"

"Foreign governments! Specifically, the British government!"

Brett was flabbergasted at the proposal.

"You're kidding! Oh my God, you want to use my brothers, our brothers, given you're in with us, to spy?"

"That's about the crux of it. Yes!"

"The British though! What about this *special* relationship we all keep harking on about? Why would you need to spy on us Brits?" queried Brett, coming from England himself.

"Things change, you Brits still have huge influence and power on the world stage. Amazing frankly, for such a small island! We feel a bit of additional intel on what our *partners* are up to can only help oil the wheels eh. And your so-called special relationship only goes back to the days of Maggie and Ronald. So what do you say?"

"You're asking me to possibly betray my country?"

"In return for allowing you to continue with your illegal Hades sect, yes."

"I'll need to think about this," squirmed Brett.

"By all means, I can wait. I can't leave without an answer. Let's face it, it's not a hard decision."

Brett wasn't used to being put under pressure by anyone, least of all one of his supposed followers. He started towards Brandon as if intending to take him on.

Brandon quickly raised both hands up. "I'm CIA in case you've forgotten, I can have twenty agents up here in a flash, then it's all over for you, no more options."

"And only you and your boss know about this?" checked Brett.

Brandon nodded. "Once we start providing any worthwhile intel, my Director will then have some chips to play with at the big table, that's what he needs to protect you and this arrangement from further scrutiny."

Brett sighed. "Okay!"

"Wonderful," said Brandon, relieved the ordeal was over. "Can you now tell me what potential members you already have in positions that might interest us?"

Brett frowned, reticent to give up such valuable information.

"I do have one person that will meet your expectations, however, I'd need to think about how we set them up to start sharing such sensitive information. I'd want to prep them myself, I wouldn't want anyone else being involved in this. They're pretty high up."

"How high up?" inquired Brandon eagerly.

"A minister in the Cabinet! So about as high up as you could get!"

Lisa Ely was a senior consultant at Brookshaw's and had known Gillian since they were at college together. Her boss had called her earlier and asked for a certain deal she was working on, to now be finalised. This wasn't a consulting contract though. This particular deal was about recruiting someone, bringing them into the fold. Something Lisa had already done once before and received a sizeable bonus for.

Not only was Lisa a clever, discerning and persuasive young lady, but she also had a weapon of influence whenever she needed to press home her advantage. She had what men had told her was the optimum mix of beauty, combined with a flirty, open allure conveying 'I'm yours'! Few men could resist her charms. She'd been seeing someone for a couple of weeks, flirting, teasing and allowing some tantalising foreplay, but his pleas for more had been pushed aside.

With her new instructions, she'd decided that tonight was his lucky night. She would give herself over to him, but only in return for something big... his integrity!

The doorbell rang of her plush apartment near Putney Bridge. She could see him on the videophone and buzzed him through, adding, "Come straight up darling."

The table was laid for the two of them and plenty of wine was on hand. She deliberately wanted to have him survey the goods on offer for most of the evening. She wore a stunning, tight off the shoulder dress with a slit down the side, which whenever she moved, revealed the tiniest of knickers and her long, smooth legs and bare feet. Her attire, charm, flirting and just the right amount of alcohol, would have him literally begging for the bedroom prize later on.

On her way to answer the door, she started the hidden camera recording device.

She greeted him with a lingering kiss straight off, moving his hands down to her bottom, a teasing taster, Then before he knew it, she pulled away and led him inside, allowing him to take in all the curves and imagine what could be if he could get her to make love to him.

Wine glasses were poured, more in his, and they chatted and flirted while she finished preparing the dinner. She led him over to the table, constantly fussing, touching, dropping innuendos, leading him on.

They enjoyed smoked salmon with capers and finely chopped onion for starters, followed by a delicious creamy fish pie, with large prawns, scallops and cod chunks, with accompanying vegetables. The wine flowed and he became more and more pliable, like putty in her hands.

"So you're starting your new job on Monday, how exciting, you are clever," she said, but then sighed.

"What's the matter?" he asked, suddenly terribly concerned. He didn't want anything to ruin the moment.

Lisa should have been a Hollywood movie star. "Oh, it's nothing really, bit awkward, nah, just forget it."

He instantly took the bait. "No, come on, what is it, tell me?"

"It's just that I've been working on a pitch for a big

contract for my firm and I'm worried that if we don't win it, I might be asked to leave! It's a really big deal."

"Well, who's this deal with?"

"That's the awkward bit," she paused for effect, "it's with your new organisation!"

"Oh, I see."

"I don't want there to be any problems for you. I guess because you've dealt with Brookshaw's in previous roles, they may ask you to exclude yourself from the final decision?"

"They wouldn't do that," he contested, bravado kicking in. "I'll be running the procurement function there, so I'll have a big say in who gets the award."

"Oh would you," Lisa held his hand across the small table. "We'll probably win anyway, you know we always do a great job, but if you could make sure we get appointed, I'd be ever so grateful!" Her eyes ever so slightly flicked in the direction of the bedroom, just for a split second. He caught it.

"Leave it with me," he said, concentrating now not to slur his words. "I'll make sure you win it!"

"That would be wonderful! But I kinda feel you should be properly rewarded, not just being with me tonight, if you know what I mean. No, you deserve to be financially rewarded." She pressed for the kill. "I know how you could get hundreds of thousands of pounds out of it, into an offshore account. Would you be interested in that?" she teased.

She got up and pulled her chair round to sit next to him, her hands fussing around his face, head and shoulders.

He pondered for a moment through the haze of the wine and her distractions.

"Bloody right I would," he announced, "you've gotta grab these things when they're offered eh!"

"My thoughts exactly," she agreed, with more caressing down his chest.

"How does it work then?"

"I can get you invited into this secret business network. Members are all very influential people, like you. Everyone helps one another and the firm, Brookshaw's, to win contracts. And everyone then benefits from all the deals done by all members, and a few times a year, bonuses are paid out according to how much you help bring in."

She checked him and he looked keen, so pressed on. One of her hands got lower.

"Someone like you I reckon would earn maybe a million in the first year. A million pounds. Think what you could do with that! That would be impressive!"

He gazed into space imagining the money, then some part of his conscience stirred in him and he grabbed her hand now at his belt buckle.

"Hang on a minute." Lisa thought maybe he'd changed his mind. "What's the catch to all this?"

She kept control. "No catch. Once you're in the club, you keep putting business you're able to influence our way, for the rest of your career and take the payments. The only rules, which absolutely cannot be broken, ever, are that you maintain complete secrecy about the organisation you'll be joining, and you can never leave."

He seemed relieved. "So I don't have to kill anyone?" he said jokingly, relaxing again and taking his hand off hers to let her continue.

She now started undoing his trousers. "No of course not. Just help Brookshaw's get the deals, and take the money!"

"I'm in," he asserted, kissing her.

"Promise?" she checked. "No going back on this?"

"Promise. Set up the intro for me to join and don't worry about Brookshaw's winning at my new job, I'll make sure of that. Now let's go to the bedroom and celebrate?"

He rose and she let him lead her towards the large bed. She waited until they were settling down on the bed itself, before playing her final card. Holding his busy hands still for a moment, she whispered apologetically to him.

"We must have just one amazing night together. But it can only be the once!"

"What! How come?" he frowned, fighting back his frustration again.

"It's simply too risky for us to carry on seeing one another, you understand that don't you," pushed Lisa. "What with me at Brookshaw's and you awarding us contracts, there'd be an obvious conflict of interest between us, we could both lose our jobs. Not to mention we can't ruin the amazing opportunity you'll have with this new club you'll be in!"

He thought for a moment, taking in her words, knowing that Lisa was right. He was now torn between sacrificing a possible longer-term relationship with this attractive woman, which might in the end come to nothing, for finally having sex with her right now and untold riches by joining this club she'd talked about.

Lisa lifted up the bottom of her dress and pulled off her skimpy knickers. His mind was made up.

"I understand. But let's make the most of it for the rest of the night eh?"

"Whatever you say darling!" She lay back to enjoy the night ahead, knowing the tiny recording device was capturing everything. Just in case he had any change of mind in the future, the video would be used to remind him he was now committed to his side of the bargain.

Lisa would tell Gillian in the morning, their new recruit for the Hades sect was ready to be joined-up!

Joe Patterson felt he'd won again. He'd got the girl, and the cash!

9

Max took the five-minute London taxi from Millbank, north-west up Vauxhall Bridge Road, to the main offices of Brookshaw Consulting.

The four-storey building overlooked the entrance to Victoria station. Surrounded by newer blocks, the old façade looked out of place in the bustling transport hub district undergoing lots of modern construction.

Max checked in with reception and could see that all the floors of the building were occupied by Brookshaw Consulting. The lobby had a steady flow of keen young and older experienced management consultants and clients pouring past him as he waited in the corner seating area. Moments later a young woman emerged from the passing throng.

"Mr Sargent is it? I'm Penny, Gillian Brookshaw's PA, would you like to follow me and I can take you up to her offices?"

Max smiled as she pressed the fourth-floor button in the lift. 'It had to be the top floor for the boss' he mused. They exited and walked through a large open-plan office teaming with staff hot-desking for that day, waiting for meeting rooms to become vacant for their next urgent strategy discussion or presentation to clients. Towards the end, the openness crowded in with glass-walled offices for individual senior staff sitting at their desks. Max guessed correctly that they were heading to the largest office at the end.

Penny introduced Max to Gillian, then departed without offering any drinks, having been told by her boss not to bother on this occasion.

"Well Mr Sargent, this is a surprise," she opened with.

"MI5 Cyber indeed! Can't say I've ever met a real spy!"

"You probably have Ms Brookshaw, you just wouldn't have realised it," joked Max, trying to make light of the situation.

Gillian struck Max as a slightly unwilling executive, perhaps obliged to follow her father and brother into the business world. She was confident and professional, but probably only because she knew she had to be. It didn't seem as though she was naturally an extrovert leader, but simply knew what was expected of her and followed the 'top executive rulebook'.

In her early forties, she carried a slim figure, a bit too slim, caused by stress and worry from the huge role she filled and the expectations and antics of her older brother Brett. Her brown hair was meticulously styled short, for ease of maintenance, but looked impeccable and trendy.

Her blue-green eyes portrayed cautious wisdom unlikely to be easily impressed and her face showed signs of weary experience beyond her years. A smart blouse, jacket and pencil skirt only accentuated her apparent poor diet, or at least the infrequency of it often due to work commitments. She was long since married and divorced, and in her own words, had 'thankfully, no children'.

"Do you live in town?" asked Max, attempting to begin with some light chit chat.

Gillian betrayed a tiny sigh. Time was precious and she was awful at chit chat.

"Yes I do, well, that is I have a flat nearby, but my proper home is in Forest Row, down in Sussex. I can be there in an hour on the train, less in a car." Smiling she refocused the conversation. "So how on earth can I possibly help you?"

"Well, I can see you're very busy so if you don't mind me cutting to it…"

"Please do."

"It's about a David Durham. Do you know him?"

She gave a quizzical look and quickly replied. "Why yes,

we've dealt with him a few times I think. By that I mean he's used Brookshaw's. Heads up Gaslec doesn't he?" Max couldn't detect any anxiety from the cool woman in front of him.

"He did indeed, but he was recently murdered," Max imparted matter of factly.

"Oh my goodness, that's awful," she replied looking shocked. "Wouldn't that be a police matter, not MI5?"

"Normally yes, but when it involves such a key figure in charge of over a quarter of the UK's utilities, we get involved, you know, in case it's a terrorist threat or something. Did you meet him yourself?"

"I can't believe someone would want to kill him, such a nice man. Yes, I had dinner with him twice, both were after the tender process had been won by us, fair and square. Just to say thank you to him and his firm for putting their trust in our expertise."

"Were you involved in the courtship process?" Max clarified, "the pitch, to win the business?"

Gillian frowned at the use of the word 'courtship'. "No, I have plenty of great staff capable of handling pitches and tender responses. I try not to get too closely involved. Best to be whiter than white and all that," she said proudly.

"Do you have a gifts and hospitality policy here," asked Max out of the blue.

"That's a strange question from an MI5 officer?"

"I've had experience before in business and procurement. Do you then?"

"Yes of course. It includes all the usual things like only accepting gifts below fifty pounds value and registering them in a book with manager approval. We have a whistleblowing hotline and rule of nothing offered or accepted when chasing or negotiating any business awards. There's no room for any bribery here!" She looked satisfied she'd been able to parry away another question. "You're not suggesting anyone here had anything to do with Mr Durham's terrible murder?"

"What makes you think it was a terrible murder," asked Max quickly.

Gillian didn't miss a beat either. "Surely *all* murders are terrible Mr Sargent?"

"We have to look into every possibility. I simply want to rule out a business-related crime, as opposed to something that happened in his personal life. It's one of the two, as this was certainly no accident."

"Of course," she agreed.

"Would it be possible to see your firm's full accounts, just to corroborate there aren't any strange payments being made anywhere?"

"I assure you that wouldn't happen. In any case, we are a privately owned company registered offshore. I'm sorry, we're not obliged to share such detail, with anyone." Gillian's remark had a hint of sarcasm in it that merely drew Max into wanting to find out more about their accounting details. But that was not for today it seemed.

"I gather the main owners of the firm are you and your brother?"

"That's right. Our father founded the company and when he retired, we took it over for him. Brett, my brother, now works in New York on the US business, and me here in the UK."

"I also understand your brother is part of the Freemasons, as was your father. Do you think they might have something to do with all this, or bring any influence to bear on Durham's death?"

Gillian looked surprised again, then quickly regrouped to reply. "Really Mr Sargent, you're clutching at straws now? Masons, conspiracy theories, secret handshakes. Nonsense. They served the masons for charitable causes. Anyway, I never got involved in any of that, it's for boys only, all sounded very dull to me!"

"Just a thought. They do seem entirely legit," concurred Max. "I'm right in saying you own a house in Venice of all places, you and your brother that is?"

"My brother owns it. I get to use it."

Max didn't skirt round his questions now. "What do you make of the basement there? That kind of shrine? The wall murals?"

"I've been in that dirty old boathouse once Mr Sargent, when Brett showed me and my Dad around." Finally, Max thought he detected Gillian beginning to shift and look uncomfortable. "Barely noticed the old pictures on the wall. Didn't mean anything to me at all I'm afraid! How would you know about the basement anyway?"

Max held his gaze on her for a moment, waiting for her to flinch. She knew the 'silence' tactic and smiled back at him, but said nothing more, not allowing herself to feel as though she had to fill the gap and say something stupid.

"You've been most helpful Ms Brookshaw," concluded Max ignoring her last question and starting for the door, where Penny jumped up from her desk to meet him. "One last question. Do you have any big contracts coming up, you know, with really big firms or government agencies, large banks, internet providers, the important stuff in our infrastructure?"

Gillian ushered him to the door. "Not that I can think of right now, we're always pitching for new business, but if I come up with anything I'll ask Penny to call it through to you at MI5. Nice meeting you Mr Sargent!"

Penny escorted Max through the office to the lifts. Gillian waited until the elevator doors had closed, then picked up her phone.

"Brett. I'm not happy. I've just had MI5 snooping around here about Durham's murder!"

Brett paused. "It was only a matter of time before they found out we're one of his repeat consulting suppliers. Nothing illegal about that. What did you tell them?"

"Nothing. Only that we've worked for his firm a few times, may as well give that, they can easily check it out."

"Anything else?"

"Nothing. He asked about our gifts policy, the masons and if he could see our accounts, to which I said no, they're private."

"Do you think he had anything? Do you expect to see him again?" asked Brett more pointedly.

"No, he's got nothing," snapped Gillian, probably won't ever see him again."

"Let's hope not, for his sake!"

"From what you've said Max there's definitely something we need to look into further about this Brookshaw lot." Si Lawson shook his head. "They've gone and bought the Venetian house of their somewhat dubious ancestor, where there are some ominous underworld murals in a basement cavern. Appleby, father and son Brookshaw all have question marks against their masonic records. Plus they've done business with Durham twice, so there is a connection, but you can't see their accounts nor can the daughter who runs the firm here tell you what big contracts they're bidding for right now!"

"I know, I know," agreed Max, "there's something fishy going on but I'm not sure what yet, maybe nothing. What else can I do?"

Si was clear. "For now, I'll start asking around in the corridors of power, if anyone has come across this firm Brookshaw's. We need some first-hand views about them, how they work."

"And me?" asked Max.

"You need to interrogate their company's accounts. Not just Brookshaw's, but also this holding company, Headshell wasn't it?"

"But Si, they're registered offshore, in St Kitts and Nevis for crying out loud."

"Then you'd better get on out there hadn't you!"

"Really?"

"Unless you've got something better to do? Go. But you'll need to figure out a way of seeing their accounts, they won't just hand over a printout, not even to MI5. You'll have to think of something else. I'll get you the details of our MI5 contact out there, they can meet you at the airport. Maybe they'll have some ideas. As it's a long-haul flight you go business class, you probably only need a couple of days there. See what you can come up with!"

The next day Max was on the ten-hour British Airways flight from London Gatwick to St Kitts in the West Indies, originally called St Christopher Island.

St Kitts and Nevis is a dual-island country in the eastern Caribbean Sea with a population of just fifty-five thousand people, with African, British, French and Caribbean influences. Both islands were formed by volcanic activity and have cloud-shrouded mountains. They joined the Commonwealth in 1983 following independence from Britain.

St Kitts is a fertile island with black sandy beaches, while Nevis is surrounded by coral reefs and silver beaches. Many former sugar plantations are now inns or fascinating ruins. The larger island being St Kitts is dominated by the dormant Mount Liamuiga volcano with its crater lake, surrounded by rainforests inhabited by green vervet monkeys.

However, the beautiful landscape isn't what attracts businesses and the rich. St Kitts and Nevis offer a citizenship investment program, with benefits. Investors can obtain a local passport to gain tax residency at the financial tax haven, with lenient anti-avoidance rules, corporation tax exemption, no transfer nor exit taxes.

St Kitts and Nevis have a strong reputation for offering financial privacy for legitimate business owners, directors and much of their accounts. This includes trusts incorporated in Nevis, the main island for such tax avoidance and company secrecy, which are exempt from tax on income earned worldwide beyond the island's shores.

After the flight above the North Atlantic Ocean, Max's plane descended from the clouds revealing the beautiful sight of the north island, St Kitts. The plane passed down its short length and landed at The Robert Llewellyn Bradshaw International Airport just northeast of the capital Basseterre.

Max was travelling straight onto the southern island of Nevis and so waited two hours to catch his much smaller twin-prop plane. This took him over to Vance W Amory airport on the northern tip of Nevis, with its single runway stretching alongside the water's edge. It was a typical day, with the sun shining through light cloud cover and a pleasant twenty-eight degrees.

He emerged from the terminal to find a handful of taxis waiting and a single person holding up a piece of paper, with simply 'Max' written on it. The older man recognised him from his MI5 photo and came over to greet him with a big, perfect-teeth smile.

"Max? I'm Camilo, Camilo Samuels. Your contact here, with the 'Box' like you," using a colloquial term for MI5, "the car's just over here," as he led Max over to a Toyota Rav4.

Camilo wasn't the military type Max had for some reason expected. Near retirement, he had thinning, grey hair, was overweight in his light linen and slightly dishevelled suit, but made up for everything with his bright eyes, amazing smile and enthusiasm. Having someone visit Nevis from MI5 London was a big deal for him, on this quiet financial outpost.

"What brought you here Camilo?" asked Max as they drove away from the airport.

"Crikey, long story short, otherwise it would take a while," beamed Camilo. "My descendent from Blighty settled here when us Brits colonised Nevis around 1650, married a local, most of our family's been here ever since. I joined the police here, during which I had four years exchange with the Met back in London. It was then I applied to MI5 for a vacancy they were looking to fill for St Kitts and Nevis. Perfect as I knew I was coming back home, so did six months training with the 'Box', then became our contact out here about ten years ago, having left the force."

"Married, family?"

"Yes, twenty years ago to my dream girl, a local, childhood sweetheart." He paused and gazed out across the sea as if remembering better times. "She was killed a few years later in a car accident. Can you believe that, of all things, here on quiet, sleepy Nevis, a car accident. We have a beautiful daughter who I brought up myself."

"I'm sorry," consoled Max. "Is your daughter here with you?"

Camilo shook his head. "Miami. She has a rare genetic disorder, had it from birth but wasn't diagnosed 'til five years ago. An awful concoction of physical deterioration and mental health problems. Miami was the best place for her to be. She's full-time residency in a specialist clinic there, it's the best place for her, they look after all her needs. I visit her most months for a weekend."

Max felt for the man and after a respectful silence, changed the topic back to work. "So does much happen out here involving our agency?"

"Not much to be honest," laughed Camilo. "I have to find the odd fleeing lightweight criminal, turn them into the police for extradition. It's mainly financial criminality, but again we don't get much of that either. Nevis isn't known for tolerating openly dodgy offshore funds, there are plenty of other islands around to accommodate all that stuff."

"So how do I get to see the detailed accounts for Headshell or Brookshaw's? We've got their registered address at Nevis Island Bank, Charlestown."

Camilo forced a frown, not a facial expression he used much with his happy lifestyle. "Not going to be easy I'm afraid, but I know where the bank is that they use to handle all their legal and financial registration admin. That's where it'll all be held. We can go through an idea I have over dinner at your hotel?" he offered eagerly.

"Great."

They'd driven from New Castle where the airport was, down the western coastal road and within ten minutes had reached Jessup's Village where Max's hotel was.

"Nice, the Four Seasons," said Camilo as they drove in, "right on Pinney's Beach. Charlestown, where the banks are, is just south of here."

He parked up and walked Max up to the entrance.

"You freshen up and I'll be back for our dinner. Meet you in the Crowned Monkey Rum Bar at six."

With that Camilo ambled off and was immediately intercepted by several of the hotel's staff who seemed pleased to see him.

Max checked into the luxurious hotel, freshened up in his room and had a walk around the site before meeting up with Camilo again. There were several large pool areas, with happy staff fussing around the guests and a selection of restaurants to choose from. For those wanting more privacy, there were some private villas with their own pools. The main sandy beach had a man-made swimming lagoon with a sea wall of volcanic rocks, alongside a long jetty leading to a large floating platform for boating activities and tours. It all felt a million miles away from city life. 'Perfect to hide away your accounts if that's what you wanted', thought Max.

Camilo was already in the bar laughing and chatting with staff and some guests. Max was starting to see how affable his fellow agent was and clearly well connected on these two small islands in the middle of nowhere.

They had a couple of drinks and Camilo led them to the more relaxed Mango restaurant, surrounded by rocks on the water's edge. He knew the staff again.

"You seem to know everyone?" noted Max.

"Yes indeed, mostly everyone," admitted Camilo, "having spent my life here and being in the local police, bar my stint in London, one comes across lots of people. It's a blessing, but unfortunately for our purposes, a curse."

"How do you mean?"

"Firstly I can't be seen doing anything shady or illegal, given people know who I am," he waved at the staff serving their starters. Max had a Nevis salad with a fine selection of roasted pumpkin, feta, cucumber, corn and balsamic.

"Yes that could pose a problem if I'm trying to be discreet," agreed Max.

"Which also means I can't help make inquiries at the Nevis Island Bank. Even I can't force them to disclose private accounts and just by me asking, will set off alarm bells all over, not least of which it'll alert the company's owners."

"Do people here know you're MI5, or have you managed to keep that under wraps, posing as a private investigator or something?" Max asked, starting to feel like his colleague was going to be more of a hindrance.

Camilo frowned. "Kept it a secret for about a year, then had a bit too much of the ol' rum one night with friends, it just came out!" Shaking his head, "I'm afraid some will know I'm with the 'Box'!"

Max sighed. "So what is your idea for me to check out these infamous accounts?"

Camilo leant forward and lowered his tone, as if about to impart highly sensitive information.

"I think the best way would be for you to go in as a businessman looking to set up your new firm's account with them. Ask for the details to be explained, you can play dumb, find out where they keep company accounts, then decide how best to lookup Headshell when staff aren't looking!"

Max was quite stunned. He gazed at Camilo wondering if he was joking, but he appeared quite serious.

"Is that it?" he asked, "You're big idea! Camilo, surely with your knowledge of this place you can come up with something a little more inventive?"

Camilo was visibly upset. "Well steady on Max, I'll help as best I can, but what you're asking isn't easy at all. These firms bank in Nevis for a reason, their privacy is pretty much water-tight here. What do you suggest then?"

Suddenly Max didn't feel like sharing his thoughts with the over-friendly, sociable and perhaps indiscreet agent he'd been foisted on. Nonetheless, he was going to need his help no doubt, so smiling, he covered his frustration.

"Sounds like a plan, I'll visit them tomorrow," said Max, much to Camilo's relief. "I'll get a taxi from here."

"Wouldn't hear of it, I'll pick you up say ten AM and drop you round there. They won't open 'til then anyway."

"You won't be able to come in with me though," asserted Max, "as you say, they'll know something's up if they see me with you won't they?"

"Absolutely, I'll just wait in the car for you," assured Camilo.

The main course arrived, Max had gone for the Nevisian lemon sticky chicken dish and steered the conversation back onto Camilo's time in London with the Met. At the end of the meal, Max asked him more about the Nevis Island Bank, how they worked and where such company accounts might be held.

Max went to bed feeling like he was clutching at straws, with a half-cock plan with the bank and a contact that would probably have been more helpful if he'd stayed in London all those years ago! He needed some luck.

The next morning Camilo collected Max and they took the short drive south and parked up just down the road from the registered office address in Main Street. Max strolled over expecting to find a busy frontage open to the public with bank tellers lined up behind their barred screens. Instead, the frontage was bricked over, likely where a shop once existed, leaving just a marble surrounded doorway, trying to look expensive. A small brass sign said 'Nevis Island Bank. Discretion Assured. Established 1990'. The building was detached with a small car park to the rear and dense shrubbery beyond.

Max could see the two floors above had offices inside, with

blinds partially obscuring the windows. This was clearly just a legal, banking and administrative service for private businesses and not open to the public.

He rang the doorbell and a voice shouted out from inside.

"Just come on in, it's open."

Max entered, thinking to himself, 'not so discreet given I can just walk in with no appointment!'.

A flustered looking young woman sat busily behind a large 'L' shaped desk thumbing through paperwork, tutting as she went. She gave Max an irritable look as if to say, 'what do you want then?'.

"My name is Max Sargent," he pitched, "I'm looking to set up a new business in the UK and wondered if I can speak to someone about incorporating my company here with you?"

The woman's demeanour instantly switched into sales mode, probably on commission Max thought, and she stopped the paperwork and now smiled up at him.

"Oh, yes, of course, we can certainly handle all that for you, that's what we do here. Do have a seat?"

Just then, an older man in a suit descended the stairs behind the desk and upon seeing Max about to sit down, interjected.

"Mr Sargent was it? I couldn't help overhearing you, a UK business, we'd be delighted to help. Maria, I'll look after Mr Sargent thank you. Do come upstairs to my office, may I call you Max?"

The woman frowned, huffed, then returned to her pile of paperwork once more.

"My name is Simon Benedict, I run this establishment. Took over from my father fifteen years ago."

He was in his early sixties and wore a dark pin-striped suit that would have been at home in the Bank of England, but here on this tropical paradise looked quite out of place. His wavy, grey hair was slicked back revealing a tanned, weathered face with dark, distrustful eyes, looking Max up and down eagerly trying to get the measure of this surprise potential client.

Max wanted to avoid too many questions so steered the discussion towards what he was after.

"Perhaps Mr Benedict, before we get into the details of my business, it may save time if you'd firstly be good enough to tell me more about what services you provide?"

The older man looked startled for a moment, as he led Max through the office past eight staff and into his private room. He gestured for them to be seated, then settled into his well-worn sales patter. This he'd done many times before, to clients who almost always had no idea about what offshore registration and banking was all about.

Max listened patiently, wondering where Headshell's accounts were in this building, while Simon explained the investment program allowing St Kitts and Nevis citizenship and passport. He went through the company registration services they offered, handling all the legal work, banking, doing the company accounts and being able to fill non-executive directorships or other duties like appointing a company secretary, lawyers and accountancy firms.

"We can provide the full wrap-around service you require, end to end, against a price list of services." Simon was about to turn the conversation back to Max but was beaten to it by his visitor.

"And where will you keep my firm's accounts, digitally I mean of course?" asked Max.

Simon showed a hint of anxiety in his eyes. "All safe and sound here in our computer system, which is backed up every hour."

"Who has access to such accounts, surely not all of your staff? I must be assured complete privacy of my firm's numbers you understand?"

Now Simon's eyes betrayed a lapse of suspicion. Max knew he was pushing his luck, but he needed more information if his idea was going to work.

"No not all staff have access," replied Simon more cautiously now. "Just myself," nodding to his large Apple computer on the desk, "and three of my management team upstairs."

"So my firm's accounts would be on those four computers and the cloud?"

Simon's patience was waning. "You seem very interested in where your accounts would be held Mr Sargent, why is that?"

Max feigned surprise. "Of course I am. Isn't that one of the reasons why I'd come to you? Your sign says it all, 'discretion assured'. I'm sorry if you feel I'm being over-cautious?"

Simon stood. "Maybe Mr Sargent we aren't the right banking service for you after all!" He pretended to look at his calendar on the computer screen. "I have another appointment so shall we leave it there for today," ushering Max out now, much to his surprise.

Max rather playfully now offered, "Didn't you want to know more about my new business?"

"Another time," Simon parried, starting to gently escort Max out through the office to the stairway back down to reception.

Max relented. "Thank you for your time Mr Benedict, I'll be in touch perhaps."

"Maria, would you show Mr Sargent out please?" Simon called down, as Max descended the stairs.

He could see Simon's tone concerned the woman who looked at him worriedly, wondering what he'd done to upset her boss.

As soon as Max got outside, he walked round to the side of the building and took out his phone. He quickly punched up the Had Drive Copier app that Alan had installed back at Thames House.

He touched the 'Find wifi networks' icon and waited for the 'busy' spinning circle to detect all the networks in range. Then after a few moments, six different network labels were displayed. Max went down the list which included most of the other business's private wifi systems nearby.

There were two he concentrated on. 'NevIslBank-08', and 'NIBpriv8875'.

Max had seen Simon Benedict's pc had some kind of ethernet cable plugged into it, but he'd also noticed a wifi consul on the shelving flashing away. He guessed the 'NIBpriv8875' network was the bank's manager's private network and tapped on the label.

Alan the MI5 techie had done his homework creating this app. Max was next presented with the PC names that were currently using that wifi signal. Simon and his other three managers were shown as logged in and on the network!

Max looked down the street at Camilo waiting in the car, looking perplexed as to what he was doing standing to the side of the bank's building.

Max knew the only way of ensuring he got what he needed was to hack Simon's PC hard drive. His managers might not have access to all their accounts, they could be divided amongst them.

Back in the office Simon got back to his desk and was about to sit down, when he decided he needed a strong coffee after his meeting with the dubious, mystery visitor.

Max touched the 'Copy hard drive now' icon next to the PC username 'benedict01'. Instantly the words 'Copying Now' came up on his mobile screen with a small bar progressing along its path.

Simon Benedict turned to go and get his coffee in the outer office and chat with staff, then quickly leant back to his keyboard and logged out, as he usually did when leaving his desk for more than a few minutes.

Max watched the bar reach halfway, and then it stopped!

Camilo had now gotten out of the car and was starting to walk over to Max, looking concerned, raising his arms as he approached.

A new message appeared on Max's phone. 'Download interrupted. User logged out!'. The progress bar had got over halfway.

"What on earth are you doing?" interrupted Camilo.

Max grabbed his arm and started walking back to the Rav4. "Come on my friend, I just might have what I need!"

"Really?" Camilo looked astonished as he was bustled back to the car.

They climbed in. "Let's get back to my hotel," instructed Max.

Camilo held onto the steering wheel. "Hang on Max, what's this all about? What might you have? Are you saying you've got Headshell's accounts? How?"

Max held up his phone. "A handy little app I've got should have what I need."

Camilo hesitated before starting the car. "I'll tell you what, let's go to my assistant's house, it's nearby, then we can have a look at these accounts you so badly need to see."

Without waiting for Max to agree or not, he pulled round in the road and headed inland towards the Nevis Peak volcano. They drove up Government Road and started to wind their way into the dense forest, leaving behind the residential area as houses became less frequent.

"You'll need a proper PC to view them on, Sancho has a good PC." Camilo seemed agitated.

"Sancho?"

"Oh, he's with us," assured Camilo. "Not an MI5 employee so to say, I employ him on a freelance basis, been with me for years."

They got onto a single track winding its way through the trees and thick shrubbery. As they rounded a corner, the track opened up revealing a modest Nevetian house in the middle of nowhere, timber-framed with a red corrugated roof. A lumbering ox of a man, Sancho, stood in the doorway to greet them, forcing a welcoming smile. He waved to Camilo who nodded back.

Max didn't feel right about this, the man waiting had something unlikeable about him, but as Camilo pulled up, the large frame was already coming round the car to greet him.

It was too late. Sancho reached to the back of his belt and quickly pulled out an old US Army issue Colt M1911 semi-automatic pistol, pointing it at Max through his open window.

"What the hell! Camilo?" exclaimed Max in horror.

Camilo got out fast to put some distance between them. He looked very edgy.

"I like you, Max," he shouted. "But you just had to bloody somehow figure out a way to see those accounts! How did you manage it, with your stupid phone? No one's done that before. Now look what you've made me do!"

"Get out," ordered Sancho, half dragging Max from the car.

"Okay! You haven't done anything yet," coached Max to Camilo, "let's just talk this through before it gets out of hand? We're on the same team you and I?"

Camilo fidgeted. "We're meant to be yes. But you've gone and put me in a bad situation, with my other employer. I can't let you see whatever you've got on your phone, if it has Headshell's accounts!"

"Why not," asked Max. "It's just a load of numbers, they're not worth all this surely?" looking at the gun trained on him. "What's all this about Camilo?"

"If I let you have those accounts, he'll have me killed!" complained Camilo. "I have to do this, for my daughter, don't you see. MI5 wages don't cover the care she needs in Miami, or the flights there every month."

"So, you sell your services to businessmen, like Headshell, to ensure anyone snooping around is put off the trail?" sighed Max. "Let me guess, Benedict's an old mate of yours?"

"Not really, but we know one another, enough for me to tell him to entertain you, then send you on your way empty-handed," admitted Camilo. He nodded to Sancho who flicked his gun at Max for him to put his hands up and move towards the house.

"Don't do anything stupid," warned Max. "If anything happens to me you'll have an army of agents over here."

"I'll take the phone now thank you," Camilo demanded, ignoring the comment and holding out his hand.

Max figured that after their brief discussion, Camilo now had no choice but to have him killed and presumably never to be found, hidden somewhere amongst this dense tropical forest.

The three of them were still close together. He felt this might be his only chance to turn the situation around.

"Well I can't exactly get it out for you with my hands up, can I?" Max nodded to his jacket pocket, "Take it then?"

Satisfied that Sancho had Max covered with his gun, Camilo stepped forward and leant in to slip his hand into Max's inside jacket pocket. He fumbled for a moment, then smiled as he felt and grabbed the phone.

Wack!

Max brought down his fist as fast and as hard as he could muster, onto Sancho's wrist, sending the gun flying to the ground. The large man cried out, more from shock than pain.

Camilo's hand was still stuck in Max's pocket, presenting him with an easy target now the gun was out of play. Max immediately brought down his elbow into the centre of Camilo's forearm.

There was a dull 'crack!' as both the ulna and radius bones fractured. Camilo's hand wrenched away from the pocket tearing it open, sending Max's phone flying away from them to the ground.

Camilo let out an agonising cry of pain and crumpled to the floor nursing his broken arm.

As Max turned back to Sancho, a large fist came flying at his face, which he mostly ducked under, as it brushed onto his head. In the lowered position and with an open torso right in front of him, Max made sure his blow hit home. He punched hard and up into the man's solar plexus, breaking one side of the costal cartilage on the lower ribs.

The single strike was debilitating for Sancho, disorientating much of his central nervous system and causing excruciating pain. He too fell to the ground in agony.

Just as Max thought he'd done enough and had intended to retrieve the gun, he realised the large man had fallen near to where the Colt was lying!

Both men realised at the same moment and although Sancho was in a lot of pain, his anger and adrenaline drove him to reach out for the gun.

He grasped it and swung his arm round whilst lying on his side on the ground.

Max had already started to go over to him but knew he wasn't going to reach out for the gun in time, so lunged forward with his leading leg, like a footballer doing a sliding tackle.

Sancho raised the gun and as it lined up with Max lunging at him, started to squeeze the trigger. But the momentum of his arm carried his aim on past Max and it was then that Max's foot, now kicking out, smashed into Sancho's hand.

Bang!

Both Max and Sancho froze, checking to see if they had been hit.

It was Sancho who then reeled back onto the ground, with a red bleeding hole in his other arm.

"Sancho!" yelled Camilo.

Max shuffled over to Sancho and grabbed the gun he'd dropped after firing it. He then moved to the large man who was already drifting into unconsciousness, with the shock of Max's blow and now the gunshot wound, he was shutting down. The bullet had passed clean through his axillary artery, the largest going down the arm. Blood seeped through the large fingers, now loosening their pressure on the wound.

Max went over to check on Camilo, who was cursing to himself for the whole mess he now found himself in. He collected up his mobile phone as Camilo watched on helplessly. They looked over to Sancho who now lay motionless. The trauma of the various wounds had taken hold of him and he'd drifted off, permanently.

"You won't get away with this Sargent!" said Camilo. "I'll make sure you never leave the island. I'll have everyone after you, this doesn't end here!" he said threateningly.

Max leant over him and checked his pockets for his mobile, then remembered he'd put it in the car's centre console. He retrieved it then checked the large man's body, gathering up his phone as well. Deliberately in front of Camilo, Max removed the sim card and battery from each phone, then smashed them underfoot. He ran into the house and seeing just one old landline telephone, went over and pulled the cord out of its wall socket breaking the small wired connection.

Walking back out of the house he looked at Camilo. "You, my friend, are the one who hasn't heard the last of this! I'm guessing it'll take you half an hour in the state you're in, to get to the nearest house with a phone."

Looking at Camilo, Max figured he was in no state to walk even that fast. Max got into the Rav4 and found the keys in the ignition slot. He started up the engine and leaned out the window at Camilo.

"You, are in big trouble!"

Max reversed back and gave the old man one last look, before pulling off.

Camilo watched, then muttered, "Not me. But you are!"

10

"You're joking right?" said Si Lawson incredulously over the phone's speaker.

"I'm afraid not Si," shouted Max at his phone on the Rav4's dash. "Camilo Samuels, our MI5 agent on the islands here, has gone rogue! Likely works for Headshell but no hard proof I'm afraid. Tried to have me bumped off as soon as he realised I might have the accounts. I haven't been able to look at the download yet from the bank's office to see if I've got anything yet, but that'll have to wait."

"Why?"

"I've got a more pressing problem," said Max. "I've just left our Samuels chap injured but mobile, along with his deceased goon. He seems to know everyone here and I suspect won't want me leaving in a hurry, if at all. I'm heading back to my hotel right now for my passport and money, then I need your help to get the hell out of here fast. I'm not sure who to trust and need to be on the next flight away from here!"

"Do you think the police there are compromised?"

"Certainly some will be, Samuels was in the police here for decades."

"Okay Max, understood. Give me ten minutes to sort something and I'll call you straight back. Stand by!" said Si efficiently, calling off.

Max headed back the way they'd come and soon emerged onto Main Street. He drove up the coast road towards the Four Seasons, wondering what Samuels was up to back at the house in the forest.

Camilo Samuels had watched the Rav4 disappear off down the track, then hauled himself up and staggered into the house, carefully nursing his broken arm, cursing all the way.

He saw the telephone line in the lounge had been ripped out and assumed Max had done the same to the other phone in Sancho's downstairs bedroom. Astonishingly he found it still intact and plugged in, underneath the bedside table. Max had missed it. The turn of fate in his favour re-energised him and his determination to stop Max from leaving. He knew a lot of people who could instantly help him.

He figured Max would likely try to leave St Kitts and Nevis as soon as he could, after getting his things from the hotel. He'd have to fly out of one of the two airports whatever. He lowered himself to the bedroom floor next to the phone and using his free hand, picked up the receiver and started dialling. He had a few numbers to ring and would have to call in some big favours for this one.

Five minutes later Max arrived back at his hotel, he parked up and made his way directly to his room. His phone rang, it was Si.

"Tell me you've got something sorted boss?" asked Max eagerly.

"We tried to get straight onto the Prime Minister there to explain everything, but he was apparently unreachable. So no more messing about, I called up the Governor-General of St Kitts and Nevis. He runs the place and is appointed by our monarch. As no international flights are leaving anytime soon from the Nevis airport, you're gonna have to get yourself to St Kitts."

"How?" said Max curtly.

"Are you at your hotel now?" checked Si.

"Yes, just getting back to my room as we speak."

"Great. We've arranged for a high-powered speed boat to collect you from the hotel jetty in ten minutes. The boat's aptly called 'Lightning Fast'! They'll take you the forty-minute trip across to the St Kitts ferry terminal which is at Basseterre. It's about ten miles across the water and that's where the airport is."

"But what if Samuels has the terminal covered by his

contacts? The police, airport, customs?"

"The Governor-General should be speaking to his Captain who heads up their Defence Force, their Army, to arrange for an armed escort to meet you off the boat and take you to your flight. There's a BA plane landing right now and due to leave back for London in ninety minutes, you should be okay to catch that, your seat's booked!"

"Bloody hell Si, that's great, you've sorted it. We can have a look through the download when I'm back, it'll be easier to scroll through all the files on a big screen, it would probably take me ages on my phone."

"Let's just hope you've got something after all this trouble," said Si.

"What about Samuels?"

"The Governor-General will have the army cover the Charlestown district to look out for him, and his home address and known associates," said Si. "I'm sure they'll have him before the day's out. Sounds like he'll be wanting medical attention ASAP anyway! You'd better get off to your boat pickup."

Max gathered his things into his cabin bag and avoided the usual checking out process with reception, which could be sorted later. He didn't want to leave any trails for Samuels. He walked straight out onto the beach and down the long narrow jetty to the large platform at the end.

One of the hotel's small speed boats was returning with a couple after a water-skiing trip. The hotel water sports driver looked a little puzzled to see Max waiting on the platform with his luggage.

He pulled in and helped his guests disembark.

"Can I help you Sir?" he asked.

"No I'm good thanks, just waiting for someone to collect me thanks," replied Max, turning away to signal that was the end of the conversation.

The young lad shrugged his shoulders and carried on tying up his boat. He checked again as he strolled past Max who just nodded back that he was fine.

In the distance Max spotted a boat coming towards him and could see as it drew closer, it was travelling over the water at speed. Hoping this was his pickup, it veered in and pointed at his jetty. Max let out a sigh of relief. He was on his way.

Looking behind him a few interested guests were watching him to see what was happening and he also spotted the young lad from the guest boat chatting to a couple of his fellow water-sports staff, all looking at him alone on the jetty end.

The boat approached and was now larger than he'd thought from a distance. The black twenty-eight-foot-long twin jet Scarab 285ID, hunkered down into the water as it slowed before reaching him. Max checked for the boat name and saw it stencilled on the side in small lettering, 'Lightning Fast'! There were two men on board, both keenly smiling at Max expecting a celebrity of sorts.

"Mr Sargent?" one called out as they came alongside.

"I am," nodded Max.

"Come straight aboard Sir," he said, waving him on to join them. "VIP yes?" he asked, trying to place Max's face in a movie he might have seen him in.

"I guess so," agreed Max. "What are your instructions?"

"We just got a call from the Governor-General's office of all places, asking that we collect you at once and take you over to the Basseterre ferry terminal. Double our usual rates. You must be important! We'd just finished a family tour," he said motioning at the water skis and double inflatable ring at the rear.

"Well let's get on then, need to get there as quickly as possible. You fuelled up to go?" checked Max out of habit, to make sure nothing simple had been overlooked.

"Half a tank," said the driver, then proudly, "that's good for seventy miles and we're only going ten to Basseterre, should do it in thirty-five minutes as it's not too choppy today."

They pulled away from the platform and slowly

accelerated off, the bow rising over the water as it picked up speed.

Max settled down on one of the comfy leather seats behind the driver, thinking to himself, 'so far, so good!'.

Samuels had been busy making several calls from Sancho's forest home. He'd asked a few of his more trustworthy police officers to cover off both airport departure lounges, he'd also spoken to one of the managers at the main St Kitts airport in Customs. His last call was to the hotel, where he knew he could rely on a couple of the food and beverage staff working the bars he frequented, and a girl on reception.

Camilo established that Max hadn't checked out, which started to raise his hopes that Max had perhaps gone straight to one of the airports, or better still, was stranded on Nevis hiding out somewhere trying to work out what to do.

It was a full twenty-five minutes later when he got a call from one of the hotel barmen.

"I think the guy you're after has taken a boat from the hotel jetty!"

"What!" cried Camilo. He hadn't thought of that. "When?"

The barman checked with the water-sports staff. "Almost half an hour ago we think."

"Crikey! Damn it!" Camilo tried to gather his thoughts. "What boat?" he asked.

"Oh that's easy, Pauli's boat. We all know that one, he recently got one of the newest Scarab's, lovely craft it is."

Camilo thought. "You don't mean Pauli Lamcross do you, good God, I dated his mother when we were kids!"

"Lamcross, that's him," confirmed the barman. Camilo hung up, leaving him saying, "Hello? Camilo, are you there?"

He made a couple of calls to get the number he was after.

The Scarab had made good progress and Max could see the shoreline of Basseterre in the distance, hoping that his army escort would be there for him, he couldn't take any chances.

In front of him, the driver's mobile rang and he picked it up. He listened for a bit.

"Who?" he inquired, looking like he was trying to place the caller. "Oh yes." He listened again and Max was acutely aware of the happy face turning into a worried, concerned look.

The other man helping with the boat noticed as well. "What's up Pauli, you okay?"

Max knew something was up and quickly looked around the boat for a weapon of sorts, but there was nothing. He sat up and watched the two lads closely. Pauli put the phone down looking scared and gave Max a quick nervous glance. He then started to turn the boat about!

Camilo had told him what he thought might get them to turn back and deliver Max to him on Nevis. He'd told Pauli that he had a murderer on board trying to flee the country. That he'd be in trouble if he put him ashore on St Kitts and he should simply turn around and come back to Nevis. Make up a story, but do not engage this man, he's dangerous!

"Hey, what are you doing?" shouted Max above the noise. "We need to go over there," pointing to the harbour now in view.

Pauli hesitated but continued to turn the boat round and head back the way they'd come.

"Sorry sir, I've got a malfunction and have got to go back to my service yard, won't take long."

The poor excuse didn't cut it with Max who knew Samuels must have got to him with the phone call. He simply couldn't let them take him back.

In a single move, he grabbed the deckhand round the shoulders, lifted the surprised lad up, and threw him overboard, much to the boy's utter surprise, crying out.

Before Pauli could even think about lunging at Max, he'd already been hit with the back of Max's fist and sent sprawling over the throttle lever and half out of the boat. The craft decelerated and as the lad shouted his objections and began fumbling for the small knife in his pocket. Max lifted him up by the legs and tossed him out into the sea as well, sending the blade into the deep blue water.

He took control of the boat and seeing they were some way out from the harbour, circled back to the two young men thrashing about in the water.

"I'm sorry Mr Sargent," pleaded Pauli, "I didn't know what to do. First I'm told to take you to St Kitts, next I'm ordered to bring you back to Nevis! Don't leave us, we can't swim that far to shore!"

"Who told you to turn back?"

"Best I don't say," said Pauli spluttering, as his friend swam over to him.

"Who? Or I'll leave you both!" Max blipped the throttle.

"Camilo. It was Camilo!"

Max looked around the boat and had an idea to get them back to shore safely, without having to tie them up. They seemed to be unwilling participants of Samuels'.

A minute later Max slowly gathered speed across the water, homing in on the large jetty extending in front of the small rock-made harbour barrier by the ferry terminal. The two lads followed thirty feet behind the boat, holding onto their inflatable double-ring for dear life, bouncing about amidst the boat's wake!

As Max slowed at the harbour entrance he could see a group of four armed soldiers waiting on the jetty with a man in a suit. He shouted out before pulling alongside, to be sure.

"Who are you?" to the suited man.

"Hello, Mr Sargent? The Governor-General sent me to take you to the airport, in fact, to put you straight onto your flight. We'll bypass check-in and security. You must know people high up Mr Sargent!"

The soldiers were intrigued at the sight of this understated British agent coming alongside, towing a couple of lads on an inflatable.

"Take their details," said Max, "I don't think they meant

any harm, Samuels tried to get them to take me back to Nevis for him."

They all climbed onto the jetty and one of the soldiers stayed with the lads to wait for the local police, while Max, the suit and the other three soldiers got into the two waiting estate wagons.

Within five minutes they were being let through a secure entrance straight onto the tarmac of the Robert L Bradshaw airport runway. They pulled up next to the British Airways Boeing.

As Max got out he looked back at the terminal building wondering how many of the staff inside were waiting to intercept him. If he'd gone through there, one of Samuels' contacts would have almost certainly got to him and spirited him off to be dealt with somehow.

He thanked the suit for the Governor-General's help, and the soldiers, who were still somewhat bewildered as to what all the fuss was about. As Max climbed the steps to board his flight home, the plane's other passengers emerged from the terminal to start boarding.

Max settled into his seat, relieved to be on his way home. There was a momentary exchange between the cabin crew and a ground staff official in the doorway, holding up boarding. Max thought for a moment that maybe Samuels was still onto him and might have him taken off the plane, but was reassured to see the soldiers and suit were holding their position on the tarmac. They stayed there until all passengers were loaded and the door closed.

The pain in Camilo Samuels' arm had been unbearable and finally, he'd called for an ambulance to take him to the nearby Alexandra Hospital near Charlestown. He'd also asked the Police Chief to meet him there, where he would do his very best to talk his way out of the whole sorry affair.

Whilst waiting for the ambulance, he had one last call to make. The call he most dreaded making. The line picked up.

"Sir, it's Samuels," he said nervously. "You know, Camilo

Samuels, on St Kitts and Nevis. I keep an eye on the Nevis Island Banking arrangement," he prompted.

"Yes, of course," said the calm voice, "how is your daughter doing in Miami?"

"Good thank you, with your help which is appreciated."

"We've not spoken for a while, I hope everything's alright there?" said the voice now more questioning.

The arm fracture pain muddled Camilo's clear thinking as to how best to pitch this.

"All fine, but I thought you should be aware, I've had an MI5 chap over here wanting to look at Headshell's accounts."

"Oh dear, that doesn't sound *fine* at all." The voice was sterner now, making Camilo feel uncomfortable just being on the phone with him. "Why didn't you tell me about this earlier?"

Camilo thought quickly. "To be honest, I didn't think it would be a problem, he only got here yesterday. I'd entertain him, put him off the trail and send him off empty-handed. Then I could update you. Benedict at the bank would never disclose any information, to anyone."

"It sounds like there is a problem, what's happened?"

Camilo knew he'd run out of being able to skirt around the issue. He had to just come out with it now. He gulped.

"There is a possibility this chap might have been able to download or somehow copy your accounts!"

There was a pause that spoke volumes. The reply was clinical.

"I'm not happy about this at all! You say *possibility*, explain?"

"He claimed he'd got it on his phone, he wasn't sure though until he checked it. I don't know how he did it, must have hacked into the bank's computers somehow."

"What's this person's name?"

"Max Sargent. Seemed pretty efficient. Took out me and my man here who was armed," said Camilo, trying to make it sound as though Max was too good for them to handle and cover their inadequacies holding him.

The man on the call immediately recognised the name. "Where is he now, you'll stop him from leaving the island won't you?"

"I've tried everything," said Camilo apologetically. "He must have pulled some strings, got away from Nevis immediately by boat, then armed escort to his plane. He'll be taking off now."

"So you've failed to do the one thing I pay you for?"

"But…"

"I'll have to consider whether we continue with our arrangement."

Camilo was now fighting for his daughter's clinic funding, which meant more to him than his own welfare, both of which seemed in jeopardy.

"Now hang on," he stuttered, "I'm in a whole heap of trouble here, I've got a dead friend, a broken arm and have to mop up this mess! You're also paying me for my discretion in not bringing you into this!"

The reply was quick. "Are you threatening me?"

"No, of course not, I need your help for my daughter, whatever else happens. But I have one last chance, a slim one, to stop this guy getting home safely."

"How can that be, you've just said this Sargent bloke is taking off?"

Camilo played his final ace.

"Yes he is. But I have a contact on the same flight!" he said proudly before hanging up.

In his New York office, Brett Brookshaw put the phone down. This Max Sargent was becoming a problem, visiting his sister and now possibly stealing his firm's accounts in Nevis.

Brett knew he now needed to intervene.

The large Boeing took off and as Max looked down on the beautiful island before leaving it behind, he thought to himself 'under better circumstances, what a lovely place, but thank

God I'm getting out of there!'.

It was early afternoon local time and so the ten-hour trip back to Gatwick would be a night flight, getting them back in the early hours of the next day.

Max settled himself down in his business class seat, to make the most of a meal and a couple of movies, before getting some sleep. After the plane levelled out far above the clouds, he remembered that he wanted to have his first proper look at what Alan's hard drive copier app had managed to get from Benedict's PC.

Opening it up he touched a new icon saying 'Downloaded files' and was immediately presented with a huge list of file names which went on forever. At the top of the list was the familiar magnifying glass search field. 'Nice one Alan' he thought. He typed in 'headshell' and hit 'Enter'.

To his amazement, a single file came up for the search result entitled 'headshell_fullac_7453bb'. But as soon as Max rejoiced at the file name, his heart sank upon seeing the flag alongside which said 'Incomplete – download interrupted'!

He opened up the file anyway and started to scroll through what was shown. There were twenty pages in total and it became clear as he flicked through them, that whilst most were intact, some were just data gobbledygook and had been compromised by the transmission being cut off mid-stream. Many of the pages were legal bumf and wordy reporting of statutory requirements, but Max managed to home in on a handful of the pages with some numbers on.

He saw that Headshell's annual turnover was currently just under one billion US dollars and that they had seven thousand staff based mainly in the UK and US. There were also the usual numbers alongside headings including assets and profit, which for a one billion turnover firm, were a massive three-hundred million.

There were some director's notes, and audit notes from Nevis Island Bank. Max scrolled through more pages that were legible, then came across the heading 'Disbursements -

Notes', which often covers a wide catchall of expenses usually incurred as part of the delivery of services.

Buried within a long explanatory paragraph, Max's attention was drawn to a particular sentence and number. It read 'Some target linked exceptional item bonus expenses were paid to select employees, agents and associates totalling US$28,223,000'!

Max had seen his fair share of company accounts, but this particular disclosure was too general and with no other supporting detail, he knew it stank! Max read the wording through again, trying to decipher what this could possibly be covering up.

He said the word 'bonuses' over and over in his mind. Then using his imagination started to replace it with other words like, 'back-handers, enticements, bribes, favours, rewards'!

Max closed the app and sat back in his seat with a knowing smile. He felt that slowly, but surely, the case of Headshell, along with Brookshaw Consulting, was starting to point in the direction of suspect business dealings and potentially a corrupt network involving money, coercion and murder!

Max set down his mobile on the shelf in front of him, as unbeknown to him, someone was watching him closely.

Two seats back, Milo Colburn anxiously looked upon the occupant of aisle seat 14B, who had been studying his phone.

He'd been waiting at the departure gate in the airport when he'd received a call from his old police boss, Camilo Samuels.

They hadn't spoken for over a year but on such a small island, had always kept in touch even though they served together fifteen years ago. Camilo had promoted Milo and looked the other way with a couple of indiscretions that should have been serious disciplinary offences by the young policeman, so he was in debt to his old boss.

After Milo's term with St Kitts and Nevis police, he'd set up a rum business in Nevis. He was making his six-monthly trip to the UK to meet with wholesalers, retailers and secure new business orders.

Camilo had explained to him that a British spy had stolen highly sensitive information that compromised the security of their beloved dual-island country. That he had evaded security and he, Milo, was their last hope. His instructions were two-fold. Firstly, and most importantly, he was to steal and destroy passenger 14B's mobile phone, which Camilo had explained, held the country's secret files on it.

The second part of his briefing coincided with one of the airport staff handing him a small envelope saying out loud for the benefit of other passengers nearby, "Your outstanding paperwork Sir."

With Camilo on the phone, he'd opened the envelope to find a single small white tablet.

"Don't touch it!" Camilo had warned Milo. "Remember, getting the phone is the main task here, but if you get the chance to slip this into any strong drink he has, like coffee or spirits, then do it."

"What is it Sir?" asked Milo innocently.

"Potassium Cyanide!"

"What? Sir, I'm on a business trip. I don't mind taking the phone, but I won't…." Milo stopped saying it out loud.

Camilo was content his accomplice had at least agreed to deal with the phone. The poison would be a bonus but wasn't necessary. If he was honest with himself, this part of the task was mainly driven by him wanting revenge for his broken arm and Sancho's death.

"Okay, okay. Take the tablet anyway and use it only if you get a clear opportunity to drop it into his drink," conceded Camilo. "Just remember who helped you out when you were in the police, promoted you and overlooked potential gross misconduct charges!"

Camilo felt he'd said enough for Milo to think about, carefully. Milo was left shocked at being thrust into having to follow these dubious instructions and had thought about nothing else while waiting to board the flight. He'd eagerly watched to see who this mysterious character would be in seat 14B and his heart sank when the tall, strong figure of Max appeared two rows in front of him.

He stared at the phone just yards away from him as if targeting it, willing it to malfunction by itself. The flight was long, and surely this man would want to sleep at some point. He would wait until the cabin lights were dimmed and most passengers were silently tucked up under their blankets. Milo felt for the small tablet in his pocket.

Having left St Kitts in the afternoon, it wasn't until halfway through the flight that the lights were dimmed and passengers finally started to settle down. The captain reminded everyone to adjust their watches onto the new UK time, instantly gaining five hours.

Milo dare not even try to sleep and occupied himself with various movies, constantly looking up to see what Max was doing.

Finally, Max got up to go to the toilet before intending to settle down. He'd been waiting for a brandy to be brought to him by the stewardess.

Milo craned his neck as Max walked away up the aisle, and to his annoyance couldn't see that the phone had been left. Max had taken it with him. Just as Milo sank back into his seat, he watched the smart, well made-up cabin crew lady bring a plastic cup with ice in it and a small bottle of brandy.

Earlier Max had asked her to pour his last drink straight out and take the empty bottle with her, so taking the initiative, she obliged him once more.

The brandy cup now sat on his tray waiting for him. It beckoned Milo, daring him to act now before Max returned.

With his heart racing, Milo knew he wouldn't get another chance like this, so started to manoeuvre his way up to stand, whilst grabbing for the tablet in his pocket. He scanned the rows of sleeping passengers, checking to see if anyone nearby was watching or might possibly see him. The person in 14A next to Max's seat stirred, trying to get comfortable in the awkward position his business class seat offered.

Unable to linger anymore, Milo stepped into the aisle and got the tablet ready in his left hand. As he passed by the drink on the tray, he dropped it into the cup without making any obvious movement and continued to walk on.

Just as Milo turned to look forward again, Max was in front of him! Milo jumped, coming face to face with his target, fearing he'd been seen.

But Max politely stepped aside to let him pass by and on to the toilet.

Milo couldn't wait to get to the false safety of the tiny lavatory and shut the door. He sat down on the seat, wondering if the man in 14B was drinking his brandy, right now. How would he react? What would the cabin staff do? Could he be implicated in any way? He would wait a few minutes.

Max was tired and warily approached his row. With both his seat and the one in front fully reclined, the gap to squeeze in to was narrow. As he swung round the top edge of the seat ahead of his, committing himself to slump into his chair, he saw the lowered tray with the waiting drink on it.

It was too late to react. His thigh squashed into the tray and as he lowered his full weight down, it bent with him, then sprung free, sending the light plastic drink flying off before he could grab it.

The brandy holding its deadly poison, fell onto the floor and instantly soaked into the course carpet. Max cursed, briefly stirring the man in the neighbouring seat. Max collected up the empty cup and placed it on his armrest. He was tired and started to settle himself, taking the phone out of his pocket and lodging it into the magazine holder on the back of the seat facing him.

Milo appeared down the aisle, nervously wondering what had happened whilst in the toilet. He eyed Max back in his seat, then saw the empty plastic cup on the chair arm.

'Oh my God! He's had it!' he thought to himself.

He settled back into his seat and kept his head down, watching to see when his target would start to cough, or choke, or vomit.

The stewardess came down the aisle and seeing Max's empty cup, gathered it up and asked him if he wanted anything else.

Max was too tired to explain he hadn't actually got to have the brandy and couldn't be bothered to order another, he wanted to sleep. He thanked her but shook his head.

Milo waited, and watched. The minutes passed and he was starting to wonder how long potassium cyanide would take to see any effects.

After five minutes, he was questioning whether the tablet was indeed poison. He waited.

After fifteen minutes it was clear something was up. Maybe it had been spilt? Perhaps it takes longer to have any effect? It could be there were no effects and the passenger, the spy, would have a heart attack overnight.

Milo tried to move on from the agonising wait for any reaction to the tablet he'd so carefully placed in the drink. He now still needed to get the phone, having seen Max put it in the seat pouch right in front of him.

Milo watched Max pull a blanket over himself, place the yellow buds into his ears and adjust the nighttime blindfold over his eyes. Flight rules stipulated that passengers should fasten their safety belts over their blanket, so that they wouldn't be disturbed if the cabin crew needed to check them.

Milo was feeling tired as several more hours passed by. The emotional stress and anxiety took their toll on him, wondering if this man might slump into the aisle dead at any moment, along with knowing he still had to get the phone!

Max had fallen asleep, or as best possible in a plane seat, along with most of the other passengers around him. Just the occasional cough or shuffle punctuated the still cabin.

Milo looked up and planned through in his mind what he must do and found himself overthinking it. He decided to simply get on and do it quickly, with the alibi that if caught, he would say that he merely picked the phone up off the floor to replace it in the pouch of the sleeping passenger.

He rose and slid into the aisle once more, charged with another task, his main task.

As he came alongside 14B, Milo checked that the passenger was indeed asleep, as was the man next to him, and those in the row opposite. In a single movement, whilst continuing down the aisle, he leant in just enough to carefully extract Max's mobile from the magazine pouch above his knees.

The thin phone easily slipped out.

Max stirred.

Milo was committed and withdrew the phone and continued on down the aisle, not looking back to see if Max or anyone else had watched his thieving deed.

He only looked back once he got to the toilet. All was still. He locked the door and sat down once more, tingling with nerves and stress.

'Jesus! Bloody Camilo, you owe me big time for all this!' he thought.

The brief interest in what might be so important in this phone quickly passed, as he wanted to just get on with the job. He first took out the sim card and cracked it in two, then threw it into the toilet bowl and flushed it. The vacuum flush took it away making his ears pop with the change in pressure. The sim had gone!

Next, he took out the battery. He didn't know why, but it was the only other item he could 'remove'. Looking around the tiny space for any ideas as to how to break or dispose of it, he placed it under the seat. Then standing on the seat to hold it, he managed to bend the battery enough to render it useless. He tossed it into the bin within the sink unit.

Fumbling with the phone now, he knew he had to destroy it so anything stored on its hard drive was irretrievable. He did the same as before, managing to bend the phone, cracking the screen. But that wasn't enough. Desperate, he smashed the device several times hard on the edge of the metal tap, until he was satisfied it was well and truly bust beyond repair. It wouldn't fit down the narrow toilet pipe, so all he could do was bury it in the bottom of the bin again.

He washed his hands trying to rid himself of the whole sorry affair, took a deep breath and returned to his seat, passing Max still sleeping. Exhaustion finally took over and Milo fell asleep five minutes later.

Max would never know he would have died an excruciating death on the flight if he hadn't spilt his poisoned brandy. He later assumed his phone had fallen onto the floor and been kept by another passenger, who wouldn't be able to gain password access anyway. He hadn't been able to share the Headshell private accounts with Si Lawson before losing his phone, but he'd seen them.

They now knew the spurious twenty-eight million dollars of 'private expenses payments' was probably either bribes, money laundering, or both!

11

Si Lawson waved at Max for him to pop into his office. Max had flown in early that morning and had gone straight into Thames House and given a full debrief to him about the whole St Kitts and Nevis trip.

"Any update yet from St Kitts about our unhelpful agent Samuels?" Max asked.

"I've just heard from the Governor-General out there," said Si. "Your Camilo Samuels turned himself into the police chief at the hospital on Nevis. Practically passing out with the pain of the broken arm you gave him."

"Samuels and his goon were about to shoot me, Sir!"

"He's lucky that's all he got then eh! Apparently, he tried to talk his way out of the whole thing but the chief was having none of it. Friendships only stretch so far, but not it seems beyond MI5's involvement and a dead body. He'll be taken into custardy later today and with your testimony, be charged on quite a few counts. Probably spend most of the rest of his life inside the St Kitts prison in Basseterre."

"Just one thing," said Max, "I gather he has a daughter in a Miami hospital with some genetic condition or something."

"So?"

"Well can you ask them to cut him some slack, or rather her? He's all she's got, I know he's done wrong, but she shouldn't be punished because of his stupidity. He thought he was onto a cushy number to help pay for it all."

"Until you turned up Max," pointed out Si. "You're all heart. Yes, I'll put in a word, maybe they can let him do the odd accompanied visit along with full access to Facetime calls with her."

"Thanks."

"Couple of things you should know Max. Firstly we've been waiting to hear from David Durham's accountant, so we understand exactly how he was living such a charmed lifestyle. We've got a copy of the report he's issuing to his wife Angela who you met." Si pulled a face. "She's in for a shock!"

"Why?"

"Their main asset, the big riverside mansion you met her at, isn't in her name! Nor is it in his name!"

"I don't understand?"

"The deeds have been registered to a shell company, then before the made-up firm's first set of accounts are required after eighteen months, it's transferred to another shell company. Each of them led back to David Durham no doubt."

"Why would he do that?" asked Max naively.

"To hide where the money's come from, that bought the house. There's more. It seems that he bought many other large purchases, sports cars, boats, a large extension, all using bitcoin. Amazing what you can get now with cryptocurrency, either using it as payment or just buying euros or pounds with it. Simply another way of turning ill-gotten funds into seemingly legit spending money. Washing it so to say! There are people on the dark web who'll clean you're already hard-to-trace crypto and make it almost completely untraceable, like cash."

"Aren't there organisations that look out for that kind of laundering?" checked Max.

"Absolutely, if you know who's suspected of laundering money in the first place! The Financial Crimes Enforcement Agency get over a million SAR's every year, suspicious activity reports. These come in from car dealers, banks, casinos, estate agents, lawyers, everywhere. The FCEA can't follow-up every slightly dubious transaction or cash payment, they have to pick out their targets."

"Good grief," conceded Max.

Si went on. "Likewise, the National Crime Agency get

thousands of DAML's every month, defence against money laundering, from anyone suspecting criminality by an entity they intend dealing with. It's just too much to handle. No one would investigate your average, high earning Chief Exec unless there'd been a tipoff."

"So where does that leave Durham's money?"

"Well, his wife will keep the clean funds, what there is of them. Any suspected assets or cash will be frozen or confiscated, including their house. She'll be able to continue living there whilst it all gets sorted out, the lawyers and accountants will get richer, and maybe she'll be allowed to sell up to pay off debts and costs, then keep what's left over. Maybe."

"Poor lady, she didn't have a clue what was going on," said Max.

"That leaves us with a more than high probability that David Durham was receiving payments under the table, then using a well-oiled laundering system to bring it from offshore accounts back into the UK as spending money."

Max nodded. "Ties up nicely with Headshell's accounts and the mystery payments worth millions, to *select staff, agents and associates*!"

"Precisely Max, but it's not yet water-tight evidence. Whilst Headshell is the over-arching owner, I suspect the front-line for any dubious business dealings…"

"Would be through Brookshaw Consulting!" interjected Max.

"Right. So onto my next topic. I asked Vince to see what tenders and new business this Brookshaw's firm might be pitching for."

"But there's no way of us finding that out from all the potential client firms that could be including them in tenders?"

"Not unless we have access to those firms' procurement heads or management," noted Si with a smile.

"Which firms could MI5 possible be able to immediately access?"

"We can at least start with every company across the government's network! We are part of the government here, so it wouldn't seem odd to inquire about a list of all suppliers currently tendering for any business across government-owned or associated businesses, would it!"

Max was impressed. "It's a start! When will Vince get replies back?"

"He already has!" said Si with pride. "He sent out an email to every single government business Chief Exec, procurement head or senior contact we have on file, requesting an *immediate* response."

"Asking what?"

"Simple. Return a spreadsheet listing every supplier currently pitching or tendering for business. We disguised it by having it sent from a governmental due diligence office email address, checking on best practices etc. Vince had over five hundred responses within an hour this morning."

"Five-hundred! I didn't know the government had so many organisations?"

"Think about it. You've got over twenty ministerial departments, cabinet, energy, transport, health service, education, treasury, housing and so on. Then there are another twenty non-ministerial departments like forestry, land registry, tax and customs, Ofsted, courts and so forth."

Max nodded as Si drew breath and continued.

"There are about four hundred agencies and other public bodies including advisory committees, commissions, standards, tribunals, councils, authorities, research and colleges, health, prisons, highways, livestock, NHS, fishing, sport and drugs to name just a few! Another hundred or so high-profile groups are covering the civil service, defence and government. Finally, you've got the part or fully owned corporations like banks, rail, post office, energy and the BBC!"

"Okay, okay, I get it," pleaded Max. "And what has Vince come up with?"

"By merging the spreadsheets and listing the suppliers in alphabetical order, we can see which suppliers come up more than once and are tendering for multiple pitches across our organisations."

"More specifically," said Max, "I assume we can see what Brookshaw Consulting are going after?"

Si handed a sheet of paper to Max. "Have a look!"

Max scanned the short list. "So they're pitching for consulting work at the BBC, the department for environment, food and rural affairs, the secretary of state for defence, some large councils, part of the NHS and a handful of other innocuous advisory committees. Busy aren't they."

"Vince called a few of them and guess which one of those has the largest consulting contract up for grabs, worth about fifty million over the next year?"

Max shrugged.

Si leant over and pointed to one of the lines. "This one here, the secretary of state for defence, in other words, the 'Ministry of Defence'."

"The MOD!" repeated Max. "You don't think they have any influence there surely?"

"Unlikely, but who knows? They have rigorous policies and procedures for tendering and contract awards, so I'd have thought it would be hard for them to sway anything. Nonetheless, Max, you should meet up with their Head of Procurement and see what you think. He's new in the role I gather, so should have a fresh, untainted view of everything."

Max casually asked, "Who's that then?"

"Joe Patterson!" said Si. "As you probably realise now, he's just come in from Durham's old firm Gaslec!"

Max looked up startled. "Patterson! You're kidding. I met him recently at Gaslec. Used to work for me. He mentioned he'd got a new job when I saw him."

"Can you trust him?"

"He was a bit slippery, had a few staff issues with him, but otherwise I've no reason to doubt he'd do a good job," pondered Max.

"But can you trust him," insisted Si. "Because you really need him on your side, as your eyes and ears in the MOD. As head of procurement, he'll have a good view of what's going on there and could help you determine if anyone's bringing undue influence on contract awards? In particular, this big consulting deal which Brookshaw's are pitching for?"

"Got it," agreed Max somewhat reluctantly. The thought of having to deal with Joe Patterson wasn't ideal, but it was the best chance they had of getting the inside track on this if something was going on there.

Max contacted Joe and suggested they had dinner as a congratulatory gesture for his new appointment in the MOD. Flattery did the trick and he accepted. Then Max mentioned he also had some developments on the Durham case he wanted to get Joe's views on. Max was careful to pitch it as though he needed Joe's help, and not that he had anything to worry about. He wanted him on-side.

Joe was spending his induction up at the Westminster London MOD offices, before going on to be based at the procurement office in Bristol. They met up in the evening at the exclusive Clos Maggiore restaurant in Covent Garden.

After some pleasantries and polite chit chat, Max turned the conversation to the purpose of the meet.

"Well done with your new role Joe. Quite a coup!" offered Max.

"Thanks, sorry I couldn't say anything before, sworn to secrecy and all that," said Joe with bravado.

"I understand. I have a delicate matter of some importance I've been authorised to discuss with you."

"Authorised? By whom?" probed Joe playing hard to get.

"By MI5. We'd like your help on something," declared Max.

"MI5 want my help? Crikey, I am in demand, aren't I? What for?"

Joe was starting to wonder if this might have anything to

do with what the beautiful temptress Lisa Ely had proposed to him. The 'business networking club'?

"The MOD are about to award a large consulting contract, maybe worth over forty million. We just want to ensure the process is handled transparently, fairly and there's no one bringing any pressure to bear on the decision." Max decided not to share that Brookshaw's was his main target of concern.

"Ah yes," acknowledged Joe. "I'm already getting involved with that one, as it's so big of course. I'll be included in the final stakeholder and committee reviews, and the decisions."

"Perfect. So would you agree to help us, keep your eye on the process and more importantly anyone with a strong view on which supplier should win?"

Joe was now torn. This investigation could well be about Brookshaw's influencing decision-makers to win contracts. Which was exactly what he was about to get himself into, but on the other side. He also figured that maybe his old Gaslec boss David Durham might have been wrapped up in all this. Was that what got him killed?

"Well?" Max snapped him out of his thoughts.

Joe looked carefully at Max, trying to get some visual assurances he could trust him. He had a decision to make. He could tell Max everything he knew, which wasn't much and now that he thought about it, he had no real proof of anything yet. Or he could go ahead with the offer of earning a lot of money for this secret business sect.

Max was conscious of Joe's apparent deliberations.

"You okay Joe? Is there something you want to tell me?" he asked.

There were too many uncertainties for Joe. He would stick with his original plan and see how things transpired.

Styling out his procrastination he replied, "Sorry Max. It's just such a big call, being asked to help you, MI5, all a bit of a shock, you understand." He smiled and offered out a hand to shake. "Of course I'll help. You can rely on me, Max. If anything looks awry, I'll call you!"

The two men enjoyed the rest of their meal, reminiscing about times when they worked together, with Max avoiding any mention of the staff complaints made against Joe. When they went their separate ways that night, Max couldn't help feel something had been up with Joe. Years of reading the subtle body language of suppliers, managers, staff and stakeholders, were telling him Joe struggled with the simple request of watching due process being done.

He reported back to Si Lawson that whilst Joe Patterson was now on board and would keep his eyes open for anything odd, he had some concerns about trusting him.

"We can put a tail on him for a few days," suggested Si, "just for when he leaves the office and a watch on him once he's home. That'll cover off him meeting up with anyone."

"Agreed, let's do that."

"If you feel he's up to something I can get his phones tapped, but I'll need a little more to go on to get that signed off quickly by our magistrate?"

"No, that's fine," said Max. "Don't bother with the phones. It's just a feeling."

"Maybe your chap will come up with something already going on in the MOD," suggested Si. "After all, he's only just joined them, so he'll be on his best behaviour, trying to impress everyone. It's unlikely he'll be involved with anything odd!"

"I'm afraid we have another problem!" said Brett Brookshaw.

"Really?"

"Someone asking too many questions about our organisation and what we do."

Brett didn't want to tell his assassin the new target was with MI5, though he suspected Ed Davies might figure it out from talking to Gillian. He'd dispatched the last two brothers without question, seeing them more as challenges for him and his trusty weapon of choice. The stiletto.

"Each time we do one of these, it does increase the chances of something going wrong." Ed was already up for the next assignment, he just wanted to make the point that Brett was in it with him. "Is it the last solution with this person?" he checked.

Brett contemplated other options he could pursue to put the man from MI5 off the trail. He concluded there were none. This was the easiest, the cleanest. The longer Max Sargent was allowed to snoop around, the more likely he was to find enough evidence to bring down the whole organisation.

Sargent was clearly onto them having travelled to Venice and then St Kitts, though that trail seemed to have closed with his phone being destroyed. Brett had also promised to continue funding Camilo Samuels' daughter in Miami and pay for a top lawyer to minimise his sentence, in return for his silence about the secret sect and his involvement.

"Unfortunately Ed I don't think there's any other way. Just be careful with this one," warned Brett.

"Got it," replied Ed, who had indeed guessed it was likely to be the man who visited Gillian from MI5. He knew though that even men from such infamous organisations, were unlikely to be carrying a gun amongst the British public unless they were on a special op.

"I'll send you his address, but I suggest you don't go there, he's bound to have alarm systems and maybe CCTV. Any ideas how you might handle this?" asked Brett, not really wanting to know any details.

"Like I usually do," dismissed Ed. "Out in plain sight!"

Ed Davies drove to Clapham Common early the next morning and parked several hundred yards up the road from Max's home, nestled amongst other residents' cars. With his mini night vision binoculars, he could clearly see the large, gated house in the small off-shoot road at one end of the Common. He wanted to know just one thing. Figuring that Max likely worked at the Millbank Thames House establishment, Ed wanted to see if he travelled there by using his own car, or by taxi, or using the one mode of transport that would play nicely into his hands. A walk to the underground station on the far side of Clapham Common!

He waited, minimising the use of the binoculars just in case anyone saw him. It was a gloomy morning and well before sunrise, he noticed lights coming on inside Max's house. Alert, he now watched more intently.

At six-thirty the front door opened and Ed got his first sight of Max Sargent. The scenarios and killing options raced through his mind as he studied the man, imagining how he would dispose of this person. What was immediately clear from the glimpse he got, before Max descended the steps and disappeared behind the gates, was that he was a strong, fit man, aware of his surroundings.

Ed watched as the gates slowly opened, expecting to see Max drive out through them. He was rewarded when Max walked through them, crossed the road and set off across Clapham Common.

'Great!', thought Ed.

But as he continued to watch, lowering himself into his seat a little, the strong, determined posture and walk were not lost on him. He played through a scene of him walking towards Max in the open space, then just as they came level with one another, his stiletto was swiftly drawn and activated. Max would crumple to the ground as he walked on. There were only a few other people on the common, so it was unlikely anyone would recognise him as he faded into the poorly lit expanse.

Watching Max walk on, Ed quickly dismissed the idea. Max would undoubtedly clock him as he approached, and either avoid him or be ready. Too risky to try that and it did rely on no one else being around. If they got into a tussle, he didn't like his chances against this man. No, he would go for the alternative idea. He watched Max disappear into the distance across the common, towards the tube station.

Joe Patterson had been thinking about his dinner with Max. His old boss of long since, now with MI5, suspected foul play at his new employer, the MOD. This had brought into sharp focus the risks he now faced. It made him nervous, but at the same time, that defiance he'd always had in him, spurred him on.

The senior directors of his inherited MOD procurement team had just taken him through a summary of the most comprehensive consulting tender process he'd ever known. It was a run-through, in preparation for an important update meeting, where procurement and other stakeholders would present an interim update to senior officials including the top person of the whole organisation. Today, they would be presenting to their UK government cabinet boss, the Secretary of State for Defence!

It was unusual for the minister to be involved in such matters, but given the value of this contract, almost fifty million pounds in the first year, he wanted to make sure the process was being undertaken with perfect professionalism and transparency. When it was decided, his name would be associated with the award. If it went wrong in any way, the British press would hound him for answers and explanations.

The procurement process had started with an open invitation for consulting firms to submit their intention to tender for the business. Following strict timings throughout the review, suppliers were then sent terms and conditions to sign up to, before then receiving the pre-tender pack. This took the form of a detailed and lengthy request for information, asking everything about the supplier, their accounts, management, other customers, any conflicts of interest, background checks, financial credit rating, expertise, capabilities and so on.

Once firms got through the basic checks and balances showing they had the experience, status, size and record to potentially take on the assignment with the MOD, they were sent the tender pack.

Suppliers were given the precise details of the consulting work that was expected across the MOD. This was broken down into six separate workstreams covering staff improvement, cost-cutting, media and communications, policies, strategy and quality.

Bidders were then marshalled through another long set of documents inviting them to outline what work would be proposed to tackle each workstream. This included consulting staff profiles and the number of days allocated, individual day rates, key performance indicators, measurement, timings, delivery criteria, escalation of issues, review mechanisms along with every part of how the MOD's expectations would be met and costed.

Joe's previous experience in the sharp, agile private sector allowed him to make some astute suggestions to enhance the best practices and tender format for the more cumbersome public entity. On the whole, though, he told his team it was a first-class tender process and they were ready to show it off to the senior stakeholders and the minister.

The deputy procurement head offered to lead the presentation, given Joe was new in the role. Joe quickly made it clear that he would front the meeting for procurement, knowing that his deputy had applied for his top job and was likely wanting to show everyone he should have got it! Joe was a force to be reckoned with when it came to office point-scoring tactics.

As the meeting approached, he was surprised at the sheer number of people filing into the large conference room. It seemed that such a sizable contract enticed everyone wanting to be associated with the hard work stakeholders and procurement had done.

Joe had already been briefed on their target audience, whose reserved seats in the front row lay empty, waiting for other high-ranking officials to arrive. Once everyone else was seated, a secretary checked that they could begin, then rushed off to collect the top brass.

The pretence and formality of it all even started to make Joe feel a little nervous. This really was a big deal!

Finally, they entered the large room in single file and made their way to their seats. Some acknowledged the waiting audience, a couple of them smiled and nodded, others looked serious and threatening, exacerbating the gravity of the meeting even more.

The men and women in the front row represented the three leadership streams of the Ministry of Defence. From the Defence Board, the highest committee, the cabinet minister Secretary of State for Defence was accompanied by the Permanent Secretary and the Minister of State for Defence Procurement, who was Joe's boss. The Defence Council had a couple of knighted high-ranking servicemen attending, an Admiral and an Air Chief Marshal. Finally, there were four members of the MOD's Executive Committee representing operations, information technology, finance and the Chief of Defence Staff.

As agreed beforehand, Joe's boss stood up and briefly addressed the entire room, setting the scene with assurances of best practice, stakeholder engagement, due diligence and transparency. The meeting was then begun with presentations from IT, Operations, Human Resources and Finance. Each of these was designed to show that all parts of the organisation had been involved with defining what was required and had been involved in the process. This all led up to united support of the procurement segment at the end.

Joe was ready. He went to the front and for a few moments, smiled and surveyed the forty or so people in the audience, gathering their full attention with the brief silence. When he felt they were all engaged, he opened his presentation.

"You know the thing I love about procurement, is that it will always find improvements. It's infinite. We do the very best deal we can today... and tomorrow we want to improve it again. By applying a professional procurement process to the review of any product or service, we will find improvements, maybe in costs, quality, process, delivery, account management, technology, efficiency or the legal contract. I am proud of what my team here have achieved with this important review, which has been conducted with the utmost integrity. Now that we are nearing the final pitches and selection stages, I'm delighted to give you all an update on where we are including the front-runners!"

Joe pitched his opener with passion and confidence, checking the front row. They were hooked. Nods of appreciation and confident smiles broke through the steely faces. His boss smiled, feeling that his choice of Joe for the role was vindicated. Joe's disgruntled deputy also nodded in appreciation of his new leader's performance.

Over the next forty-five minutes, he went through the steps of the tender process, with more assurances of a thorough and fair review process. Towards the end of which even one of the minister's cut in.

"Mr Patterson. I think I can say on behalf of the panel we are totally behind you and how your team have conducted the review. Why don't you now cut to the shortlisted suppliers, as I know some of us have time constraints."

Joe then went through each of the top suppliers that had made it through the stages so far and were closing in on the contract prize.

There were the usual large, household name firms, mostly with financial backgrounds who had expanded their services to cover all aspects of businesses and industries. Consulting was big money, charging clients anything between £700 and £5,000 per day for their varying hierarchy of consultants.

There were also several niche management firms, and then there was what was becoming known as the 'giant slayer'... Brookshaw Consulting! The fast-expanding, up and coming, hungry new kids on the block.

Joe was incredibly subtle in the way he pushed

Brookshaw's forward, making little comparisons with the others, extolling the benefits of picking not the largest, nor the smallest, a firm that would be flexible in it's approach, that wanted success for their customer more than racking up chargeable days.

He ended the presentation explaining what the final steps in the process would be, including pitches to stakeholders by the top suppliers, scoring them against detailed criteria and then contract negotiations including service delivery and overall price.

At the end, the Secretary of State for Defence stood up and thanked everyone for their time and hard work. Everyone began to leave the room, chatting about what they'd heard, shaking hands with members of the team and introducing new faces.

The Secretary of State for Defence approached Joe who was still standing up front by the screen. His words were hushed and precisely chosen.

"Good to have you on board Joe. I'd say Brookshaw's are looking good, wouldn't you?"

He smiled, pausing for a moment before his hovering entourage ushed him out, leaving Joe to his thoughts.

12

The next morning Max set off across Clapham Common from his home. The sun was just starting to appear, bringing much-needed light and warmth to the cool, damp London morning. He passed the bandstand in the centre of the common and then the small lake called the Long Pond, a favourite of model boating enthusiasts, before exiting the one kilometre long common onto the street called The Pavement.

The West entrance to Clapham Common Station was unlike most other large, obvious Underground entrances. The small domed roof above the stairway down to the station, sat apologetically in the middle of a cross-section of two busy roads by a small clock tower.

It was a simple station, with two small entrances, one way to get to and from the trains via the stairs or escalators, and a single island platform between both the north and south bound lines.

Despite the early hour, commuters were already converging at the entrance and filing down the stairs. Max made his way down to the platform which stood between the two lines and edged towards the northbound side. It was already busy with travellers piling up waiting for the next train.

The rush of air being pushed through the tunnel signalled its approach and people folded newspapers and picked up briefcases, starting to jostle for position ready to board. The seasoned amongst them would calmly stand exactly where they knew the carriage doors would come to a stop, ready to be the first on with a better chance of a seat.

Max was relaxed and never joined in the unseen battle to secure a much sought-after seat. He only had six stops to

Embankment, then a change and one more stop to get to Westminster, one of the nearest undergrounds to Thames House at Millbank.

Despite the station being near the bottom end of the Northern line, the train was already full of commuters that had boarded in Wimbledon, Tooting and South Clapham. People would huff and puff and tut as they got on, starting their days being grumpy about the crowded trains. But this was London rush hour and Max had long since decided that the best way to deal with the mad rat race, was to simply go with the flow, keep to yourself and embrace the inevitability of it all! It was a pain.

He managed to carefully squeeze himself into the centre of the carriage and pressed between other bodies, held onto the handrail above them running the length of the crowded space.

The last few people pushed in battling with both unwilling bodies reluctant to move over again and the determined closing doors of the train. Everyone stood subtly bracing themselves as the train started, careful not to swing or fall into someone else.

Most people in the confined space would fix a gaze onto something nearby, a shoulder, an advertising poster, a light, anything but look someone else in the face or meet another's stare. Max had an inbuilt caution, perhaps from his brief service in the Commandos some twenty years ago, and always liked to survey his surroundings. He casually glanced at the people around him, just a quick check on how they looked, how they stood, their demeanour.

'The usual odd mix of people', Max thought to himself. With one exception. All of their pale skin complexions were punctuated by one tanned, handsome man, with dark eyes and hair. Max envied the sun-kissed look but then thought nothing more of it and began studying one of the ad boards.

The train stopped at Clapham North where a couple of people pushed out onto the platform, past many more trying to get onto the train. Bodies were pressed together more.

Ed Davies had been waiting on the Clapham Common platform for half-an-hour, before Max appeared, mingling in with commuters but refraining from boarding a train. Finally, he'd spotted Max descending onto the platform. He'd then surreptitiously blended into the crowd as he manoeuvred himself nearer, to ensure he got through the same doorway of the train. He'd wanted to be close, but not right next to Max.

As the train pulled into Stockwell, Ed took advantage of the ebb and flow of passengers leaving and getting on, others jostling for better positions or grabbing a vacated seat. He positioned himself one person away from Max ensuring that he was lined up behind two other people to Max's side. The doors closed and the train lurched on.

"Do you mind! Stop pushing!"

The silence was broken by an irate passenger who'd had enough of being pushed by another. The distraction allowed Ed to take the stiletto handle from his pocket and cup it in his hand. He quickly glanced at Max and the path he would need to take between two other people pressed together.

He knew he needed to make the move just as they approached a station, so he could exit quickly before anyone realised what had happened.

The train started to decelerate as it came towards Oval station. Ed decided to go for it, trying to mask his heightening tension, as he threaded his arm between the two people in front of him.

In his peripheral vision, Max just caught the look of anxiety in the eyes of the dark stranger.

The woman next to him swayed back as the train slowed, then looked down.

"What are you doing!" she exclaimed, turning her stare onto the dark figure.

In the same instant, Max's eyes dropped from the man's face, now looking determined, down his shoulder and arm, which then disappeared between the neighbouring passengers.

Just as Max looked down to his side, he caught a glimpse

of the tanned hand.

Max pushed out at the two people between him and the man holding the knife handle, just as Ed pressed the button and sent the long blade shooting out of its retaining handle.

Max had been just in time to create the few inches of distance needed to avoid a fatal stab and as he simultaneously spun round, the blade's tip sliced through his shirt and cut a harsh two-inch graze into his side.

Ed saw that he'd missed and with the flashing blade still extended, started to lunge forward again aiming more mercilessly now at Max's heart.

The woman saw the knife and screamed, as other nearby passengers were also startled by the furore.

As Ed lunged the stiletto forward, Max dodged back to avoid the jab, pushing several more people behind him into one another, protesting their anger out loud. One man fell into the lap of a seated woman.

Whilst Ed's hand was still outstretched with the knife, Max took his chance in the crowded space and punched the back of his attacker's hand, making sure his second knuckle made contact first, to inflict a disabling blow.

Ed cried out and involuntarily let go of the stiletto. It fell to the floor, as the train pulled up alongside the next platform.

For a moment, whilst both gathering themselves, the eyes of Max and Ed met, assessing one another, judging options. They both came to the same conclusion now the stiletto advantage was lost.

Ed was first to move. He violently shoved the closest commuter aside, clearing his path towards the opening doors. As he exited the carriage, Max was already weaving his way through people, making his way to the same opening.

He burst out onto the northbound platform at the Oval, just in time to see the knifeman running into the passageway linking the two separate platforms at the station.

Max ignored more cries from people and ran after him.

Ed could see a train getting ready to leave the southbound

platform ahead. He came out of the short tunnel and ran halfway down the platform to put some distance between him and Max. Just as the beeping noise signalled that the doors were closing, Ed dived into the next opening, just as the doors shut.

The train heading away from the City was half empty. Ed fell into a seat in time to watch Max stop running on the platform and look at him in despair. Ed allowed himself a smile as his carriage in the middle of the train, passed by Max then left him behind. He'd got away.

Max watched the train slowly accelerate as it passed him. He instantly judged its speed and started scanning the carriages for anything to grab onto. The sides had no protruding rails or handles.

He started running down the platform in the same direction as the train. By the time the rear of the train came level with him, he was sprinting at almost the same speed as the final carriage. But he was about to run out of platform!

The back of the train had both a small ledge in front of the closed door at the end and also several bars for maintenance men to climb onto the roof for inspections.

Max launched himself off the edge of the last few yards of platform, just in time to grasp one of the hand-bars above him and land on the small foot ledge. The train disappeared from the station's light into the dark tunnel.

Max grappled with the door handle and upon realising it was locked from the inside, started banging on the window. Several seated and shocked passengers got up and came over to the door.

"Let me in, please? I'm police!" shouted Max, knowing the 'police' card usually got people to follow instructions. They opened the door, as the train went back to the previous station at Stockwell. Max started to make his way through the first carriage. He reckoned the knifeman was about three carriages ahead.

Ed sat back in his seat relieved the whole thing was over.

He was angry he hadn't got his target and was starting to wonder if he should go back to life in Italy. People had seen him and CCTV might have captured him somewhere, but he didn't have any official criminal record.

Toying with the idea of going home or staying in London with Gillian, he looked up at the tube map. Morden was at the end of the line, but what if Max had managed to call the police, then that was the most likely station they'd get to in time to meet him. He needed to get off sooner, so randomly picked Tooting Bec to get off at, in five stops time.

Max approached the interconnecting door to the next carriage and peered through to survey the passengers, before going through. He moved down the centre aisle, watched by surprised commuters wondering why on earth someone needed to change carriages for a short journey.

Each time the train stopped at the station, Max found his way to the nearest doorway and stuck his head out, looking up the platform at the carriage exits, checking to see if his attacker got off. He didn't. He must still be on the train.

He came up to the next interconnecting door with more caution, knowing he would soon see the man he was after. As he glanced through the small door's dirty window, he immediately spotted the suave, tanned, young man seated halfway down the carriage, staring forwards. There were about eight yards between them.

Max moved back from the door as the train pulled into Balham station. He quickly looked through the small door's window again to make sure the man didn't leave the train. He remained seated.

As the train pulled away, Max grasped the door handle, took a deep breath, then burst through!

As he focused on the seat the man had been sitting in, he was shocked to see it was now empty, which momentarily put him off his stride.

Ed had just gotten up and was moving to the exit doors just beyond his seat in readiness to swiftly get off at the next stop.

Hearing the interconnecting door behind him burst open slamming against the side of a seat, he turned.

With the surprise shock of seeing Max running into the carriage, he froze for a second, trying to take in the sight of his chaser now confronting him. Then he turned and ran!

Max followed more slowly, assuring commuters that there was nothing to worry about, police matter, knowing there were only a few carriages left before they would be stopped by the driver's locked door at the front. He watched the man disappear through the next end door and off along the aisle.

Max proceeded through the same door and the next carriage and peered through the following window. Ed wasn't anywhere to be seen, he must have already got into the last carriage beyond. He went through the narrow door.

Smash!

Ed's fist came cracking down into the side of Max's face as he emerged from the doorway.

Ed had jumped up onto the seat behind the door, pressing himself into the corner, waiting for Max to come through.

The blow was a good one and along with the stunning shock of it, sent Max onto his knees, reeling over an empty seat opposite Ed. But this put a few feet between them, which gave Max just enough time to recover and see the next blow coming at him. He swerved his head to the side avoiding the strike, then grabbed Ed's extended arm, lifted it and hit home a hard punch into the man's gut. He doubled up and staggered back down the aisle.

The few passengers in the carriage cried out alarmed and started to get up and move away from the two fighting men. A couple of them called out for help ineffectively, in the sealed metal space inside a dark tunnel. The driver ahead couldn't hear them.

Max got to his feet and beckoned them to move to the far end of the carriage.

"Stay back please, this man is dangerous!" Max advised with authority.

He then looked at Ed and allowed himself to comment glibly, "Though perhaps not quite so dangerous, now you've lost your stiletto eh?"

Ed stood up straight, sneering at the sarcastic jibe. He was cornered. No more running. Time to fight.

He lowered his hand to the large belt buckle he was wearing, pressed on a clip and slowly, deliberately withdrew a short-bladed knife!

Max watched on and realised he'd taken the man for granted too soon. The shiny blade was less only a couple of inches long and an inch wide, but was still capable of slicing deep gashes into him. Ed gripped the small handle tightly and now waited for Max to make the next move.

"Listen, we don't have to do this," offered Max, hoping to avoid any continuation of the brawl, with the appearance of this new weapon. "You know we'll find you sooner or later. I'll let you off at the next stop?" he suggested, hopefully.

Ed backed up towards the exit doors as the train began to slow up.

"Not such a smartass with the comments now, are you?" sneered Ed. "Yes I'm getting off now, and if I see you exit this train onto the platform behind me, I'll start using this on some of the other commuters!" he threatened, waving the blade briefly at the huddled passengers at the far end.

Max knew he had to concede, there were too many people in the carriage and station, to become a passing target for this madman to hurt. A quick slash of that blade would change someone's life forever, if it didn't end up killing them.

Max held his hands up. "Okay! Go! Just don't hurt anyone. I'll stay on the train." Max seethed with anger and frustration having to give in to the situation, but was conscious of the audience at the other end of the aisle watching and listening to everything being said. He had to put the public's safety first now. This fish could hopefully be caught another time.

The carriage pierced into the lighting of Tooting Bec's underground station and slowed to a halt. Ed kept the small knife held up at Max and backed into the doors waiting for them to open.

Nodding he said, "Persistent, aren't you! I'll give you that." The doors opened. "Until next time!"

With that, Ed stepped back onto the platform and then ran towards the exit.

Max gritted his teeth as he watched the man disappear. "Until next time!" he said under his breath.

The passengers at the far end remained frozen, not wanting to get involved, nor risk exiting the train with the knifeman outside. They all stared at Max, not a word was spoken. The doors closed and together, with Max, they pulled out of the station back into the blackness of the tunnel.

Joe's phone rang, showing 'Caller Unknown' on the screen. He answered. "Hello?"

"Joe Patterson?" checked the other man's voice.

"Yes. Who's this?"

"You recently had a conversation with a certain attractive young lady, about joining a special kind of club, yes?"

"Oh yes, that's right." Joe's heart rate increased. This was it. The call he'd been expecting. The secret business networking sect.

"Are you still fully committed to joining?"

"Yes. Well, at least I'd like to understand more about it, what I'm getting into," suggested Joe tentatively.

"Of course, that's understandable. We'd like to invite you to the induction, before which you can meet the leader and he'll explain everything and answer any questions you might have."

"Sounds fair, then I can decide if I want to join or not?"

"No, I'm afraid it doesn't work like that, you'll be committed by then. You must decide now, one way or the other. Your lady-friend would have told you what you need to know."

"Well, that wasn't much. How do you know you want me in this club?"

"A close colleague of yours was part of our organisation. He recommended you, highly. The lady you had a brief liaison with thinks you're suitable. And you've already started to show you can do your part with your presentation and recommendations at the MOD!"

Joe was flattered though trying to assimilate all that was being said.

"Colleague, who? And how do you know about what I presented at the MOD? It's confidential!" Joe started to feel a little disconcerted about this club knowing so much about him. He figured the colleague had to be his old Gaslec Chief Exec David Durham, especially as the caller said *was* with us!

The reply skipped over directly answering his first question. "We are far-reaching and have a lot of prestigious, senior members. We look out for one another. And when you contribute to the organisation, the rewards are significant. You will become a wealthy man Mr Patterson!"

Joe quickly weighed up everything as best he could. Part of him had alarm bells ringing loudly. This was clearly a dangerous and no doubt illegal, immoral enterprise. But the flattery of being chosen for this elite club, the excitement of it all, the challenge, and most of all the promise of big money, had won him over.

"I'm in!" he announced.

"Excellent. Do you have a pen and I'll give you the address of where to go and when. Please remember our first rule. Total secrecy. You are not to speak of this to anyone, ever!"

Later that day Max spent time at Thames House with the identity team, piecing together a digital photofit of the knifeman on the tube. Having spent hours compiling what he felt to be a good image, they ran through the available record searches MI5 had access to which included passports, driving licences and a bunch of internet and social media mediums where face images are used for registration or user profile purposes.

Max pointed out that the man had the tiniest hint of a foreign, vivacious accent when he spoke, possibly Spanish or Italian, much to the identification analyst's frustration.

"Well of course that explains why I can't track him down. Your stiletto man has no criminal record, no apparent UK footprint and is probably not even from this country. He's likely under a foreign passport!"

Eduardo Davies had indeed escaped initial identification, as he still went under his Italian passport and documents.

Max inquired with the Met and Transport police as to whether the infamous stiletto knife had been found and handed in. This might at least link the owner to David Durham's murder.

However, neither had any reports of the knife and suggested that someone had probably picked it up and was either intending to hand it in, or unfortunately might have decided to keep the rare and powerful automatic switchblade.

"Sometimes these things take time to fall into place," said Si Lawson, seeing that Max was frustrated.

"This is crazy, the knifeman almost killed me this morning, there were witnesses the police can get by appealing to commuters at the station. But I'm guessing we won't bother with that, given we can't even get the identity of the bloke, who then gets away because I let him!" huffed Max.

"I understand," said Si sympathetically. "We can all agree it's highly likely your man was David Durham's killer, and it's not too long a stretch to now conclude he could be working for Headshell, or Brookshaw. More than likely by the sounds of it, they're bribing and influencing business for their own gain. We're onto them Max, just keep going and the evidence will start dropping out, it always does. We need evidence, hard proof."

"Unless this ends up being one of those cases that get

added to the 'unsolved' pile!" said Max angrily.

Si put his hand on Max's shoulder. "Here at MI5 we don't have many cases in that *unsolved* pile. Look, why don't you take the rest of the day off," he said half-jokingly as it was already gone three in the afternoon. "You've had a close call this morning, almost got yourself assassinated for crying out loud, but no-one got hurt thanks to you. You've spent the rest of the day fretting about his identity and this whole case not going fast enough. Go home and I'll see you tomorrow?"

Max sighed and decided the boss was right.

"Thanks, Si."

Max got back to his Clapham home by four and settled down for a chilled evening in front of the TV. At six he got himself cheese on toast with a couple of boiled eggs on top. But he couldn't stop thinking about the case. Images kept swirling round his mind, of the murals on the walls of the Venetian house, of the glimpse he got of the Headshell accounts and the strange twenty-eight million expenses, and of what he could have done differently on the underground train.

He needed to clear his head, so went out to his garage, a rarity in Clapham. The roller door lifted revealing his two supercar investments sitting menacingly on the car lift system he'd had installed, to accommodate one car above the other inside the garage pit.

His Vector W8 American supercar and Ferrari F40, both had powerful V8 twin-turbo engines, both were left-hand drive. Only seventeen of this model Vector were made, before the inventor entrepreneur's firm ran into financial difficulty and production ceased. With its wedged shape, it was modelled on a fighter jet. Opening the upward scissor doors, similar to many Lamborghini's, revealed a dash and gear level resembling that of a fighter plane, with an LED display panel and controls.

Above the Vector sat the Ferrari F40, one of the most iconic supercars in the world, with its distinctive large rear aerofoil and perspex covered engine bay. Only thirteen hundred were made and since Max bought his for several hundred thousand some years ago, they were now changing hands for a cool million.

The design, effort and cost of the F40 went into its mechanics and certainly not the sparse, unimaginative interior. With hard bucket seats, no electric windows or air con or carpets, the driver rightly felt as though they were in a stripped-out racing car, for good reason. It was a useful and constant reminder of what the powerful car was capable of and demanded respect when driving it.

Max drove the F40 out and through the gates, as the garage door closed behind him. A blast down the A3 would help clear his mind of Venice, Brookshaw's and stiletto knives!

Max passed through Wandsworth then opened the car up as he approached the Wimbledon area. Twilight set in. Max's phone rang, it was Si.

"Max, got some news for you and by the sounds of it, you're in your car which is good."

"What's up Si?"

"Graham Satchel just called in, our guy assigned to keep tabs on Joe Patterson. He's on the move!" said Si enthusiastically.

"Oh yeah, where to?"

"He doesn't know the end location yet, they've just turned off the M23 at Copthorne West Sussex and are now heading towards East Grinstead."

"What on earth would Joe be doing down there tonight?" muttered Max to himself.

"Graham thought you'd be interested and might want to join him? He'll guide you in, to wherever they end up."

"What, now?"

"Yes! You should go, Max, where are you?"

"Coming out of London on the A3, just went for a drive to clear my head."

"Perfect," said Si. "You're probably less than forty-five

minutes behind them, so keep going down to East Grinstead and I'll get Graham to liaise with you directly on what's happening. Could be nothing of course."

"So just follow, watch and observe, and standby?" checked Max.

"Yes, unless you've got something better to do! You never know Max. Graham should have binoculars and maybe his long-range listening pointer with him. Keep me updated okay and stay out of sight?"

Ten minutes later Max's phone rang again.

"Max? It's Graham. Si updated you?"

"Hi Graham, where are you, still on the move?"

"He's just pulled off a road called Hindleap Lane in Wych Cross. I drove on past him, hang on, I'm going to take the next turnoff, it's called Twyford Lane. Put that in your SatNav."

"What if he's continuing on somewhere else?" asked Max.

"Unlikely," replied Graham, "I can see on the map the road he went into is a dead end. Looks like it only leads to a large residential estate with a long driveway." He flipped his map onto Satellite' view. "Big place and grounds, with its own lake by the look of it!"

"On my way," said Max, "should be with you in half an hour or so."

"I'll find somewhere to park that'll get us near to a good observation point. Keep on down this lane and park up when you come across my dark blue Audi," instructed Graham. "Call me when you're here and I'll tell you where I am, it's all trees and ferns here so we've got good cover to observe from."

"How will we see anything in the dark?"

"No worries Max, I've got a couple of night vision binoculars!"

"What the hell can he be doing down here in the middle of Ashdown Forest?" posed Max.

Graham just shrugged at his phone then rang off.

13

Joe Patterson drove up the long driveway through the trees, wondering what awaited him. He was nervous. The commitment and the apparent dangers of joining this organisation were now clear to him. It was a risk. But he was also excited. Flattered at being asked to join this elite businessman's club, along with other senior people of industry, he imagined himself to be one of the younger participants. His fast career rise and positions of power would stand him in good stead, to contribute to the greater cause, and more importantly, benefit him from the contributions of others like him. He clenched the steering wheel and nodded to himself that he was doing the right thing. If he did what they asked, they would surely protect him.

He rounded a bend and was then afforded his first view of the magnificent open grounds surrounding the large country house. It was stunning. An oasis hidden away from the world on Ashdown Forest, in well-to-do West Sussex.

The grounds showed signs of being meticulously kept in order by a team of full-time gardeners. Lawns were mowed with straight lines, flowerbeds weeded, trees pruned, and leaves cleared. There were a couple of ornate fountains, a rose garden and a few statues scattered around, all serving to build the expectations of who lived here.

The manor house was a large square-shaped three-storey building straight out of a period novel or movie. Joe half expected the maids and butlers to dash out to greet him. Some of the lights inside were on and he could see figures standing and moving about. There was a single-story extension on the rear of the building for the indoor swimming pool and in the distance, he could see a tennis court.

The driveway swept round to the front of the house and opened into a vast expanse, where about seven cars of various prestige marques were parked up under the feint moonlight. Joe pulled up amongst them, his anticipation rising, he took a deep breath before getting out.

A man in a black suit emerged from the large entrance and beckoned Joe to come over to him. It was Liam Welling, Brett Brookshaw's bodyguard and 'enforcer'.

Liam was in his late forties, medium height, medium build, unremarkable looks with short, plain hair, a forgettable neutral face, grey-green eyes set deep in their sockets and a strong jawline. An unremarkable man in every way and someone you might briefly talk to at a party, then by the end of the evening, have completely forgotten.

Part of a large family brought up on a council estate near Croydon, getting any airtime with his wayward parents was near impossible, with six other siblings fighting for their meagre attention. They all went to the local comprehensive school and half of them had left education by the time they reached sixteen.

Liam battled on to get a couple of poor grades at A level, but enough to give him a start, to break away from their family's destitute destiny. Like his brother and sisters, they all headed out into the world in different and separate directions.

Liam tried a few jobs including bricklaying, then a plumber's apprentice and finally a dull administrative office job for the local council. Nothing seemed to spark his interest but he realised that he didn't want to sit behind a desk. Seeking outdoor excitement, he applied to join the London Fire Brigade.

He sailed through the preliminary medicals, tests and interviews and went on to excel in the six-week pre-course learning scheme. After an eleven-week training course, he was appointed as a Firefighter stationed at his local depot in

Croydon.

Liam spent fifteen years in the fire service, working his way up through Leading Firefighter to Sub Officer, but not to Station Officer or Commander. Those roles were taken by remarkable people and Liam was not one of them. He was a good firefighter, cut a few corners, not one to take station pranks well and preferred to stay clear of drunken boy's nights out with colleagues.

Instead, he'd been wooed by another firefighter into a far more exciting hobby. One that held the carrot of riches in front of your nose every day, but the carrot was held by a demon. Liam started gambling!

At first, it was the ever-expanding choice of instant, daily and weekly lottery related cards and tickets. Then with his friend, they'd become regular visitors at one of the high street betting shops, where they would place their hard-earned pay on horses they knew nothing about and football scores they had a feeling about.

As fast as Liam earned money from his firefighting, it went on rent, food and gambling. Sometimes he'd win big, hundreds and a few times, thousands. But this only served to fuel the addiction, teasing him with the brief delights of winning and urging him to bet more to keep on winning.

Eventually, the miserable lifestyle began to take its toll on his mental health and emotions, which in turn led him to the demon's other enticement, alcohol. Once he began drinking regularly to escape his misfortunes and drown his sorrows, it wasn't long before his hangovers and lingering intoxication were seen at work.

His Station Officer had high regard for Liam, who had been a solid firefighter, saving many lives and buildings during his career. But the boss had no option and was forced to hand down verbal, then written warnings. Liam kicked both habits, for a while, but the draw was engrained in him now and as soon as he returned to the gambling, the losing and then the drink, he was hauled up in front of the Station Commander and told he would be fired. His bosses took pity on their colleague whom they'd served alongside for a decade and a half, and gave him the unspoken option of resigning, before being formally dismissed. Liam walked out with a small pension and a modest payment for his fifteen years' service.

Distraught, dejected and seething with anger at himself, he went into London to enjoy his money and make it work for him. He went to one of the many casinos he now frequented, the Hippodrome by Leicester Square.

That same evening a certain Brett Brookshaw was also inside the Hippodrome casino with some guests, potential clients, having taken them to a late afternoon theatre show. They'd dined at the casino's Heliot steak house and were now playing at the roulette tables.

Opened in 1900, the Hippodrome was the most innovative theatre in London, with ballet's, circus acts with live animals and a large pool. A long string of top performers displayed their crafts at the Hippodrome, including the escape artist Harry Houdini and Judy Garland. The famous site latterly became one of the 'in' nightclubs, Stringfellows, before being reclaimed back into the entertainment and casino complex it is now.

Liam's fortune that night consisted of a long-drawn-out financial death. He won a little, then lost it, ate into his money more, won some, lost again. The house odds stacked against him, gradually and painfully clawed away at the last of his worldly wealth. Fuelled by the complimentary drinks on offer, encouraging players to remain at the gambling tables, he got louder and angrier.

One of the other players at the same roulette wheel was a Chinese man, who took his gambling very seriously. Annoyed at the drunk Englishman disrupting his evening's pleasure, he started politely muttering his disapproval of Liam's behaviour. The mutterings became open criticism, then complaint, and finally, when Liam accidentally knocked over his pile of chips, he shouted at him.

"What are you doing, you stupid drunk man. Leave the table, you are ruining everyone's night and bringing us all bad luck!" Looking at the croupier, "Why can't you ask him to leave?"

Liam fought back. "Listen here you, I'm a member of this club and have just as much right to play, as you do. Who do you think you are coming over here and speaking to me like that!"

"Stupid gweilo!"

Liam was incensed and clumsily shoved the man back away from the table. Now insulted, the Chinese man grabbed the nearest glass, which happened to be Brett's drink, smashed it on the edge of the roulette table and held it up, threatening to lunge at Liam.

Just as he started to move at him, a strong arm locked into the Chinese man's thrusting arm, gripping it in a vice hold. At the same time, his other arm was wrenched behind his back momentarily disabling him.

Brett had watched on as these two players' argument had escalated and instinctively stepped in when his glass had been grabbed.

"Okay, okay, I think that's gone far enough," shouted Brett holding the struggling Oriental. "He's just had a few drinks, there's no need for any violence is there!"

The casino security guards descended and wrestled the man away from Brett who obligingly handed him over. One man in a suit also guided Liam away from the table and towards the exit. Everyone around the roulette wheel was stunned by the ruckus. The croupier broke the silence with those words that got their attention and brought gamblers excitement and hope.

"Place your bets ladies and gentlemen!"

And within moments normality was restored.

Later than night Brett escorted his guests to the exit and noticed the drunk man from his table whom he'd saved, slumped outside on the pavement, being laughed at by some passing revellers. He ushered his guests into taxis and approached the poor soul, waving away the group making fun of him.

"What a state we're in eh ol' pal, you okay?" said Brett sympathetically.

Liam looked up and recognised Brett from the roulette table. "Bloody gambling! Lost the lot!" he slurred angrily.

"They always win don't they," empathised Brett looking back at the casino. "Best stay away so you don't lose anymore eh."

Brett's large black chauffeur-driven Mercedes pulled up alongside them.

"No, I've lost the lot! I mean everything I have! I'm finished! I won't even be able to meet the rent anymore!"

Liam's head sunk down in shame. Brett felt for the man. He could sense he was a good person and something inside inexplicably urged him to help this man. He'd often given money to down-and-outs, but this person had more to him than met the eye. Without really thinking about it, he made Liam an offer that would change his life.

"Listen, why don't you come back home with me just now, have a good night's sleep and we can help you sort things out in the morning? It's a short drive, but I've got a little place down in the countryside, nice and quiet away from all this."

Liam rewarded Brett with an appreciative smile and nodded, heaving himself up onto his feet with Brett's help. He fell asleep in the back of the car and barely woke once they arrived at the Manor House near Forest Row, which Brett had recently acquired for him and his sister Gillian.

Over the next few days, Brett allowed Liam to stay at the house to sober up, get to know him, and assess him as to how to help him. Grateful to Brett for his help, Liam repaid him by asking what work he could do around the estate, anything his saviour wanted of him was willingly undertaken.

It soon became clear to Brett that this fallen angel had been sent to him for a reason, which they could both benefit from.

As the weeks and months passed, Brett got used to Liam being around, filling in for sick or absent gardeners, his chauffeur or looking after the pool. He could have sent him on his way with a fresh start, money for a rental and food, but it seemed far easier to employ him within his fast-expanding empire.

Four months after that fateful night at the casino, Brett trusted Liam more than anyone beyond his sister. The ex-firefighter would now literally do anything for him, anything. He suggested Liam became his 'special assistant' with duties including chauffeur, porter, bodyguard, helper, fixer and some years later, he became his enforcer!

When Brett decided to move to New York to grow the business in the US, Liam accompanied him out there as his dutiful, loyal servant. When Brett introduced him to his dissident sect exploiting the business world, he fell into the role of Brett's guard dog without question. He'd also play the role of Brett's very own Charon, the ferryman and gatekeeper to his underworld!

"Joe Patterson?" checked Liam, "welcome to the Manor House."

As Joe walked over to the entrance, he could now see the splendid vista the large house faced to the left. Adorned by the moonlight glimpsing through the sparse cloud covering, long terraced lawns led down to a small lake at the bottom. The expanse of water glistened amongst its darker surrounding forest with dense trees and a couple of smaller lawns.

"Wow, quite a place you have here! Who owns all this?"

"We do," said Liam. "By that, I mean the Brookshaw's, Brett and Gillian. Manor House is predominantly the home of Gillian, but we use it from time to time for special occasions, like tonight."

"For me?" asked Joe, expecting to be told something else grand was taking place.

"Indeed. For your ceremony Joe," said Liam sternly. "We

take such things quite seriously. The induction of a new brother into the sect is a huge commitment for us, and of course even more so for you! And a celebration, you're lucky to have been chosen to join," he added awkwardly.

They admired the view for a moment, then Liam led Joe into the hallway.

"Please wait here for a moment," instructed Liam pointing to a chair. He then carried on towards one of the many doorways off the large hall.

Joe could see through into what appeared to be a lounge, where several men were gathered, talking in hushed whispers. But it was what they were wearing that spiked his interest.

Each wore a jet black, silken full-length robe, like an ancient monk's, covering their entire body. Their hood cowls were pulled back and draped around the shoulders. He thought he recognised one of the men but couldn't quite place him. Perhaps he'd seen him on TV or something? Joe found the sight of the men dressed in ominous black robes both intriguing and a little disconcerting.

"Come through please to meet the Grand Master!" announced Liam from the doorway. Watched by the men in the adjoining room, he led Joe into a large library office. Another man rose from one of the leather seats by a coffee table. "Joe Patterson. Meet Grand Master Brett Brookshaw!"

"Mr Brookshaw," greeted Joe shaking his hand. "It's an honour to meet you. I've dealt with your firm several times before, but we've never met."

"No, my sister handles the consulting firm here in the UK, I now cover the US," replied Brett, eying Joe up and down assessing him. "We're delighted you're joining us. Welcome!"

He waved Joe into one of the other leather chairs. Liam sat in a seat to the side of the room, slightly apart from them.

At the far end of the room there was another door and a large, modern chrome legged desk with several piles of paperwork on its glass top. All three internal walls were completely covered with floor to ceiling shelves full of books, neatly arranged into groups, sections, cover types and colours. Many were new looking books, some old, and others extremely old in appearance. Three leather chairs faced the glass coffee table, and light fittings and switches had been replaced with shiny modern chrome fixtures. The room looked like old and modern had clashed and neither had won.

"Before we get into the evening's proceedings Joe, I wanted to explain in clear terms how we run things here," explained Brett. Without waiting for any response, "You're committing yourself to abide by the traditions and rules of a business networking sect that was established almost two hundred years ago. If the rules are followed, the risks are minimal, but the rewards are consistent and most worthwhile!"

"I was told the rewards could be as much as seven figures?" asked Joe greedily.

Brett liked the young man's appetite for wealth. "Yes, we have brothers earning much more than a mere million pounds. Last year we paid our members a total of almost thirty million! We take care of setting up your offshore account which is untouchable except by you and we'll help you clean any money you wish to withdraw back into the UK through our various channels, all of which are entirely secure from authorities and the tax man."

"Sounds great!"

"What you earn is entirely up to you, the more you bring in, the bigger your rewards. Under your old boss at Gaslec you've already been helping us appoint Brookshaw's and with your new role with the MOD you are well placed to now profit personally from continuing to support the firm."

Joe looked at Liam and before thinking about what he was about to say, just blurted it out.

"Did you kill my boss David Durham?" He instantly regretted the question, desperately hoping the answer to be in the negative.

Liam returned the intense stare and without missing a beat, answered.

"No!"

Liam was at least able to tell the truth, knowing full well that his UK counterpart Eduardo had performed that service, not him. Joe looked relieved, happy to believe that the sect he was joining had nothing to do with David Durham's unfortunate accident.

"So how did this all start, you said almost two-hundred years ago?" asked Joe, happy to change the subject back to the organisation's history. Brett replied.

"One of my ancestors, Thomas Appleby, was among the earliest generations of freemasons in London. The masons adopted age-old traditions, all developed to bind fellow masons together into a tight, organised club of craftsmen. The values they hold promote self-improvement, education, high standards, traditions, advancement and charity. Over time they accepted people from all walks of life and business, and so created the opportunity of utilising its huge network of allegiance and contacts."

"I thought the masons were legit though?" queried Joe.

Brett nodded. "Yes. That was the problem. They didn't believe in their brothers' personal financial advancement! The potential to profit from their impressive network was always and still is overlooked. My ancestor tried to persuade them to change. When they wouldn't, he tried to establish money-orientated alliances, but the values of masonry were already set in stone, excuse the pun!"

"So I'm guessing he left," ventured Joe.

"He did. He moved to Venice, one of the big trading hubs of Europe, and inspired by the God of wealth and riches, Pluto, he set up his own organisation, which we are continuing today." Brett gestured at the building and gardens outside.

"So this has nothing to do with the freemasons?"

"Some of our brothers are still masons, including myself. What we do here is completely separate from masonry, though it serves our purposes to keep links into their organisation for recruiting new members of influence. There will always be masons like my ancestor and myself, who feel the business networking potential within the freemasons isn't being utilised to benefit individuals. Ironically, the public think the masons are all about favouritism, helping one another to advance and get promoted, when in truth none of that happens."

"So you've taken masonry to the next level?"

"You could say that," nodded Brett. "We still borrow some of their traditions and labels. Members are called brothers, I am the Grand Master, we have symbols and ceremonies like the one tonight you'll go through, to ensure people are committed to the cause."

Joe looked over at Liam, about to ask what role he played. Brett interjected.

"Liam here also plays a masonic role of sorts. In the freemasons they have people called Tylers, who guard the doors to ensure no one can eavesdrop on their meetings and learn about the secrets of masonry, kind of like their security." Brett smiled at Joe. "Liam is both my bodyguard and shall we say, one of my enforcers!"

"Enforcers?" repeated Joe with some concern.

"Yes of course," assured Brett, "the success of our organisation depends on its secrecy, loyalty, determination and rules. For the sake of all brothers, including yourself, we can't have anyone threatening the sanctity of what we have established. Liam sees to that! Without tight policing, people might think they could do what they please."

Outside, down the sloping lawns and across the lake on the far side, Graham Satchel had taken up position in the undergrowth. He'd only needed to make his way several hundred yards through the tress from his parked car, to get a clear view across the lake to the manor house beyond.

Before setting up the directional listening device, he held up the night vision binoculars to see what was going on. A few cars were arriving at the parking area and several room's lights were on inside the house. He could see into what looked like a library where a couple of figures sat talking, but too far away to see who.

Just then a large dark figure passed across his view!

Graham jerked his head back and lowered the binoculars, to see a man walking between him and the edge of the lake, about forty yards in front of him. Graham ducked down hoping he hadn't been spotted, then slowly raised his head to check. The man was holding a shotgun and was dressed like a gamekeeper. He appeared to be looking in his direction. This was a guard!

He froze. Watching closely, the man paused, then casually strolled on, occasionally glancing around to check that all was quiet, not expecting to find anything. He moved on and disappeared into the trees to skirt around the far side of the lake.

Graham now frantically looked around the grounds and in the distance, picked out two other similarly armed 'gamekeepers' walking the perimeter some way off. He took out the second set of mini binoculars and laid them on the ground ready for Max and began to set up the small directional microphone, as he called him.

"Max, I'll be brief as guards are patrolling so keep down when you approach. I'm 200yds northwest of my car when you come across it and have a good sight of grounds and house," he reported.

"Copy, out," said Max.

Graham aimed the mic pointer at the room where he'd seen people talking. Although the doors were closed there was a window open, he could just about make out most of what was being said. He listened carefully.

In the library office, Joe steered the topic away from 'enforcers'.

"So are we worshipping the God Pluto?"

"Not worshipping as such. And we use the other name

Pluto goes by. We call ourselves the Hades sect!"

"Isn't he the God of the underworld?"

"You know your mythology. But that isn't referring to hell before we get carried away into thinking we're devil worshippers. In ancient times, all wealth and riches came from the earth... metals, diamonds, gold and the like. Hence God of wealth. Those that worshipped him, also wanted their souls to join him in the afterlife and be with him and all his riches. You've probably heard stories about the souls of ancient Greeks paying Charon, who was Hades' ferryman, to get across the river Styx to join him in the underworld of riches?"

Joe nodded. "You have to pay the ferryman," reciting the age-old quote.

"Absolutely, so this forms part of your induction ceremony. You will simulate this by paying our ferryman and crossing the lake here to be accepted into the Hades sect by myself and fellow brethren." Brett picked up an old coin and passed it over for Joe to take. "Look after this! It's a sign of your membership and you'll need it tonight to, as you rightly say, pay the ferryman!"

Joe studied the thin metal disc which had a bee on one side and a stag on the other. "Looks old?"

"About 350BC, so yes, very old," replied Brett proudly. "It's an obolus coin from the time the worshipping of the Greek Gods was at its peak, and one of the coins that would have been used, in mythology, by dead souls to pay the ferryman to get to Hades."

Joe looked impressed and gripped the coin tightly.

"The brethren you mention, I saw some of them starting to gather, can I know who they all are, for networking purposes?" asked Joe cautiously.

Brett frowned. "Brothers are free to communicate how they wish to with others within our gatherings. Some are happy to talk freely, others want to limit their contact, understandable if they hold positions of public notoriety and fame. We ask that you respect how each person wishes to conduct themselves, be it openly or anonymously. It's your call, as long as you adhere to the rules, and we ask that even those who are happy to converse, never mention names or anything which would openly identify themselves. We regularly sweep our premises for bugs but you can never be too careful!"

As if on cue, Liam got up and retrieved a black robe from a chest of drawers and brought it over to Joe, holding it out, waiting for him to take it.

"Your robe, which must be worn with hood up for the ceremony and other such meetings," said Brett, "mainly for tradition, but also to respect those who wish not to be seen." Brett leant forward and patted an old looking book on the table between them. "Only I know the identity of all the member brethren!"

Joe took the robe as if it were a piece of priceless art. He looked upon the golden motif embroidered onto the black cloth on the top of the garment. Joe looked up at Liam questioningly and Brett allowed him to explain.

"Our most sacrosanct rules are represented by our Hades sect's sign," said Liam as he sat back down again. "These show the bident of Hades, the two-pronged spear, denoting our resolve, determination and loyalty to creating wealth for one another. The motif of the helmet is the cap of invisibility Hades was given. This represents the absolute secrecy we demand of everyone. You are never to speak of our existence to anyone, ever!" Liam looked resolute and threatening.

"Understood! Without being a smartass," ventured Joe, "didn't Hades also have some three-headed dog as well?"

"You really do know your stuff," congratulated Brett. "Yes, he was called Cerberus. He protected the gates of Hades and ensured souls didn't escape." He laughed and waved towards Liam. "Kind of like what Liam does!"

Joe looked back at the old book on the table. "So will I get added to this?"

"Indeed you will," replied Brett picking the book up and

patting it gently. "This book was started by my ancestor in Venice and has a log of every brother that's ever been part of the Hades sect, from around 1840 up to the present day. It was originally used to note down each brother's contributions to the organisation from favoured business dealings and also what kickbacks they were then paid in return. It's shown on the wall mural in the basement of his Venetian home, which I now own. I obviously keep a soft file copy of everyone's 'financials', but it seemed right to continue his original tradition of entering each brother's name and dealings in this book. Your name will be entered as part of the ceremony later."

"I'm honoured," said Joe with a slight bow.

"Good, you should be, you'll be amongst exalted and impressive company."

"The book of names," mused Joe.

"I prefer to call it, the book of souls!" corrected Brett. "Seems more befitting under the circumstances."

Liam stood up and beckoned Joe to follow him out.

"Liam will take you through how we expect the ceremony to go and explain everything you need to know," Brett said. "That'll take about twenty minutes and then I'll see you soon afterwards during the proceedings. Glad to have you on board Joe!"

Outside, down the lawns and across the lake, Graham had heard most of what had been discussed in the office library, feeling like he'd struck gold. He'd also been watching as best he could through his binoculars and was about to call Si Lawson when he heard a twig snap to his side!

He moved his face away from the eyepieces to check the sound and flinched in shock, to discover he was now looking into two shotgun barrels! With his nose against the cold metal barrel ends, he could smell the burnt shot and gunpowder from previous discharges.

"Don't move a bloody inch, or I'll blow your head clean off!" said the uncompromising man's stern voice.

The gamekeeper guard had caught sight of Graham and doubled back round once out of sight, then slowly and stealthily crept up on the MI5 agent, to ensure there was no chance of him escaping or drawing a gun.

"Hand over your phone, that aerial listening thing and the field glasses gadget you've got there!" he demanded, levelling the barrels at Graham's midriff as he slowly got to his feet with his hands held up high. The man leant forward still holding the gun against him and gave a few cursory pats, checking for any weapons. While he was being frisked and handing over the other items, Graham took the opportunity to cover the spare mini binoculars with his foot.

"Okay, okay, easy," pleaded Graham, "we can sort this out, I don't want any trouble."

"Too late for that my friend," said the gunman, "you're already in a heap load of trouble as it is!"

14

Ten minutes later Max pulled up alongside Grahams' Audi, as quietly as he could in the F40. He cursed to himself that he was in a bright red, loud supercar for such an assignment, when stealth was needed, so kept the revs as low as possible without stalling.

He got out of the car and using his phone carefully headed off north-west for about one hundred yards, searching all the time for his colleague. He came to a spot which suddenly afforded a view of the magnificent lake, lawns and the huge house beyond. Looking down he noticed the foliage and bracken had been compressed and as his attention focused on the area, he spotted the small black binoculars on the ground that Graham had left. His colleague had been there, but where was he now?

Max decided the best thing to do was see what was going on whilst waiting there for Graham to return. Kneeling, he picked up the night-vision binoculars and scanned the estate as far as he could see. There were lights on in the house with figures moving about. Strange he thought, the people appeared to be wearing black cloaks? A couple of people were talking outside at the top end of the elegant sloping lawns, also both wearing the black robes, this time with hoods over their heads.

Max could see some fancy cars parked in the main courtyard to the side and watched as another new unusual reddish looking Mercedes E class pulled in. The driver got out but was too far away for Max to see who it was. Searching around the outer parts of the grounds, Max could see one man resembling a gamekeeper with a shotgun patrolling and figured this was one of the guards Graham had mentioned!

Max moved his gaze back to the house and the people now starting to come outside, just as the lights placed around the grounds came on. Their soft glow dimly lit the house, lawns, pathways and lake, bringing everything to life out of the darkness.

The midazolam that Liam had injected into Graham Satchel's arm worked quickly, making him drowsy and ambivalent to what was happening to him. After the gamekeeper guard had brought him inside the rear of the house, Liam had searched his wallet and phone. Brett walked in.

"What is he, police, press?"

Liam replied. "I'm afraid he's MI5, got an ID card. Graham Satchel."

"MI5? Again?" Brett's tone betrayed some incredulity. "First we have this Max Sargent bloke snooping around, now this guy! I've had enough of all this! Was he with anyone, sent any messages recently?"

"No texts since earlier today to his wife it looks like," said Liam, then glancing to the guard.

"No sir, he was definitely alone. Me and the others will continue to sweep the estate and we'll find his car or motorbike later, it must be somewhere nearby."

Brett nodded to the gamekeeper to go, then turned to his loyal confidant propping up the dazed Graham.

"Liam, it's too risky to let this chap go, with his mic and lenses he's probably already seen and heard too much. I can't have this affecting anything, we need to start the ceremony now."

He leant into his friend, "This is what we'll do…" He gave Liam instructions in hushed tones.

Liam wasn't easily surprised, but on listening to his boss, even he allowed his expression to show a glimmer of consternation and surprise!

Max watched on as more cloaked attendees came out of the house and started to make their way down the lawns towards the lake. One carried a small wooden lectern. Some chatted, others remained silent and separated from the rest. Max counted about fifteen people as they all headed in his direction down the lawns towards the lake.

As they approached the water, three figures peeled off to the side and began skirting around the lakeside, coming in his direction. He lowered himself down so as not to be seen. It looked like two of the cloaked, hooded people were supporting the one between them, who appeared to be slightly drunk, staggering and tripping as they went.

Graham, who had tape across his mouth and his wrists tied, was being held by Joe and Liam. Joe had only been told this other person would accompany them during the ceremony, but had no idea why or who this somewhat intoxicated brother was!

Max watched in amazement as the main gathering on the far side of the lake began taking up random positions along the water's edge, encircling what appeared to be the leader who stood behind the wooden stand, placing an old book on top of it and opening up the pages. With his binoculars Max could make out some kind of badge or motif on the front of all of the robes, resembling a two-pronged spear around a helmet. Adjusting the zoom he strained to get a look at any of their faces, but quickly realised they were all covered with black veils or masks.

The three figures nearest to him momentarily disappeared out of view. Max craned his head up to locate them, fearing they might suddenly appear close by. He saw them again. They were getting into a small boat that had been moored alongside a rickety wooden jetty, previously out of view, hidden by the overgrown foliage. One of the cloaked men boarding, handed something to another, then helping the other passenger, they both sat down on a bench seat in the middle.

Part of the ritual involved Joe paying the ferryman to cross the lake, symbolising the Styx. So he was handing over his obolus coin to Liam, in the role of Charon, boatman for Hades.

Max looked on as the third man stood on a small platform on the rear of the boat and gripped what looked like a gondola paddle. He looked across the lake and waited.

The leader paused then spoke to the gathering. Max didn't recognise the faint voice across the lake but could just make out a few clips of what he was saying. He heard mention of "as is our tradition when welcoming a new brother into Hades," and "will abide by the sacred and uncompromising rules of the sect," and "he will now travel to us across the Styx. Charon?"

On cue, the boatman near Max started to manipulate his rear paddle, moving the small boat off from the jetty, with its two passengers sitting still in its centre, one occasionally nodding off it seemed, as his head started to lower then jolt back up.

Max was stunned by the bizarre ritual and with the mention of Hades and the Styx, had now gathered this was some weird induction ceremony that had something to do with worshipping Hades, God of the underworld! Still unaware that the estate was owned by Brett and Gillian Brookshaw, he thought his colleague Graham must have followed Joe Patterson to some strange satanic cult he belonged to. He checked around the gathered hooded figures one more time, desperately trying to identify which one might be Joe, but all faces remained covered.

The cool, damp night air had started to create an eerie mist just inches above the lake's water, adding to the mysterious façade unravelling in front of Max and the gathered disciples. Apart from the distant sound of planes flying into Gatwick airport some ten miles away, everything and everyone there was silent, transfixed on the boat drifting slowly across the lake.

It was about halfway now and without explanation, the ferryman let go of his oar leaving it dangling in its holder. He stepped down from the raised platform into the boat just behind the two seated figures and pulled something from under his robe.

Zapp!

The crackling blast of voltage from his taser sounded across the lake, flickering against the back of one of the seated passenger's necks! The instantaneous sparking momentarily lit up the scene inside the boat, showing the hooded ferryman standing over the pathetic passenger. Then as quickly as it was shown to all, the sight disappeared back into the night's gloom and the soft lighting around the grounds.

Max and some of the hooded onlookers by the lake jumped with a start, caught off guard by the shocking incident.

"Jesus!" Max hissed under his breath dropping the binoculars, then immediately hoping he hadn't been heard. He picked them up and continued to watch, shaken by what he'd seen, unaware there was more to come!

He could see the man tasered in the boat was writhing in agony and confusion, muscles contracted, fingers contorting, slumping down towards the edge of the boat. The other passenger had jumped back and away from him in horror and was staying well clear of both the victim and the ferryman!

Liam moved over to the squirming man. Then grabbing his legs, hauled them up onto the edge of the boat. With a heave, he pushed the dark figure overboard and into the lake!

Max froze in horror, as did several of the brothers watching the horrifying event unfold, mentally retreating deeper into their hoods, glad of the covering and anonymity. None of them moved however, they all stood firm, forced to watch.

With his night vision and magnifying lenses, Max had seen something the others on the lakeside hadn't. Just as the robed victim had gone overboard, his hood and black veil had fallen back uncovering his face!

Max couldn't believe his eyes, as he just caught a split-second glimpse of the man's face before he fell into the water.

He recognised that face. It was Graham Satchel!

The shock of fifty-thousand volts combined with the mild anaesthetic drug in his system, tied hands and the freezing cold water engulfing him, was too much for Graham.

The water instantly closed around him penetrating his nose, mouth, ears and eyes. Even in his bound state of shock and drowsiness, adrenalin instinctively kicked in, urging him to fight for his life. He struggled and fought his way back up to the surface and as he opened his mouth gasping for breath, the edge of the tape unstuck. He took in the cold air, and some of the colder water. It made him choke. His brain told him he was fighting to stay on the surface, but unable to summon his electrocuted muscles to perform, he was actually sinking down into the water.

He'd taken his final breath.

Just before he drowned, his brain registered looking up through the darkening water as he sank, and seeing the watery outline of the ferryman looking down at him!

Max was beside himself with anger and shock. Should he run from his cover and stop this madness? Could he save Graham if he dived in? What would they do to him if he was caught? He knew the answers were all negative with bad repercussions if he tried anything. The gamekeepers had shotguns! He couldn't believe he'd just witnessed Graham's murder, and that he couldn't do anything about it.

Instinctively wanting to share his predicament, he grabbed his phone and brought up Si Lawson's number. His finger hovered above the screen, but he stopped short of pressing down. There was nothing he could do for Graham now, so the priority was to find out more about what was going on here and who these people were. His attention was drawn back to the lake, where the leader was speaking again. The boat was now approaching the jetty on the other side by the gathered ensemble.

"Our sect cannot allow outsiders to infiltrate our brethren. We will protect all brothers and our identities." Brett was resolute, committed, commanding. His words started to give some reassurance to the gathering, calming nerves, bringing them back together. Brett continued.

"As with souls who try to leave Hades, Charon the ferryman and Cerberus the hound will not allow intruders to cross over into our organisation. The ferryman has to be paid, one way or the other!" Brett wanted to use this drama as a warning to others, of the consequences of thinking they could opt out once they'd made their fortune, as well as show brethren their anonymity was safe and infiltrators would be dealt with.

"What the hell!" murmured Max under his breath.

The boatman now handed back the obolus coin to the remaining passenger.

Joe was still shaken by what had just happened. With the threatening black-robed audience and the Grand Master's total control, he felt compelled to just get through it and not cause any fuss. He stumbled onto the jetty, wishing he'd never met Lisa Ely, the beautiful temptress from Brookshaw Consulting! He was in it now though, up to his neck!

Brett gestured a welcome by holding out his arms. Joe approached him and dutifully placed his obolus coin onto the open pages of the old book on the lectern, then quickly stood back again. He could now see Brett's eyes staring at him from behind his black mask under his hood. He knew he was being assessed following the awful scene on the lake, so did his best to pull himself together and look confident and collected. It was hard though. He had to will his body to be strong and stand firm.

Brett wasn't surprised that his little show had shocked the young man, and likely some of the others here. He now spoke more softly, calmly, just loud enough for the figures around him to hear. Across the lake, Max strained to listen to what was being said but was too far away to understand.

Brett looked round to the dark figures encircling him. "Tonight we are honoured to accept a new brother into our brethren. He brings with him position, power and influence, which in turn will contribute considerable and sustained wealth creation for Hades and all those within our sect."

Brett looked back to Joe. "Do you swear to uphold the values and rules of Hades, the complete secrecy of our organisation and everyone within it, and with resolve and determination, actively influence others and contribute to our riches, a share of which you will receive?"

Joe gulped. "I swear on my life to do these things, forever more!"

Brett handed back the obolus to Joe. "Take the coin you used to cross over into Hades as a memento and reminder of the commitment you have sworn to and a sign to other brethren."

"I accept this coin in agreement and will abide by your wishes in matters relating to our organisation and its dealings." Joe glanced back at Liam just to check he was still by the jetty. He was. Remembering his lines, he continued. "I now ask for your final consideration to be accepted as your brother, and entered into, the book of souls!"

Brett raised his arms again and looked from left to right at his congregation. "If anyone here has any reason or objection, to this man now being indoctrinated into our sect, speak now?"

Joe tensed, sensing this was a potential danger point should someone challenge him joining for whatever reason. He glanced around the others trying to judge if any of them were about to raise a hand or speak. All was quiet, everyone there standing still. One person coughed.

Brett waited, then satisfied all had played their part, picked up the fountain pen on the lectern.

"So it is done. I will now enter your name into the sacred ledger where your contribution and rewards will be noted." He wrote Joe's name in the old book, waited a few moments for the ink to dry, then carefully closed it. "Congratulations," he said, offering out his hand.

To the relief of Joe and the brethren gathered, the mood lifted. Most of the dark figures started clapping tentatively, a couple came over to shake the newcomer's hand.

Max had been watching carefully and remembered the mural on the wall of the Venetian boathouse depicting the ledger book of souls entering Hades. Having now seen the enactment with the leader writing the inductee's name into the old book on the lectern, he knew it was too much of a coincidence for this not to be connected with Headshell and the Brookshaw's.

As the gathering started to break up and make their way up the dimly lit lawns back towards the house, Max decided it was time to make a hasty departure. He'd seen enough and wanted to report into Si before calling in a full raid. He was also conscious that he hadn't caught sight of any of the gamekeeper guards whilst watching the ritual and didn't know where they were. He slowly made his way back to the cars, careful not to make any noise as he picked his way through the bracken and trees.

As he circled round the small pull-in where the Audi and his Ferrari were parked, he spotted movement some way off amongst the trees, on the opposite side of the cars!

He immediately crouched down, searching the area for somewhere to hide. But he'd left the tree-line and was now out in the open. The gamekeeper was starting to make their way towards the cars, having now spotted them.

Max had only one place to go for cover and keeping low, shuffled quickly over to the Audi! He instantly regretted the choice, knowing he was now effectively trapped there and would inevitably have to confront the armed man making his way over.

Should he stand up and talk his way out of it? Unlikely the guard would send him on his way as a night-time walker! He looked round for anything he could use as a weapon and thankfully spotted a short, thick piece of a branch. Using the car to hide himself, he scurried to retrieve it.

He could now hear the man trudging through the undergrowth, getting closer to the cars.

"Jonny," said the man into his radio, "found the car, in fact there's two cars here!"

"Do you think one of them belongs to our chap?" crackled the reply.

"There's an Audi here, probably his. Bit odd though, the other car's some expensive red Ferrari!"

"What out here in the middle of the night? Well, that definitely ain't police! Anyone nearby?"

"All quiet here."

"Where are you?"

"The first pull-in on Twyford Lane, southerly end of the estate."

"Okay, I'll be there within ten minutes in the Land Rover with the tow bar. Wait for me there!"

The gamekeeper was now on the other side of the Audi to Max, who remained silent and was watching the guard's feet move under the car. As expected he continued walking down the side of the Audi, making his way to the rare supercar parked behind. Max had to do something, he couldn't let the second gamekeeper arrive, but was conscious the man near him had a shotgun!

With no time to weigh up other options, the moment presented itself as the guard rounded the back of the Audi, barrels first, pointing down. Max edged round the same car, crouched poised to spring, then as the shotgun came into reach, leapt up at the man, swinging the wooden branch!

There was a loud bang, as both barrels fired into the ground, spraying up dirt and stones. The piece of wood connected with the side of the man's head, with the rotting bark on it breaking off into pieces. The shotgun fell to the ground, followed by the man holding his head and crying out.

Over at the manor house, everyone heard the double gunshot. Brett and Liam looked at one another and without a word, Liam bolted off in the direction of the noise that came from beyond the trees past the lake.

Max eyed the gamekeeper closely as he fell, to see if he was out cold and going to stay down. Unfortunately not!

Cursing now and shaking his head to gather his orientation, the guard looked up in disbelief at Max and started to get up.

Max flung himself onto the man still holding the piece of wood and simultaneously swung another punch at his face. It smacked him in the jaw and flew from Max's grip. They grappled with one another, grasping at one another's face and flaying arms, trying to get a pin-hold. Max knew wrestling was no good, he needed to put this guy out cold, but was finding it hard to get the room for another good punch.

He started to work his way round the side of the man's body, gripping him between his legs to reduce the writing and soon got behind him on the ground, with his arms crossed over his shoulders and around his neck. Max gently applied more pressure and started to squeeze, dodging and resisting the guard's attempts to lash out behind him.

The choke hold started to take effect, reducing his ability to breathe freely and compressing the spine and airways. Max knew he had to be careful not to break the man's neck. Despite what he'd seen, the gamekeeper didn't deserve to die, he just wanted him out.

The man's thrashing decreased and moments later, he went limp. Max held on for a while longer, then released him. He picked himself up, looked around, then quickly got into his car and fired it up. Deliberately not turning on the lights, he wheel-spun the powerful Ferrari round and back onto the narrow road.

Liam had passed the bottom of the lake and ran into the treeline near to where Max had watched the proceedings. He could hear a sporty car start then wheel-spinning on the dirt ahead of him.

The F40 shot off down the road, its large rear tyres unable yet to get the grip they sought, just as Liam emerged from the trees into the layby. He strained his eyes through the darkness trying to ascertain the car's number plate, but with no lights on, it was gone into the night before he got anything.

Max cleared the area, making his way back towards the

M23 motorway, before calling up Si on speaker. Once he got through he went on a rant telling his boss everything that had happened since he got there and watched events unfold.

"What should we do Si, we can't just leave Graham there, in that lake? Do we go in full blast with police, agents and armed response teams while they're still there? I mean like now!" Max demanded.

"Do you know who lives at the Manor House?" asked Si. "Vince got Graham's location after he'd got there just so we knew where you were both heading."

"No idea, who?"

"The Manor House estate's registered owner is the Headshell corporation! It's Gillian Brookshaw's home! Called the Manor House!"

"What! Well that's it then, we should go in?"

"Steady on Max. I'm afraid that's exactly why we *shouldn't* go in tonight. Most of those people will have gone by now, there's more in play here than a quick unfruitful bust. Unfortunately, there's nothing we can do to help Graham now." Si calmed his voice. "Look, Max, go home now and I'll see you first thing in the morning. I'll need to take this to the Deputy Director General! Maybe you tag along with me eh?"

Max agreed.

Back at the Manor House most of the brethren had left, including a weary Joe Patterson. The unconscious gamekeeper had come round but couldn't give Liam any decent description of the intruder. With the other guard, they'd hooked up the Audi and would return it to the manor house garages. From there it would be disposed of in the morning, using one of the car-crushing plants nearby happy to take cash, no questions asked.

Brett caught one of the last robed guests in the hallway, about to leave.

"Do you have a moment, just before you go." It wasn't a question.

They went into the library but Brett didn't take a seat, he

wanted to keep this brief and not entertain a protracted discussion.

"I'm sorry about the kerfuffle earlier, out on the lake," said Brett almost apologetically, eyeing the brother before him, gauging his reaction. "I must protect those of us here who go above and beyond to serve our cause. If one of us falls, we all fall!"

The other man frowned, but conceded, "Unfortunate, most unfortunate, but understandable I guess. As you say, once we're into this, we're well and truly in, come what may!"

Brett was happy with the pragmatic response, it was just what he needed for his proposal.

"I have an exciting opportunity for us. For you. To make significantly more bonus money. And, more frequently than the business you put towards Brookshaw's every few years."

The man looked intrigued. "Oh yes, how's that then?"

Brett smiled. "It's somewhat of a departure from influencing contract awards for consulting across your remit. It involves simply passing on information."

"Who to?"

"You'll pass anything you have of interest onto myself, to start with anyway. I will then broker it onto a foreign party, to protect your identity you see," explained Brett.

The man looked concerned.

"More specifically, the information will go to one of our Hades brothers in America."

"Why would someone in the US want information from me?"

Brett drew in a breath. "He works for the government. They will pay a great deal for information you come across… minister!"

The man looked horrified for a moment, thinking quickly, taking on the repercussions of what he thought was being asked of him.

"Crikey! I'm guessing you mean the CIA right?" he concluded.

Brett nodded. "Nothing betraying our country's security of course, just any tittle-tattle and plans, talks and so on that our US friends might be interested in. As I say, they'll pay well to establish a connection."

The other man wasn't happy, but thinking of the money and the man going into the lake, gave a reluctant nod.

"After all," said Brett, "you're present at all the PM's cabinet meetings! I'm sure there are all sorts of interesting stuff you get to hear about!"

15

"I'll do the talking," instructed Si Lawson to Max as they took the lift up in MI5's Thames House at Millbank. "Unless he asks you something directly, then keep it short and factual."

"Got it," Max confirmed, telling himself the Deputy Director General was just a human being and not someone to be feared. But the stories of the DDG's record, in politics and the services, his astuteness, ability to grasp the facts and cut through the nonsense to get to a decision, were legendary. He was a sharp man, he had to be in this job, ensuring the Director General and in turn the Prime Minister were kept up-to-date and prompted to make the right calls on sensitive security, financial and criminal operations.

They exited the lift and walked down the corridor, capturing glances of interest as to what they were doing on that floor and who they were seeing.

The DDG's assistant Chuck saw them and pointed to a couple of chairs outside the large glass, sound-proofed office of their boss.

The DDG was on the phone to the Chief Constable of Sussex police and his District Commander covering the West Sussex area where the Manor House at Wych Cross resided. When he saw the two men from his Cyber team waiting, he cut short the call, eager to get them in. This was a big deal!

Si introduced Max as they sat down.

"You're scoring quite a tally for these big corporate type criminal operations," he opened with. "Good job with the last few, this one seems a bit tricky?"

"Did you manage to look at the report I sent you earlier this morning Sir?" asked Si.

"Of course," came the curt reply. "I've jotted down a few

things, so let me make sure I understand everything? I've got to make my recommendations to the DG in twenty minutes."

"Yes sir."

The DDG referred to a piece of paper on the expanse of his desktop.

"So, we believe this Brookshaw Consulting firm owned by Headshell, Brett and Gillian, with offshore banking in Nevis, potentially have a business networking organisation of influential industry leads, they're bribing to the tune of thirty million per annum, to award their company contracts?"

Max and Si answered together. "Yes sir."

"And you feel they may have been responsible for David Durham's murder, and also attempted to kill yourself, Max, in Nevis and on the tube, and are responsible for the murder of our agent Graham Satchel last night?" The DDG spoke efficiently, sparing the compassion.

"We do sir."

Looking at Si the DDG suggested, "On that point, as Max has had a couple of run-ins with this lot, you might think about giving him some extra protection if you know what I mean."

"I agree," said Si.

"You believe this organisation calls itself Hades, is likely led by Brett Brookshaw, ancestor of the founder from the eighteen-hundreds, an ex-mason, however, the freemasons of today have nothing to do with all this?"

"Correct sir."

"How many people are in this sect?"

"We don't know for sure sir, there were about fifteen people present last night but given Brookshaws' size in both the UK and US, I suspect there are considerably more members we don't know about," said Max.

"Hmm, that brings me to my first point," said the DDG. "You don't know who any of the members are," checking his notes, "oh yes, except for this procurement chap Joe Patterson, who Graham and then you followed to this ritual last night. But you didn't actually see him there, in person, or anyone in fact, because they all had hooded cloaks on!"

Max and Si frowned, realising that despite the circumstantial evidence, they didn't yet have a watertight case at all.

"But sir, I watched as they killed Graham," pleaded Max, getting a sideways look from Si.

"Max," the DDG turned his full attention to him, "I'm not suggesting I don't believe you, I do, but I suspect his body has been removed from this lake along with his car and any trace he'd ever been there, rest his soul. You don't know who killed him do you. Which brings me to my next point."

"Sir?"

"This book of souls, on the mural, but more importantly mentioned by Durham just before he died, 'it's all in the book of souls'. Presumably what you saw last night, this ledger the leader wrote in after inducting someone, might contain the names of all the so-called Hades members?"

Max and Si now realised what the DDG was driving at.

"That's a likely assumption sir, yes," said Si.

The DDG sat back. "Then that's what we're after, isn't it!" He waited for both of them to nod in agreement. "We'd be wasting our time smashing in there raiding houses and offices, they're just buildings! If their sect's membership spreads far and wide, we'd never find out who they all were. No gentlemen, I suggest what we're after are the names in that bloody book, that we're all calling the 'book of souls'. It's a best guess, but worth trying for if we want to catch the whole haul of them, here and in the US?"

The DDG looked determined as Max and Si both nodded again in agreement.

"It's unfortunate about Graham, but we can't have any busts or raids yet, not until we have a try at the big prize. I want to mop this whole thing up in one go, not by piece-meal taking forever more. That's what I'll be telling the DG who will include it on his daily update to the PM. We'll have to tell the CIA something about all this but for now, I'll keep it brief.

I want to maintain control and not have the Yanks charging in like a bunch of cowboys! Back over to you guys, follow the one lead you have?"

Max and Si looked at one another in the hope one of them would say out loud what the lead was.

The DDG huffed, "This Joe Patterson for Christ's sake!"

Max and Si went to the door, "Yes sir."

"I suppose you've already spotted one of the anagram's you can get from their corporation's name Headshell?" Before the two men could look bemused again, the DDG spared them. "Hades hell! Someone's either got a warped sense of humour, or they're just taking the mick out of everyone!"

Just as they were exiting his office, the DDG grabbed a picture of a car off his desk. "Oh yes, Max. Your report mentioned that you saw a Mercedes E class arrive at the Manor House last night, 'in an unusual red colour' you say." He showed Max the colour photo of a reddish E class with the colour printed underneath stating 'Hyacinth red metallic'. "Anything like this?"

Max studied the picture. "It was dark and I was mainly watching through the night vision binoculars, everything was tinted green!"

"But your report said you were constantly looking up from your field glasses to check for guards and see what was going on around you?"

"That's right," said Max. He looked again. "It does look quite like the car I saw, the colour I mean, couldn't be sure though. Why?"

"No reason, just a stupid niggle," said the DDG. "I just remember thinking it was an unusual red colour myself when I saw it six months ago. It's the same unusual red and car model the PM chose for the new ministerial fleet cars!" He shrugged. "I might just have Chuck see if they're fitted with trackers, I suspect not though. Probably nothing! On you get guys."

As they walked back to their team's offices, Si picked up

on one of the suggestions the DDG had made.

"Go have a chat with ordnance. I'll call them. I think as you've had two attempts on your life, you could do with a little extra defence. It doesn't warrant you carrying a firearm, but we can get you a couple of bits to have with you at all times from now on."

"Like what," asked Max.

"Didn't you say the stiletto chap had a belt buckle knife or something? Maybe one of them and perhaps a mini pepper spray, we'll sort something out anyway!"

Brett Brookshaw was concerned. He'd never intended people to die. He merely wanted his enforcers Liam and Eduardo to be available as bodyguards for him and Gillian if he felt the need arise. Maybe also occasionally strong-arm anyone who needed reminding or persuading to uphold the rules of the sect. Secrecy was paramount.

Thomas Appleby's Hades organisation had remained active for a generation after his death, into the early nineteen-hundreds. Then, for no obvious reason, it had disbanded, simply fizzled out. Perhaps members had left, or trade wasn't as bountiful as it used to be, or maybe the police were closing in on them.

The desire to push the boundaries in business and leverage influence, swinging decisions in your favour was always in Brett's genes. He'd already seen the opportunity to utilise his connection amongst the freemasons, as his ancestor had before him, for personal gain.

His father had set aside his loft as an overflow space for his library, where he relegated the older and less desirable books to. There must have been several thousand books up there, stacked into tall, precarious piles, gathering dust.

They'd been talking about leadership skills and his father mentioned to Brett that there was a superb book on the subject he should read. Having looked for it in the main library and not been able to find it, his father told Brett to look up in the loft.

Intrigued by the haul of literature hidden away, whilst hunting for the leadership book, Brett spent several hours up there sifting through almost every book there was. It was a treasure trove of literature, with books on business, sports, cars, movies, farming, cities, politics, best sellers, first editions, new and old.

Whilst examining one particular pile of books, Brett went down the spines searching for the leadership title and was drawn to a particularly old looking book with no title or labelling. He almost passed over it having searched through so many books that evening, but it pulled him back. Carefully removing it from the pile, he could see the old, tattered book had no title on the front or rear covers either.

He opened it up wondering what the subject matter could be, and immediately saw it was not a printed novel or educational book, but a large, thick notebook, like a ledger.

The handwritten ink inside was still clear and as he started to flick through the pages, he could see the contents were page after page of names and notes. Underneath each person were written a few, or in some cases, a lot of lines summarising what appeared to be a short description of a trade or business deal. Next to this were two monetary sums both dated, mainly in pounds, shillings and pence but some of the early entries were in lira. The first number was occasionally labelled with the words 'sale', 'in' or 'trade', and the second number with the tag 'return' or 'payoff'.

Looking at the line descriptions and money, it was clear to Brett that this was a trading ledger showing deals that had been done with, by or for each named person, along with the pay out, or likely bribe paid back to them!

There were well over a hundred named records in the book, some just several lines, others taking up a whole page, filling over half of the entire book. The remaining pages were still blank. There was no mention of who the bookkeeper or author was.

The discovery of the book, which Brett later called 'the book of souls', had been the catalyst for him to embark on re-establishing a properly led, organised club of business influencers. Brett would use the same book that Appleby had started nearly two hundred years ago in Venice, recording the names of each member and their financial dealings, contributions and the payments they were rewarded with. He already had the ideal channel to gather in business awards and money, in his father's growing consultancy firm, a business that could reach into all parts of industry and financial enterprises!

So after almost a hundred years of stagnation, Brett had brought his ancestor's creation back to life, using a combination of the masonic traditions he knew well from his own time with the freemasons, and blended this with what he had discovered about Appleby from his ledger and then later the murals in his Venetian home.

Having worked so hard to get the Hades organisation up and running, he simply couldn't allow anything or anyone to ruin it all!

Brett was due to fly back to New York with Liam and wanted to address what had occurred last night.

"What's happened about the clear-up?" he asked Liam.

"The boys have pulled up the body and disposed of it and the car," replied Liam. "They'll never be found, ever!"

"I don't like having this MI5 bunch on our tails, what with this chap last night and the other one, Max Sargent, over in Nevis and speaking to Gillian!"

"If they had anything, or if he'd contacted his lot last night, this place would be swarming with police," suggested Liam. "I don't see any of the ol' bill here today? They've clearly got nothing, or they'd be here!"

"What about that other car you saw, the Ferrari? What the hell was that about? They must have been the person the gamekeeper got knocked out by, so couldn't just be a member of the public?"

"No idea boss." Shrugged Liam.

"I don't like it. We need to put a stop to this. I wonder if this Sargent bloke owns the Ferrari? We know where he lives, get one of your lads to pop round there during the day and check if there's a Ferrari in his driveway will you?"

"Sure. What've you got in mind then?"

"I'm not sure yet," pondered Brett. "Somehow we need to let Eduardo have another chance to do what he should have done the first time round!"

Within an hour, one of Liam's guards drove to Max's house on Clapham Common, Eduardo had provided the address. Although it was just off the main road, all was quiet at the house and the neighbouring properties, with everyone at work in the city.

He looked around and nimbly climbed over the fence next to the closed gates. There was nothing on the driveway, so he went over to the garage which had a couple of small windows in the roller-blind doors. They were too high up for him to peer inside, so he held up his phone and took a couple of pictures into the garage.

He looked at what the camera had captured. Inside the garage, the photo showed the rear end of a red Ferrari F40 parked on a car lift, with another sports car just visible underneath in the lift-ramp pit.

He immediately sent the picture off to Liam, then climbed back over the fence and within one minute of arriving there, was gone again.

Liam and Brett now knew Max had been at the Manor House!

Joe Patterson's procurement team had sent the stakeholders an extensive assessment document to complete, marking the shortlisted suppliers for the MOD consulting tender. Designed to leave no stone unturned, the document asked each recipient to score every supplier against criteria including suitability, references, account management, fit with the MOD, culture, best practices, team profile, expertise, number of days, day rates, overall costs, guarantees, tender response, pitches and contract compliance.

Dealing with facts and weighted scoring, it left little room for subjectivity, but it did leave some. The responses were coming into procurement to collate.

Joe had already held several review meetings with his own procurement staff and felt content that he had managed to subtly cajole and persuade most of them that whilst it was close, Brookshaw Consulting was the best choice for the award.

He hadn't been there long enough to get around all the other stakeholders in HR, IT, finance, marketing or legal and whilst Brookshaw's were clearly being talked about as a front-runner, it was going to be a close call.

Joe knew this was why he'd been asked to join Hades. This was his first opportunity to show them he was worthy of the special membership, and worthy of the pay-outs that would be coming his way.

But seeing the unknown man next to him in the boat being stunned and tossed into the lake to drown, had taken its toll on him. He was torn between the simple life and career he had, going all-in with this Hades sect with its risks and rewards, or just throwing in the towel and going to the police. After all, he hadn't killed anyone, he was a valuable witness and had been unknowingly duped into attending last night. Maybe he could get away with it if he turned them in?

The sight of the robed brother disappearing into the water came back to him. He realised that if he ever went to the police, breaking the sacred rule of secrecy, he'd be a dead man!

His phone rang, jolting him from his thoughts. It was his

boss, the Minister of State for Defence Procurement.

"Max, just wanted to check in with you on the consulting award, how's it looking?"

"We're getting the score sheets in now, probably have more than half of them back," reported Joe enthusiastically, knowing how much passion in a role was infectious. "As we expected it looks like we'll have two front-runners, one of the big-four firms, and Brookshaw's."

"Interesting, we thought as much didn't we." There was a pause. "Look Max, it's usual for the Secretary of State for Defence to be seen to stay out of such decisions and let the process decide, but he seems quite clear about who should win this contract, having seen all the information that's been circulated."

"Oh," replied Joe, feigning some degree of nonchalance.

"Yes, he's asked me to pass on his off-the-record vote, so to say."

Joe wondered if his boss's minister was an ally, or whether this would all come crashing down on him should he suggest the alternative firm won.

"And who does he feel should be awarded the contract?" Joe braced himself."

"Brookshaw's!"

'Thank God', thought Joe.

"Anyway, I'll leave that with you Joe, I'm sure you can take that into consideration should things get too close, you're in a good position to make sure the minister isn't disappointed aren't you!"

They ended the call.

Joe's phone then rang again. It was Liam Welling!

16

Max put a call into his old colleague Joe Patterson. He knew he had to follow up on this one lead, even though he didn't like dealing with this man any more than he had to. Max also assumed that Joe was one of the cloaked figures gathered at the lake, who witnessed Graham being murdered! He resented Joe being part of that but didn't want to spook him away or put him in a position of having to admit to being there. He had a bigger goal, the book. He was intrigued to catch up with him and see what was happening with the MOD tender.

Joe was more reticent to have another meal with Max and be pinned down to another conversation for so long. They agreed to have a brief lunchtime catchup on Westminster Bridge, which was between Max's MI5 building at Millbank and Joe's MOD office in Whitehall.

The bridge was built in 1750 with seven large cast-iron arches spanning the Thames, predominantly painted in green, matching the colour of the seats in the House of Commons. It's one of the most recognisable bridges because it leads to the famous Big Ben clock tower and the Houses of Parliament on the Westminster side of the river.

Max waited in the centre of the bridge, looking upriver at the massive London Eye millennium wheel and the various boats and tour cruisers going up and down the waterway. He spotted Joe walking along the bridge towards him and gave him a friendly wave, thinking he may as well try and keep him on his side.

Joe was apprehensive about meeting Max again, especially after being so shocked at events on the lake. Max may have just been his old boss from many years ago in procurement, but Joe was acutely aware that he was now meeting someone from MI5. He kept reminding himself that if the police had anything on him or the Hades sect, they would have swooped in by now. He knew he was going to have to put on his best game for Max and play ignorant when asked about the consulting pitch at the MOD.

On top of everything, Joe still felt torn between sticking with Hades and the promised riches, or telling Max what he knew, maybe in return for some kind of police protection or anonymity program?

"Thanks for meeting up Joe," greeted Max.

"No worries, but if we could keep it brief, my diary at work is packed out."

"Of course," complied Max. "How is work, your new role at the MOD?"

Joe tensed slightly. "Pretty busy as you can imagine. New team, new boss, new ways of doing things and after a stint up here I'll probably have to get down to the Bristol site soon."

"I really meant how's everything with the consulting tender we talked about when we had our dinner," corrected Max. "Anything suspicious?"

Joe wondered if Max knew anything, but played it straight.

"Oh yes, the consulting tender. That's pretty much being decided on as we speak. Close, but I think we've got a winner."

"Who's that just out of interest," asked Max, suspecting he knew the answer.

"That new firm, Brookshaw Consulting!"

"Really, and you're happy with the process they've gone through?"

"Absolutely Max," said Joe confidently. "All these reviews at the MOD go through such a rigorous and transparent process, with so many stakeholders involved. It's very robust."

"No one showing any favour towards one supplier or another," checked Max again.

Joe shook his head. "No. It simply wouldn't be possible,

too many people involved." He looked away at the London Eye. "What's your concern, you seem unsure about Brookshaw's?"

Max felt they were both dancing around what each of them suspected about the other. Did Joe know he was there, at the Manor House? He decided to play his card and see what reaction he'd get.

"I'm worried Joe. For old time's sake. I'm worried about your safety!"

Joe flinched, then played it straight back. "I don't know what you mean?"

Max sighed. "We have reason to believe something's going on, related to this firm, something potentially sinister. People could easily get caught up without realising what the consequences might be?"

"What people?" Joe looked uneasy.

"People like yourself Joe."

"Caught up in what for heaven's sake?"

"The worst kind of trouble you could imagine!"

Joe was out of smart responses and for a moment they both looked out up the Thames, wondering what to say next. Max pushed on.

"Joe. If you found yourself unknowingly caught up in something you knew to be wrong, you can tell me. I'll make sure you're looked after. I, or rather MI5, can be a mighty strong ally to have if you've found yourself in a tight spot!"

Joe remained silent, frantically weighing up his options.

"Well, if I were in a spot, how could you help me?" he asked cautiously.

Max thought this could be a chink in the armour. Might he cooperate after all?

"Unless you personally have committed a crime, there's always a good case for you being coerced under pressure, being mislead and unable to act from fear of threat and your own harm." Max tried to open the door a little more, hoping Joe would see there was a way out of this for him. "Always best to get out of these things before it's too late and you're in so far we can't retrieve it for you?"

Joe thought some more.

Max put a hand on his shoulder. "This isn't for you Joe. The baddies always get caught in the end. If there's something going on, you can tell me?"

Joe turned to look at Max, seeking verification in his eyes that he could be trusted. He gulped, then suddenly looked most forlorn.

"Oh my God Max, I'm screwed! I don't know what I've got myself into, it's bloody mad, you've got to help me?"

"Okay, okay, just calm down Joe, tell me what's happened?" Max wanted to make sure they were on the same wavelength and hear him out before giving too much away himself.

Joe slumped onto the iron bridge railing and took in a deep breath, seemingly suffering from a mini anxiety attack.

"I thought it was just a harmless business club, for executives like me, kind of like a mason's to help one another progress. Then before I know it they're offering me all sorts of rewards and asking me if I'm in or not!" He turned to Max. "I didn't know whether I was coming or going, so took a chance on joining, just to see what it was all about."

"Yes." Max found himself starting to sympathise with Joe and see that maybe he hadn't known what he was getting into. Would he confess to the ritual?

"Then before I can back out, I'm trapped into doing this weird bloody ceremony down in Sussex and get inducted into this mad business cult. What the hell am I going to do Max? They not messing about either, they're dangerous!"

Max was heartened by Joe's openness. He was beginning to win him back over, perhaps?

"What about this ceremony, what was that about?" he asked.

Joe seemed to gather his thoughts before answering. "It was weird, everyone in black hooded robes, a Grand Master, promises and rules, about helping one another in business, then off we all went!"

Max wanted to be angry that Joe had left out the bit about Graham being tasered and dumped in the lake, but given what Joe had already opened up with, felt it was understandable he'd left that part out for now. He didn't want to press him on the murder, or ask pointed questions like who the Grand Master was. He needed to concentrate on the goal.

"You're doing the right thing, Joe, don't worry, we'll sort this all out. Anything else about what happened to you?"

Joe began to look like he was questioning himself about opening up to Max.

"Not really. There was a ride on a boat across a lake, I had to commit loyalty to the cause, then I got my name written into this old book, like a membership ledger or something!"

'Bingo!' thought Max.

"This book, what else do you know about it, where's it kept for instance?" asked Max carefully.

"In the house where the ceremony was held, I think it's hidden amongst all the other books in a library there." Realising Max's interest in the book, he looked excited. "Is that what you're after Max, the book, with the names in?"

Max played it down and shrugged. "If you helped me get this book, that would really support your case to get out of this mess?"

Joe looked pensive. "The house will only have a few housekeeping staff there tonight. You'd need me to get you in there, that should be possible if we go together in case they have security at the entrance. But if there's any sign of police, they'll probably have protocols to destroy the book."

Joe now looked terrified. "Max, you absolutely cannot have police or backup with us if we go in! I'm afraid if something went wrong, they'll kill me for what I'm doing. I'm sure of it. Once you've got the book and I'm completely safe, then you can do what you want! I'll need protection though."

"There's no harm in having some backup ready for us

surely?"

Joe held Max's arms. "I'm not kidding Max, I won't do this if you have police or anyone else involved, it's you and me, or not at all!" He said crossly, agitated.

Max had got much further than he thought possible and didn't want to let Joe change his mind.

"Alright, just you and me."

"Tell you what," said Joe, "give me your address and I'll pick you up at say eight tonight, then we go down there, it's near Forest Row."

"Okay," agreed Max, looking like he had no idea where this place was.

They both walked back along the bridge towards Big Ben, where Joe went right to Whitehall and Max left to Millbank.

"It'll be okay Joe," assured Max as they parted.

"I bloody well hope so," said Joe.

Back in Si's office, the boss wasn't happy.

"We could be close to sorting this Max, if we get this book we can round up everyone involved, even in the US with the help of the CIA. We must be ready to pile in!"

"Si, you've got to trust me on this, we haven't got the book yet and we'll never get it if Patterson even suspects us or the police are circling ready to pounce, then we lose everything! As the DDG said, we've got to use our one lead. Crikey, he's putting himself on the line here, just let me go in and sort this?"

"It's too risky, I don't like it one bit, Max. You're going into the viper's nest. No, I'm sending Vince down there, that's final. He can just hang out nearby somewhere in case you need help, no one will see him."

"Just Vince then," agreed Max.

"I'm going to tell the Chief Constable, just so he's aware, no action, but he's got to be in the loop.

Max nodded.

That evening, Joe pulled up outside Max's gates on Clapham Common and Max came out to join him.

"All okay Max, no cavalry?"

"Just us Joe. I hope your information about the house being quiet tonight is correct?"

"Don't worry Max, if I don't like the look of anything, we'll postpone it for another time. I ain't putting my neck on the block for all this, having said that I already have by talking to you haven't I!"

They drove down the A3, round the M25 and down the M23. Little more was said, each of them in their own thoughts about what they were doing.

"What's the story with us visiting Joe?"

"They'll recognise me, I'll just say I left something there after the ceremony and you're a work colleague I'm dropping home, let's say to Crowborough, on the other side of the Forest yes?"

"Okay, what have you left," prompted Max, wanting to make sure Joe had his story straight.

"They give us each this old Greek coin, like a kind of masonic symbol, as a reminder of the ceremony and our membership. I'll say I need to pick it up before getting into trouble about it. Should only be the housekeepers there tonight."

Max was comforted by Joe giving up another revelation in mentioning the coin he'd seen being handed around during the ritual.

"Where's the owner of this house," asked Max, pretending not to know anything about the Manor House.

"They live in London during the week."

Max was happy Joe was being straight with him, as that tied in with Gillian Brookshaw being in town most of the time.

They pulled off Hindleap Lane, familiar now to Max, into the long single-track driveway, passing a couple of large houses, before reaching the end, where there was a gated entrance with the sign 'Manor House' in their headlights.

A man came out of a small doorway in the wall beside the gates, dressed in a gamekeeper's uniform. Max stirred in his seat seeing the man, then thankfully realised it wasn't one he recognised as having wrestled with.

Joe lowered the window and explained why he was there. The man eyed Max briefly.

"Just a work colleague, taking him home," added Joe.

The warden pressed a remote in his pocket and the gates opened. "Be quick then!"

They drove down the long winding driveway and Max was treated to a different perspective of the large house he'd seen from beyond the lake. All seemed quiet, the forecourt was empty but there were a couple of cars parked to the rear which Max assumed were staff. Joe parked outside the front door.

"Come on Max, let's get on with this," getting out.

Max came round the car, thinking that this was going to be very straightforward. It seemed quite surreal, with the house so empty of life, so normal, as if what he'd witnessed here never actually happened.

As they reached the front, the door was opened by a middle-aged woman dressed in a housekeeper's uniform.

"The gatehouse said you needed to retrieve something, do you know where you left it, Sir?"

"Probably in the library," replied Joe, smiling sweetly at her.

"This way," and she led them through the hall to a doorway, "do you need me to help?"

"No we're fine thanks," said Joe going in, "we'll only be a minute."

Max followed him inside the office with bookshelves covering the walls and was already imagining bringing the book of souls back to Thames House later that night, then with Si Lawson, seeing who's names were inside the sect's ledger!

"Right," said Joe, we're looking for a very old, tattered book, sort of greyish green. You start that end, I'll start here."

Max went over to the far end of the shelving and they both began to look over the bookends. They were both concentrating on the task in hand, that neither of them noticed each of the doors of the room open slowly and quietly! Until it was too late!

"Mr Sargent! We meet again," said Eduardo, holding up his stiletto handle!

Max was startled as he looked up to see the man that had tried to kill him on the underground, enter the room, immediately followed by the barrel of a shotgun. One of the gamekeepers!

Max and Joe both looked to the other door and to their dismay, another gamekeeper entered the room, shotgun levelled at them. It was the same man Max had fought with and choked unconscious. He sneered at Max, sporting the bruises Max had given him.

"You've been a lucky chap so far," said Eduardo, "but I think maybe your luck's just run out!"

Max's first thought was for Joe. He held up his hand to him, "Just stay calm Joe, we'll sort this out."

Then Joe starting to shake his head. Max studied him closely as he looked frightened, then his expression seemed more apologetic!

"No… I'm sorry Max, really I am," he stammered.

"What?" questioned Max.

"I had to. You can't protect me from them, they're too powerful, too well connected!"

Max stared back at him, the feeling of abandonment swept through his body.

"You're kidding me, Joe? Don't tell me you've led me here, for them!" He gasped out loud in exasperation and disappointment. "After all we talked about, I thought you'd seen sense?"

Joe moved backwards towards Eduardo. "Sorry Max. I've worked my way up to the top, and want to use my influence to make some money. A Chief Procurement Officer's pay might be good, but it's nowhere near what I deserve."

"Go now!" ordered Eduardo.

With that, Joe left the room and ran to his car, to leave as quickly as he could.

"So which one of these is the famous book your leader uses?" asked Max.

Eduardo looked at the rows of shelves. "I suppose it doesn't really matter now, you knowing. It's not here at all, it's with the boss halfway to New York with him on a private jet!" He held up the handle of his knife.

"Going to try using that on me again are you?"

Eduardo pressed the button on his stiletto and the long blade instantly lashed out into position, gleaming. "What this? No, far too simple, and quick. We have something else in mind." He nodded towards the patio doors and one of the men went over to open them.

"They'll come for me," said Max holding up his hands, as the two shotguns ushered him to the doors and out.

Eduardo collected Max's phone and performed a quick search. "I'm reckoning that's not going to happen, is it!" He pulled out a plastic zip-tie and fastened it around Max's wrists in front of him.

Max looked unsure of where the three men wanted him to go.

"Down the lawns, slowly," said one of the men, now walking each side of him, guns raised. Eduardo followed.

"You're gonna wish you hadn't come back here, how stupid!" he hissed.

Max heard the stiletto spring retract the blade back into its handle behind him.

They made their way down the several open lawns, stepping carefully through the darkness. No moon was visible and a cloud covering made the dark eerie estate almost invisible.

As they neared the bottom Max could see through the gloom, the small boat used in the ritual was still tied to the nearest jetty. He had a bad feeling about what they had planned for him!

"The bodies seem to be piling up, why make it worse with

mine, you still have a chance to let me go, I can make sure no one comes after you tonight? You can get abroad before this all blows up." Max was clutching at straws now and surveying the lake frantically looking for anything that gave him options.

"One more body isn't going to make much difference," replied Eduardo dispassionately. "Over there, to the boat, get in it," he ordered.

As Max stepped into the small boat he saw something that made his heart skip a beat! On the floor lay a large rock with a climbing rope tied around it!

Max looked around appealing to the two gamekeepers.

"Guy's, this is cold-blooded murder! I'm with MI5, you'll be hunted down and spend the rest of your life in a maximum-security prison."

"Shut it arsehole," replied the man with bruises on his face.

They all clambered into the boat and the other gunman went to the rear and started familiarising himself with the gondola-style paddle.

"Bloody hell, this stupid thing's impossible to use," he complained.

"Just get us out a little way for God's sake," said Eduardo, while the other man tied the end of the rope tightly around Max's ankles, knotting it many times. Once he'd finished he pulled at it to make sure it held fast, leaving only a couple of feet rope between Max and the rock.

Max tried one last time. "Guys, you can all go to Spain or South America and live long happy lives with all your money. If you kill me, you have no options, I promise you'll be caught!"

The men ignored him completely now, much to Max's frustration and anger. The boat waggled clumsily away from the jetty, swaying from side to side with the inept paddler. After a few moments, Eduardo had had enough. They were only five metres out, he spoke impatiently.

"Jees! Let's just get on with this!"

He stepped back and hauled up the rock, letting the two

gamekeepers grab Max and manoeuvre him to the edge of the boat. It was all happening too fast for Max to try to wriggle and stop them.

The three men looked at one another, Eduardo nodded and they pushed Max over the side with the rock!

Max hit the water with a splash, took a deep breath almost too late, then was immediately engulfed by the cold. He stayed at the surface for a moment, then felt the dreaded tug at his feet as the rock began to sink, pulling him down! He descended, his buoyant air-filled lungs losing the battle with the merciless weight.

He looked up through the water at the three shadows, but with the darkness of the night and the dirty lake water, they were gone when his head was only two feet under.

Adrenaline kicked in and Max desperately fought back the panic by trying to stay calm, giving himself just a few critical seconds of uninterrupted thought to weigh up what he could do.

His descent stopped as the rock settled into the soft, muddy bottom of the lake, which was only four metres deep. Had they taken the boat to the centre of the lake, the depth there would have been almost twice that.

A plan hit him!

With his hand's fastened to his front, Max quickly pulled at his belt buckle and withdrew the small two-inch blade now concealed there. He manipulated it carefully round, knowing that if he dropped it, he was finished. Turning it towards himself, it sliced through the single plastic zip-tie around his wrists.

With his hands now free and still holding the small knife, he immediately set to work on the rope around his ankles, furiously cutting at the nylon fibres in the cold, black water. He could feel his lungs starting to beckon for air.

The three men in the boat didn't move, continuing to stare down into the dark water below them, each imagining the suffering Max must be going through as he began taking the water into his lungs.

The small but sharp blade cut the rope free from Max's ankles! He dropped the knife and started to swim through the darkness in the direction he remembered the jetty being in. He couldn't see anything but kept low in the water, brushing through weeds and soft mud as he persevered forwards.

Finally, one of his arms hit a wooden post, which he knew must be one of the supports to the small jetty they'd left from. Almost out of breath, he quickly rose through the water, pulling himself between two more posts so he was in the middle of the structure.

He carefully broke the surface so as not to cause any water ripples and stifled a gasp for air, straining his lungs to be silent. Max had managed to get under the centre of the jetty in a concealed space with just six inches between the underside of the wooden slats and the surface of the water.

He peered through the sideboards and could see the boat with the men still looking down into the water. He cursed them under his breath but remained still and silent, happy to be alive and thankful for the tiny, innocuous blade he'd agreed to have.

A couple of minutes passed and finally, convinced Max was dead, Eduardo nudged the other two men.

"That's it! He's finished! Come on."

They paddled precariously back to the jetty, as Max lowered his head so his nose was just above the surface. They disembarked onto the jetty just inches above him.

"Nasty way to go that," said one of the gunmen.

"Had it coming to him," said the bruised man unsympathetically.

"Okay, we're done here," said Eduardo. "I'll tell the boss it's sorted! You guys can pick up the body in the next couple of days and get rid of it."

They walked along the jetty and just as Eduardo was about to step off onto the grass, he stopped, turning round.

Max remained silent, but had the terrible feeling he might

have been spotted or heard!

Eduardo looked out onto the lake. Something made him want to check that Max's body was down there, dead, so he was sure. Then he thought to himself, 'no-one could have escaped that!'. He scanned across the water one last time. All was still, then made his way back up the lawns to the house with the others.

Max waited another ten minutes, making sure everything was dark and quiet, before ducking under the jetty side planks and slowly climbing out of the lake, shivering.

Under the cover of darkness, he kept low and skirted around the lake to the far side and headed for the treeline where he'd recently watched the ritual from. Passing the very spot he'd been that night, he found the layby, then walked up the lane to the main road. He now jogged away from the manor house and soon reached Wych Cross, where after a few minutes he managed to wave down a car and ask to make one emergency call with the driver's phone. Five minutes later, Vince who was nearby, picked him up.

Max felt stupid for trusting Joe Patterson, what a fool he'd been and what an ordeal. He never wanted to lay eyes on an idyllic, beautiful lake in the woods ever again!

But despite everything, he now knew where the book of souls was. With Brett Brookshaw in New York.

And, he'd earned an advantage of sorts.

They now thought Max Sargent was dead!

17

"You want to do what Max?" exclaimed Si. "After everything you've been through!"

"Si, you know it's the best way to sort this." Max was determined. "Someone from MI5 has got to go to New York and get this bloody book, once and for all. It may as well be me! We can't just expect the Americans to finish this."

"You're crazy, they've almost killed you three times, it's too dangerous. Let's just hand it over to the FBI or even CIA, they can raid Brookshaw's place, it's their turf," insisted Si.

"What, you're happy to hand all this over to the Yanks? Really? You always say they mess things up, going in like the cavalry, all guns blazing? Anyway, Brookshaw's a Brit after all. He's our problem." Max was determined to end this himself.

"No, I don't like handing it over, oh, I don't know. I don't want to lose you, Max, I don't want that on my conscience."

"Look, you know it's the only way to conclude this? Yes, we could raid the Manor House, raid their consulting firm, arrest those we might get to know about including Joe Patterson, then what? Brett gets his lawyers involved and we have God knows how many of his Hades gang running around willy nilly, scot-free and we don't even know who they all are, probably never will!" Max was compelling, quoting back what the DDG and Si himself had said before. "We need that book!"

Si slumped back in his chair. "Damn it, Max. If you're up for it? Then I suppose," he agreed reluctantly.

"I also need another crack at their company accounts, there must be a digital record somewhere of payments being made to the offshore accounts of their members."

"Where would you find that, you've tried St Kitts and Nevis?"

"The only other place it could possibly be," said Max. "Brett Brookshaw's Headshell offices in New York!"

"You'll need help with all this."

"I'm better off alone Si."

"Oh no, sorry Max, you're going onto American soil, so I've got to inform them what we're doing. I may as well suggest they help, they'll get involved in the end anyway. If I take the initiative, I might be able to limit the so-called cavalry to just one or two of them."

"If we must, could be useful I suppose," conceded Max.

"Right then, I'll sort the necessary with the DDG. Vince can get you Brett Brookshaw's home address in the Hamptons and his office in the Chrysler Building I gather. I'll also sort things with the CIA and get your contact sorted by the time you land at JFK New York. Get a new phone and belt from Alan and sort yourself onto the next available flight!"

"By the way, Si, given I'm meant to be dead, according to the Hades bunch, is there any way I can go to the US under an alias? Just in case they've got contacts that could flag me flying over, border control or the hotel, we may as well try to hold onto my advantage."

Si thought for a moment. "You're right! We do have the facility to authorise another passport and MI5 ID here in Thames House. Let me make a call, the DDG will need to agree to it, then you can go to the guys on the second floor and they will sort it all out while you wait."

"Thanks, Si, also, let me have the details of your best MI5 agent based in the big apple," said Max. "I need someone I can trust out there. A Brit."

"Will do. We'll also now put tabs on Joe Patterson, Gillian Brookshaw and the Manor House, so they can't leave the country. We need to be ready to start picking up people if, or rather when you get that book. Got any plans for once you get there?"

"I've a few ideas which I'll have thought through properly during the eight-hour flight over. The rest of it I'll have to wing as I go along!"

"Good luck Max. If that book's got the members' names in it as we think, we need it in our hands. Preferably don't let the Yanks have it!"

Max's British Airways flight landed at JFK and he switched his phone on. A text came through from Si advising him, 'CIA agent Callum Pearce will meet you at your hotel at 9am tomorrow, I've only told them you may need assistance connecting with a suspect Brit!'.

Max queued at the airport's passport control, trusting that the new documents he'd been given at Thames House would pass muster. The border control official looked the same as his colleagues all lined up in their booth's, suspicious, serious and a little bored. He lingered on the passport.

"Ralph Cunningham," eying Max closely. "What is the purpose of your visit?"

"Pleasure," said Max, "a couple of days sightseeing."

The man checked his screen for any flags raised by the many organisations who fed through alerts on suspicious, watcher, tracing, incorrect paperwork or wanted criminals. Nothing came up. He handed back the passport and Max passed through.

He then took a yellow cab from the airport to his hotel in Manhattan, the Waldorf Astoria in Park Avenue.

Built in 1931 as two large buildings combined, the Waldorf and the Astoria, at forty-seven floors it was the tallest hotel in the world until 1963. With its grand art deco design and interiors, it is synonymous with political, business and fundraising conventions, gatherings and parties of the rich and famous.

Max checked into his room and called up the MI5 contact Si Lawson had given him. He arranged to meet up later for dinner, then left the hotel and caught another cab. He wanted to visit one special place first, to pay his respects.

On 11th September 2001, nineteen al Qaeda extremists carried out suicide attacks against targets in the United States. Two planes were flown into the twin towers of the World Trade Centre in New York, a third hit the Pentagon in Arlington Virginia and a fourth plane crashed in a field in Shanksville Pennsylvania. Almost three thousand people lost their lives during the 9/11 attacks, as a horrified world watched events unfold that day and President Bush declared his 'war on terror' to help rally his nation.

The cab took Max to lower Manhattan and dropped him off near Ground Zero. Max strolled towards the fourteen-acre memorial site and could feel the chill and grief the area symbolised, imagining the terrible events of 2001 on that very spot. The towers, the people going about their usual daily routine, the offices, then the planes, fires, the response from the brave services, police and firefighters, the deaths, the bravery, but also the helplessness. And then the awful sight of one, then the other tower crumbling downwards, engulfing the area in dust and debris.

Above him towered the recently erected One World Trade Centre, like a phoenix rising out of the ashes in defiance of the terrorist attacks.

The memorial known as 'Reflecting Absence', comprises a field of trees interrupted by the two square, black holes where the footprints of the towers once were. Max gazed into the pools of water, entranced, sharing the grief of so many affected that dreadful day.

Max caught a cab to Ninth Avenue to meet his MI5 colleague at the Old Homestead Steakhouse. Opened in 1868 it's one of America's oldest restaurants and remains one of the sought-after dining experiences in New York City.

Max spotted his contact Jeremy Hall from his photo. He was already waiting at a small table. A tall, slim figure in his late thirties and exuding a naïve keenness from his youth, inexperience and posting to this exciting overseas role based at the British Consulate on Second Avenue.

"Ralph Cunningham," he offered as he stood up, "or rather Max Sargent, which is it today?" trying to break the ice.

"Max is fine, as long as it's just the two of us."

They sat down and exchanged some preliminary background chat, before both ordering a large steak and a bottle of red wine.

"I didn't get much of a briefing from your guys at Thames House, other than to make myself available to you for whatever you needed. So, what this all about?" asked Jeremy enthusiastically, leaning forward.

"In short, we have a British businessman, Brett Brookshaw…"

"Of Brookshaw Consulting," he interrupted, "I've heard of them, doing well by all accounts."

"Perhaps a little too well," said Max. "That's the problem. He's established a networking club with influential senior figures across all walks of government, life and business, and for diverting, or favouring consulting contracts going to his firm, they share the rewards with huge payoffs!"

"So basically, insider trading, bribery and money laundering?" Jeremy said intuitively.

'Smart lad' thought Max.

"But it's all gotten a bit out of hand," continued Max. "They've killed several people we know about, plus a couple of attempts on me, hence the alias, they think I'm at the bottom of a lake!"

"Bloody hell, that has got out of hand! And they're operating here in New York as well?"

"Yes, the Hades sect as it's called, goes where the firm goes, so mainly UK and the US, here where their offices are. He also has a large estate in the Hamptons and judging from the satellite pictures, it bears a remarkable resemblance to the place they own back in the UK, large house, grounds, all overlooking a lake."

"How come?"

"Apart from wanting the best that money can buy, it seems they use these places for their indoctrination ceremonies, black robes and all," explained Max. "The lake represents the River Styx!"

"Good grief! You mean as in Hades and crossing over to the underworld, blimey!" Jeremy was quick to catch on.

"Yes, all quite fanatical, which is why it's dangerous. I plan to have my CIA contact drive me out there tomorrow so I can take a look. We believe there's a book holding the names of all the sect's members and their payments. That's what I'm after!"

"Who's your CIA contact?"

"A Callum Pearce?"

"Oh yes, I've met him a couple of times at joint UK, US agency meetings, nice guy, very much on the ball," concurred Jeremy happily showing off he'd made the brief connection.

"Okay, good. Tomorrow, I'll keep you updated when I can by text or phone, but I'll need you to follow me say a mile or two behind, so you're around if I need backup alright?"

"Of course," agreed the young agent.

The steaks arrived and were huge.

"Wow, these Yanks eat so much!" joked Max. "Let's share our locations on our phones so you know where I am. I don't fancy ending up in any more lakes! And I suggest you request a gun for tomorrow, just in case!"

"I'll get that sorted tonight after dinner." The comment took the edge of Jeremy's enthusiasm. "You don't think I'll need to use it do you Max?" he asked worriedly.

"I bloody hope not, but this lot don't muck about!" He surveyed the large filet of beef on his plate. "Come on, let's eat!"

The next morning Max went down to the Waldorf's reception just before nine. He settled in a seat admiring the art deco surroundings and the large gold and black marble columns intersecting the huge hall. He noticed an athletic-looking guy striding through reception confidently and dismissed him thinking, 'too obvious and cocky by far for CIA'. The sporty guy then looked around the room and spotting Max looking like he was waiting to meet someone, came over.

"I don't suppose you're Mr Cunningham by any chance? From the UK?"

Max stood up surprised this could indeed be his contact.

"Why yes, Ralph Cunningham, good to meet you," greeted Max. "Callum isn't it? From the agency?"

They shook hands. "CIA yes, but not Callum Pearce I'm afraid."

"Oh?"

"He was reassigned, something's he's been working on for ages flared up last night," shrugged the man, wearing a suit just slightly too small for him. "I've been asked to fill in and help you however I can."

"And you are?"

"Ah yes, sorry, should have said!" He pulled out a CIA name card and handed it over. "Cuffney, Brandon Cuffney!"

The name meant nothing to Max.

"So what's this all about, all I got told was that you needed to connect with another of your Brit's out here, whatever that means?" Brandon asked with a hint of sarcasm.

Max was already thinking he was going to struggle to spend the next few days with this American All-Star wannabe, so decided to keep it brief.

"Well I have a contact out on the end of Long Island I need to see. I'd be grateful if you wouldn't mind driving us out there, I can fill you in on the way?"

"What, right out to Montauk?"

"Not quite that far."

"Could be a good couple of hour's drive, what with traffic and all?"

"Well, if your car's nearby, let's go," prompted Max.

They drove down Lexington Avenue and passed another art deco landmark. The Chrysler building!

They both looked up at it, unknowingly for the same reason. Brett Brookshaw's head office was up there!

"I'll have to get inside for a closer look round," mentioned Max.

Brandon turned to him somewhat startled. "Why?" he asked abruptly.

Max was taken aback by the harsh tone, then shrugged, "It's one of your New York top sites, isn't it? All that art deco, like at the Waldorf."

"Like your art deco do you," Brandon said with another hint of sarcasm.

Having watched Max and Brandon drive off together, after a while, Jeremy Hall pulled away, watching Max's location ahead of him on his phone map.

They passed through the Queens Midtown tunnel and joined the I495 Long Island expressway, which would take them most of the way.

After forty minutes of light conversation, where Max felt the arrogant CIA agent was trying very hard to outdo him, Brandon once again came back to wanting to know more about Max's purpose there.

"So where is it your contact is, near the end of Long Island?"

"It's a place in the Hamptons, near Mecox Bay."

Brandon's heart missed a beat as he was stunned by hearing the location.

He tried to reassure himself, thinking 'surely this can't have anything to do with the Hades sect I've just joined, to gain access to the British government's cabinet minister? They can't be onto us?'.

The previous day, upon finding out MI5 were sending their agent Ralph Cunningham out to New York potentially after another Brit, Brandon's boss at the CIA had pulled a few strings. He'd over-ruled the team lead who'd assigned Callum

Pearce and insisted that they were working on a confidential case that could be related to MI5's line of inquiry. Brandon Cuffney was duly tasked to babysit the MI5 agent. But in the event this visit had nothing to do with their Hades infiltration, the CIA boss decided not to tell Brandon. He wanted to see how it played out, just in case it came to nothing.

Whilst Brandon knew nothing about the trouble a certain Max Sargent had been causing in the UK, nor therefore his supposed death, he was however starting to think the Brits might be onto them and Hades. Had they uncovered the cabinet minister? The repercussions were enormous if this all came tumbling down, he would be right in the middle of it all!

"The Hamptons," Brandon repeated, the sarcasm was gone. "Who exactly is this Brit contact?" He pulled his ace card. "The CIA have a right to know what you're up to over here, this is our turf!"

Max was surprised at the sudden, curt demand from his CIA escort. He, in turn, had no idea Brandon had anything to do with Brett Brookshaw or the Hades sect, so whilst he didn't take to the man, he felt it was time to give him more information. After all, he would need his help figuring out how to get access to where the book of souls might be kept, either at the Hamptons estate or the Chrysler building office.

"We have reason to believe a businessman is bribing executives across all industries, to win deals." Max kept it brief.

Brandon felt the anxiety swell inside him.

"So, who is this businessman, does he have a name?" Brandon's confident tone now had a nervous edge to it.

"He runs an up-and-coming consulting firm," said Max, checking Brandon's expression. "Brett Brookshaw. Know him?"

Brandon felt as though he'd been hit with a sledgehammer and gripped the steering wheel to gather himself. 'They know! God damn Brits! They're already onto us!' he fretted.

"Brookshaw? Yes, I've heard of them. Don't know

anything about this Brett guy though." Brandon tried his best to sound nonchalant and unphased. "Do you know who these people are that they're bribing, to win these deals?" Brandon tensed, ready for the answer. He was also starting to look out for where he could turn off the expressway if he needed to.

"We know a few members of this networking organisation, but that's the point. We can't go busting in until we have all the names of everyone involved, otherwise they'll just disappear," explained Max unknowingly.

Brandon relaxed a little. At least this Ralph guy didn't suspect him or the CIA, or he wouldn't be sharing all this with him.

"How would you ever find out who's involved?" Another key question.

"We believe they have a ledger with all the members' names in it, a book. That's really what we're after!"

Brandon could feel his pulse racing. 'Jesus, if MI5 get the book of souls, with all the name's inside, including his, it was over!' He was panicking and frantically began rolling through the options in his mind, he had to do something. Damn! Should he call his boss back at the CIA? Maybe call Brett, he'd know what to do? Should he detain this MI5 agent, or try to collaborate, but then he might find out they, the CIA were trying to spy on the British government! What a mess!

"What's the plan for today then?" asked Brandon, playing for time to pull himself together, as he looked for an exit off the highway.

"I want to have a closer look at his estate in the Hamptons, maybe see if there's some way of getting in."

Brandon started indicating right to pull off onto a service road at exit 55 after Dix Hills.

"How come we're turning off?" Max asked.

"Fuel stop," said Brandon abruptly.

Max glanced at the fuel gauge, it showed half full! Something was up? Brandon seemed suddenly tense, anxious, on alert? Max realised something he'd told him had spooked him.

They pulled off the main carriageway and into a large Shell fuel station.

Brandon got out and started towards the shop. "It's a pre-pay," he justified.

Max also got out and followed him. "Need the loo!" was his excuse, but he wanted to see what the American was up to.

Brandon frowned showing rising annoyance. He wanted some space to make a call and was getting more agitated, knowing this was coming to a head.

"Can't you wait?"

"No. Why should I, it's right there," said Max pointing to the sign showing the toilets to the rear. He could see Brandon was acting very oddly now.

"Look, I need to make a call, in private!"

"Who to? Is everything alright Brandon? You seem a little upset?" asked Max, now worried and on high alert.

Brandon cursed and panicked. "Damn it!" He came over to Max and ushering him round to the back of the building. Without warning, he then delved into his jacket for his CIA issue Glock 19 handgun!

Max was ready and instantly saw he was going for his gun. He grabbed Brandon's wrist before he could bring the weapon clear of his jacket and with his other hand, held the top of the gun and violently twisted. Brandon hadn't yet gotten a tight hold of his Glock yet and the gun came away from his fingers before he could react.

Max gathered the handgun into his grip and was now standing next to Brandon pointing his gun at him. It had all happened in an instant! They stared at one another, both in disbelief!

"Just stay calm!" ordered Max. "What the hell's going on here? Why would you pull a gun on me for God's sake?"

Brandon slowly raised his hands, trying to determine if this MI5 man would shoot him if he had to? He looked deadly serious, so any idea of calling his bluff evaporated.

"You have no idea what you're doing!" Brandon said dismissively.

"Are you referring to this?" said Max shaking the gun at him, "or us chasing after Brookshaw?"

"Both!" Brandon instantly regretted the comment.

"Oh, so you do know something about what I've been telling you? Something hit a nerve that's for sure!"

Max pulled out his phone with his free hand and called his backup Jeremy, who was less than a mile behind and had seen from the map that they'd pulled off the highway.

"Get to me, now!" instructed Max. He then rang off. "Handcuffs? Throw me the key and put them on yourself!"

"What? You're crazy!"

"You just pulled your gun on me. Put the cuffs on!" Brandon obliged and threw the key to Max. "Who were you going to call?"

Brandon shrugged, as Jeremy pulled up to them and got out, looking shocked at the sight of his fellow operative holding a gun to a CIA agent.

"What the hell Max?" Jeremy immediately realised his faux pas. Max sighed.

"Max? So Ralph Cunningham's not even your real name! Christ, you damn Brits! Don't you even trust the CIA?" exclaimed Brandon furiously.

"Apparently not it seems, for good reason!" said Max. Looking at Jeremy who now had his handgun out, "I need you to detain this guy, right here, in the gents if necessary, unless you can get covert backup and collection from your guys back at New York HQ. He absolutely must not be released or allowed to contact anyone. Which reminds me, get his phone."

Jeremy approached Brandon and retrieved his mobile and car keys, passing the phone to Max. Luckily the screen hadn't locked out from when Brandon had just opened it up to make a call moments ago.

"Get his car off the forecourt and park it up over there at the back, and search the boot," Max asked.

Max checked the texts and was instantly drawn to the contact 'BB'!

"You're kidding me!" showing the screen to Brandon. "Surely not Brett Brookshaw?"

Brandon's hope of salvaging this was disappearing, with handcuffs on, gun taken and now two MI5 agents, one going through his phone.

"Look, can we talk about all this, it's just a big misunderstanding."

But Max was already looking through the last few texts Brandon had exchanged with Brett the day before.

'BB – formal meetup 8pm tomor at mine?'

'BrandonC – will be there.'

'BrandonC – something's come up at work, won't be free now, sorry.'

'BB – ok.'

Max smiled. "Formal meetup eh? What might that be?" Brandon looked down at the ground gritting his teeth. "Let me take a wild guess," continued Max, "you're having one of your weird ceremonies, by the lake?"

Brandon looked up at him glaring, "What the…!"

Max went into the phone's settings and cancelled the passcode so he had access to it from now on.

Jeremy had driven Brandon's car over and emerged from under the rear boot lid, holding up a black hooded robe!

"Well, well, looks like you have done what you were instructed to do, by helping me," chuckled Max. Brandon looked at him, his phone, then the robe, his face reddening with anger. "I think you may have got me the invite I needed to get into the Hampton's estate after all!"

"What's going on Max?" Jeremy pleaded, desperate to understand what was unfolding.

Max took the robe from him and looked Brandon up and down.

"Just my size I reckon!"

He looked down at the motif embroidered onto the chest

lapel, showing a bronze-coloured ancient helmet between the two prongs of a bident spear.

"The symbols of Hades, God of wealth and the underworld. Invisibility and power!" He looked at Brandon and shook his head, tutting. "Not very invisible now are you? Boy, are you in so much trouble when this gets out, you'd better pray I close this whole operation down, because if I don't, then they'll be after you for sure!"

"You'll never get away with it. They'll spot you a mile off, you'll be killed!" implored Brandon. "Let's all go back to New York, get our superiors involved and sort this out round the table eh?"

"Wonder what they'd all say? I can see the headlines, CIA agent is a member of corporate corruption cash for contracts scandal!"

"You don't understand Ralph, I mean Max, I've managed to infiltrate the Hades sect for the CIA, we've been tracking them for ages, I can get all the intel for you, the book. Don't go in there now, you'll blow everything!" begged Brandon, sounding quite convincing.

Max ignored him. "Jeremy, change of plan, I'm going to need you. Wait here with him and get a couple of your colleagues to get here as fast as possible, then they'll take him back to the British Consulate and detain him there, no phone calls, no contact whatsoever. I'll call my boss in London and update him, he'll sort out the detention authorisation and paperwork, we'll likely charge him eventually, but for the next day or so I just need him held."

"What about me once I hand him over?"

"You then come to me, you'll have me on the tracker app. I'll be holed up somewhere in the Hamptons for the rest of today near Brookshaw's estate. You should be able to get to me by mid or late afternoon, still in plenty of time for the evening," said Max.

"What are we going to do?" Jeremy asked, hauling Brandon into his car to watch over him for a few hours.

"I'll fill you in later when you get to me, but we're going to gate-crash a party!"

"Huh?"

Max walked over to Brandon's car holding his phone and newly acquired Glock, which prompted a thought. He turned to Jeremy.

"One more thing I need you to get your chaps to bring with them, for you."

"What's that?"

"A sniper rifle, with night sights, laser and silencer!"

18

"Crikey Max," said Si on the call, "I'll have to get the DDG involved if we're detaining a CIA agent in New York!"

"He's one of them, a member of this Hades cult, one of Brett Brookshaw's bloody gang! Is there no end to the people he's got involved? Surely we can detain him? I can't have him on the loose for the next twenty-four hours."

"At least you've seen the evidence on his phone and that robe, maybe we should think about getting the local's involved at the Hamptons estate?" suggested Si.

"No, we can't trust the local police, frankly I don't trust anyone if he's got into the CIA, I need to go alone," reasoned Max. "Besides, we can't go blundering in, what if the book isn't there, then we've got nothing again. No Si, I'll go in, it's our best chance, you just make sure Brandon Cuffney is held until I get clear!"

"That's what I'm worried about Max, you getting the book, then getting out and away. Be careful, they may think you're dead for now, but once you start any trouble, they're capable of anything!"

Max drove the remaining hour to the Hamptons, then given he had another eight hours to kill before the evening's event, deliberately drove on past the road leading to the estate, into Bridgehampton. There, he found a roadside diner where he had a long lunch. He then drove a little way along the Montauk Highway and pulled off into a car park overlooking a small lake, Poxabogue Pond.

Looking through Brandon's mobile, he started to wonder if he should tell Brett that he, pretending to be Brandon, was coming to the ritual after all? It was a risk, what if Brett called back, it was over then. But just turning up would also be odd and inevitably draw some challenge once he got there. He decided he had no choice but to text Brett.

He typed out a short message saying simply, *'BrandonC – free now, will be there tonight, may be slightly late.'* His finger hovered over the 'Send' button, this could blow everything.

He sent the message, then held the phone with bated breath, praying Brett wouldn't call!

Five minutes passed and nothing, which Max found annoying and worrying. He waited.

Ping!

After ten minutes a reply came back. It was short but gave him the assurance his plan might work and he wouldn't get a call. It said just, *'BB – ok'*.

Max checked the Glock's magazine. It could hold fifteen rounds, but he needed to know what he had in there, just in case tonight went wrong. He counted nine rounds and one in the barrel. More than enough, he thought!

He settled down into the driver's seat and turned on the radio for company. Sleep was out of the question, he just needed to stay out of the way for another four hours or so.

After a while, Jeremy's car pulled into the car park next to Max.

"Hi Max, sorry, took a bit longer for me to explain why I needed two more guys to come and collect Cuffney and detain him back at the Consulate. We had to wait for the signoff between my lot here and your Deputy Director General back in London. All sorted now, we've got a twenty-four-hour detention, no questions asked, but then we've got to come clean and tell the CIA everything!"

Max nodded. "We'll hopefully have sorted this within the next twenty-four hours… or we'll be dead!"

"Hey, come on Max, you're kidding right?" Jeremy looked worried.

"Got the rifle?" asked Max.

"I have," replied Jeremy, "after a lot of bloody paperwork." He held it up. "The British Army's finest, the

L115A3, effective for over a kilometre, with night and thermal sights, laser targeting and suppressor. What the hell's going on Max?"

Jeremy got into Max's car and for the next hour or so, Max explained the whole story of the Hades sect and took him through the plan for tonight. The young MI5 agent listened intently, was intrigued, astonished, aghast and anxious about being thrust into the frontline so abruptly. But he was up for it!

At twenty to eight, Jeremy drove off ahead of Max, to find himself a suitable location.

As eight pm approached, Max got the black robe out of the trunk and put it on. It had a faint smell of Brandon's cologne. He looked again at the bident and helmet motif, proudly stitched onto the front. Inside the hood was a black fabric veil mask, attached by velcro, which Max was grateful for as it would hide his identity apart from his eyes.

He got back into the car with the hood down around his shoulders and with a deep breath, pulled out of the lake's car park. Heading back to Bridgehampton, he took Ocean Road south, then after a few minutes, veered off into Mecox Road. This led to Brett's Hamptons estate, on the edge of Mecox Bay.

Max realised that he couldn't stake out the place before entering. If he was seen loitering around the perimeter of the grounds, that would be that. He had to trust in his disguise and the apparent acceptance of anonymity these rituals allowed. He would have to simply turn up as if he were Brandon Cuffney!

As he drew nearer he pulled the robe's hood over his head and secured the veil across his face. He also shuffled forward in his seat and firmly jammed the Glock into the back of his belt.

The lit-up entrance glowed out of the darkness ahead! It was eight-fifteen. Max hoped he'd guessed the timings correctly. He couldn't afford to be early and have to engage in conversation with anyone, but neither could he arrive too late, after proceedings had begun.

The sign on one of the large gate posts read 'Manor House'! The same name as the similar property back in Sussex. The two men at the gate were quite different though to the guards back in the UK masquerading as gamekeepers, with their shotgun licenses. These two were dressed in smart black casual clothes and both holding automatic machine guns, as permitted by law for US citizens to own quite freely.

One of them walked to the car, alert, then relaxed once he saw the driver wearing a robe and hood.

"Brandon Cuffney," said Max confidently, safe with his guess that the gate guard would know the name but not Brandon's real voice.

"You're a bit, late sir, better hurry!" he replied, waving him on.

Max proceeded down the driveway through some trees, which then opened out just as it did in Forest Row, revealing the stately house set at one end of the vast grounds. It was quite surreal, seeing this duplicate estate in Long Island's Hamptons, with its ornate gardens, sloping lawns and twinkling in the faint moonlight, the water's of Mecox Bay. The lake!

Max could immediately see some dark, hooded figures starting to make their way out of the house, towards the lawns and in the direction of the water. He deliberately parked his car on the forecourt nearest the exit, facing back along the driveway, in case he needed to make a hasty retreat later!

He slowly strolled towards the gathering, trying to blend in with the dutiful meander of the others, not too quick, not too slow, purposefully, respectfully. Though from behind his veil, Max was frantically scanning the landscape and each of the other robed men, expecting one of them to come over and greet him. But none of them did. His attire had gained him instant acceptance, with the understanding that if a brother wished to remain anonymous, they could.

Max now started searching for anyone in authority, security, a ferryman, the Grand Master. Brett Brookshaw!

Then he recognised a face, just as the person exited the library patio door, before pulling his hood over his head. He recognised the face from photos he'd seen.

It was Brett Brookshaw himself!

Max's heart missed a beat! Not just because he was at last in the presence of his nemesis, but because he noticed what he was holding. The old, tattered book. The book of souls!

For an instant, Max toyed with the idea of simply pulling out his gun and taking the book, but it was all happening too fast. Something told him to wait for a better opportunity later on.

Too late! His procrastination beat him, as several more cloaked men followed Brett out through the doors and surrounded him, chatting as they made their way down the lawn with the others. Max glanced around totting up a quick headcount. There were eighteen people. A sizeable gathering!

He blended in again and ahead of the main group, could see several of the sinister-looking robed outlines already down near the water's edge and continuing off into the distance. Max figured they were the new joiner and the so-called ferryman, going off to their boat's starting point across one of the water inlets of the bay, representing the charade of being the River Styx!

A hand touched Max's arm! He spun round, half expecting to see a couple of guards about to haul him away.

"How are you?" said a man's deep voice from under an ominous hood and cloak.

Upon looking into Max's eyes, the man quickly said, "Oh, dear, I'm so sorry. I thought you were someone else, my apologies!" He quickly withdrew himself and continued off across the lawn, respecting the code of each other's choice as to whether to communicate with others.

Brett heard the apology and looked over, always keen to keep tabs on who was who, and which brothers were happy to stay and chat, and which preferred not to meet others, for fear of compromising their public or senior roles in business.

He caught Max's eyes, but not quite enough to ascertain which of his members was beneath the robe. He was about to move over to Max, when one of his close team, grabbed his attention to check final arrangements for the ritual, tell him the lectern was in place and that Liam Wellings had taken the inductee to the boat.

When Brett had finished talking, he looked up again for the mystery brother, but he was gone, engulfed into the throng of other figures walking down to the water. For a moment he looked across them wondering which was Brandon Cuffney, his special CIA brother. He wasn't sure. He would find him after the ceremony. He had some good news to impart. The first relay of information from their UK government cabinet minister brother had come through!

Back in the UK, at the Manor House in Wych Cross, the gamekeepers had been dragging the lake with a hook and rope, to retrieve the body of Max Sargent and dispose of it. They'd carefully covered the area they knew he had been dropped in, on the end of the rope and rock, but had found nothing. It now dawned on them that maybe somehow, Sargent had escaped, swam off into the darkness, otherwise the body would have been found?

They alerted Eduardo who in disbelief, swore at them profusely. But his anger was really at himself, for having to entertain the possibility that the MI5 agent had eluded him once more. But also, that he now had to tell his boss.

He called Brett. No answer. His phone buzzed on the desktop in the library at the Hamptons estate. Brett wouldn't get this call due to his own rule of no mobiles being allowed for the ritual ceremonies. Eduardo called Liam, whose phone was also in the Long Island Manor House. In desperation, he left them both voicemails and texts, telling them the news neither would want to hear. That Max Sargent may still be alive!

Max could feel the tension rise as they reached the water's edge and Brett took up his position behind the lectern. He placed the old book on top and opened it up carefully.

Max's nerves were tingling, for his plan had to be enacted now. He knew he needed to have the whole gathering away from the house and cars, out in the open, with little cover. He'd also figured from watching the ritual back home in Sussex, that the 'ferryman', who tasered his colleague Graham and dropped him into the lake, was likely Brett's henchman. So, he needed him as far away as possible, on the lake!

Brett started his monologue. Across the water, Max could see the two dark figures climbing into a small boat. He waited, watching them set off from the jetty and start slowly moving across the shimmering water.

He prayed his young fellow agent would come through for him!

The sixteen robed brethren standing still around the nearby wooden jetty fell silent. Lit only by a crescent moon and a few dim low-level garden lights, the scene resembled some kind of disturbing satanic cult from an old Hammer horror movie. Hooded heads moved subtly between the boat and the Grand Master waiting for them. The boat's passage was slow, with the ferryman at the back paddling the gondola oar and the sole passenger seated in the middle.

Max wondered what influential official or businessman was sat there this time, willing to sacrifice their integrity.

This was it! He had to do it now!

Max pulled out his Glock from underneath his robe and strode over to Brett Brookshaw, amidst shock and gasps from other hooded brethren!

Several figures instinctively made for him, but quickly stopped in their tracks when the gun barrel was levelled at them.

"Nobody move!" instructed Max.

The brethren were twitching with shock whilst assessing

the situation, looking round judging if they could run for cover without being shot. A reminder was needed.

"Everyone, get your hands up high where I can see them!"

In the boat, the inductee and the ferryman could just make out what was happening. They were shocked at the sight of a gunman holding up the entire gathering. Already a third of the way across the water, Liam quickly turned the boat around and started paddling furiously back to the far side jetty. With no gun, it would have been foolhardy to continue towards the mystery intruder.

Brett spoke, seemingly unconcerned. "Just calm down everyone! Whoever you are with the gun, you're making a grave mistake! Put it down and let's talk this through. I'm sure we can come to some arrangement to pay you off for whatever troubles you have?"

"I don't want your money or your bribes," exclaimed Max, moving into a position with his back to the lake, where he could see all of the cloaked figures in front of him.

'Where's Jeremy', thought Max.

"We're going to have to sort something out, you can't shoot us all, there are too many of us," negotiated Brett. "Give me the gun?"

Finally, on cue! A tiny red dot appeared on Brett's waist and as Jeremy adjusted his aim from the estate perimeter, the dot moved onto the centre of Brett's chest.

"I've got company," said Max with reinvigorated confidence, thankful to see his colleague was out there somewhere.

Brett looked down in dismay at the red laser sight dot on his front, ironically hovering around his Hades motif.

"Nice!" Brett said sarcastically. "So, what do you want?"

Max held out his hand, "That book!"

Brett churned with shock. He was always so wrapped up in dealing with people's greed for money and wealth, bribes, rewards and wanting more all the time. The realization that this brother, or intruder, was after a far more dangerous prize, his book of souls, hit him hard.

"Why would you want this book, it's just a prayer book?" Brett bluffed, but he wanted to find out if this gunman knew what it was.

Max tightened his grip on the Glock. He didn't want to discuss it, he just wanted to get out of there. The threatening eyes beneath those hoods were boring into him with hatred and malice.

"Just hand it over, now!" moving closer.

"Take it then?" challenged Brett.

Max tensed more but moved closer again. The dot remained on Brett.

"Don't forget, one stupid move and my friend shoots you!"

The reminder stopped Brett thinking he could grab the gun when Max reached out and he withdrew a step.

"Okay, okay!"

Max leant forward and collected up the old book. He felt it in his hand, tattered, crusty, imagining its use over the past hundred and eighty years. He quickly allowed it to open up at a random page, just to check it really was a ledger of members of this Hades sect. The covers fell apart revealing a page showing a name, with brief descriptions of dealings, with various monetary payments and dates recorded!

He smiled, closing the book, but then noticed some of the cloaked men around him were edging closer with intentions of rushing him. Another reminder was needed. Max raised up the hand that held the book.

Thud!

Jeremy's bullet splintered the top of one of the wooden posts of the nearby jetty. It had the desired effect, for everyone flinched back in shock.

Max put the book under his arm and pulled out his phone.

"Everyone, lower your masks and hoods! Now!" waving the gun around at them.

Tensions were now really high and this request was visibly agitating many of the brothers encircling Max. 'Perhaps a request too far' thought Max regretfully. He had the book, so pictures or video of the hostile mob would have to wait. Even insisting on Brett lowering his hood wasn't necessary if it was going to cause a riot here, Max had already seen it was him when he exited the house.

He started to edge his way through the figures towards the open lawn.

"Remember my friend out there! Any movement and he'll start shooting, on full automatic. You wouldn't stand a chance. Don't move until the red dot disappears!" warned Max, hoping to God they would obey his instructions!

On the far side of the inlet, Liam pulled the boat up alongside the other jetty and jumped out, breaking into an immediate run to get back over to Brett.

Max cleared the gathering, checked the red dot was still moving amongst the black figures, then sprinted up the lawn towards the house.

As he reached the building, he glanced behind him. They were still all standing by the water's edge, but he could hear them debating whether to make a move or not. He dived into the patio doors of the office library. As expected, it was very similar to the room back in the Sussex house. However, all the furnishings were old and traditional, clearly Brett's preference, over his sister's more modern taste.

Max quickly looked through the thousands of books lining the rows of shelving.

Liam had now reached the group, who were all frantically checking to see where the red laser dot was. They were realising no one could find it anymore!

Jeremy had left his position and was moving towards his next job in support of Max's escape.

Max ran back out of the doors onto the patio and round the side of the large house. He could see the brothers down by the water were starting to move about, shouting at one another as they realised the laser dot pinning them down was nowhere to be seen.

Max ran, jumped into Brandon's car and fired it up, immediately accelerating down the driveway, wheels screeching. He glimpsed sight of some of the dark figures running up the lawn after him!

The tyre noise alerted the guards at the gate, who both stood side by side in the middle of the exit, waiting to see what the fuss was about.

As Max emerged from the trees at speed, they raised their guns in readiness. Max slowed down and held his hands up over the steering wheel.

"Don't move!" was shouted out, but not by either of the guards. They looked round in surprise, to see a man behind them pointing a high-powered rifle at them, just twenty feet away. It was Jeremy.

"Stand aside or you're going to get hurt real bad at this range!" he threatened.

The two men quickly obliged, tossing aside their guns without being asked.

Max drove through and stopped long enough for Jeremy to climb in, then they shot off on the journey back to New York.

Brett got back into the library and saw his phone had missed calls and messages from Eduardo. He read the text out loud as Liam came in.

"Eduardo's been trying to reach us. Says, 'Lake empty, Max Sargent must still be on the loose! Sorry'." He gritted his teeth and looked at Liam. "Damn it! That must have been Sargent down there holding us up and taking the book. Get after him, I need him killed and the book back!" he ordered. Liam ran off.

The two guards at the gate had gathered their guns and radio as soon as Max and Jeremy had gone, jumped into their pickup truck and given chase. They could make out the taillights of the car ahead and radioed Liam with what had happened and where they were heading. Liam discarded his robe and with another guard, followed in a car.

"Fastest way back to New York and the Consulate,"

shouted Jeremy to Max driving.

"I'm with you on that!" agreed Max. "Nice work back there, jees, I can't tell you how glad I was to see that bloody red dot appear!"

They pulled onto the Montauk Highway then at Southampton joined the 27.

"I think we've done it Max," celebrated Jeremy, looking through the book. "It's all here, back to the seventeen hundreds, names, dates, payments including in Venice, London and here in the US!"

Max was conscious of a particular set of shaped headlights trailing him in the distance of his rear-view mirror.

"Not yet. I think we may have company! Let's face it, they probably know we have to make it back to New York for safety so I'm guessing they're after us!"

He punched in Si Lawson's number.

"Max! Thank God! We've all been wondering what's happened out there?" Si greeted them with relief in his voice.

"I'll be brief Si," said Max hurriedly. "We've got the book, with all the names. I haven't had a chance to look at it but Jeremy confirms it's what we expected, the ledger of all members and payments."

"Great!"

"We're clear of the Hamptons estate but have a tail, though they're not moving up on us, so I suspect they might be waiting for more to follow or for a particular point on the journey to make their move! Any chance of some local backup here?" Max asked.

"Crikey Max, that's just not going to be possible," said Si apologetically. "We're so far beyond our remit, all hell will break loose at the top if we try to involve the local authorities, plus we're not sure we can trust them. If Brookshaw has just one of them on his side, they could be all that's needed to finish you and lose the book!"

Max suspected that would be the answer, though Jeremy looked disheartened by the news they were on their own.

"We'll get back to the Consulate with the book as fast as we can!" said Max determinedly.

There was a pause. Max knew it wasn't good.

Si came back on. "Er Max, sorry, but we need you to do one more thing before coming in!"

"What? You're kidding Si, we've kind of got our hands full right now trying to avoid being caught and disposed of in the middle of bloody Long Island, with no help whatsoever!"

"The book Max…"

"What about the book? We've got it I said!"

"It might not be enough," said Si. Max and Jeremy looked at one another.

"What do you mean sir," asked Jeremy, a worried look on his face.

"The legal guy's are saying that this ledger alone might not be enough to ensure charges stick against Brookshaw, not to mention cases against all the names in the book. Mere notes it seems, don't prove the transactions actually happened!"

"I don't believe this!" exclaimed Max. "What more do they want?"

"If we could somehow get hard, digital evidence of the monies paid out or received, then we've got them. Like what we were after at St Kitts. Undeniable proof of the bribes, the fraud, money laundering, the payments."

"So what are you asking us to do Si?"

"Before you return to the Consulate, assuming you'll lose any tails you have, you must go to Brookshaw's office and see what you can find there? He's got to have a record somewhere there of what he's paying these guys, in his Hades organisation! If he has, he'll probably try to destroy it all maybe in the morning before any police get in there."

"You mean his Chrysler Building office? It'll be closed up, we won't get there until about ten tonight, assuming as you say we get rid of the tail!" argued Max. Though he already knew they only had this one chance to try this, before Brett either got someone to destroy any evidence or got to the office himself.

"Sorry Max. You're a clever chap, you'll figure out a way of getting in there. Jeremy, you need to help Max with this. We've got to have sight of those transactions Max, as well as the book!"

Back at the Hamptons estate, Brett had been getting updates from Liam and the guards following Max. He felt helpless just receiving reports whilst doing nothing himself. Max Sargent had evaded his efforts to silence him and he was starting to wonder if his guys would be able to stop him before he presumably returned to the city.

Having assured his brethren the matter would be resolved that night and they should go home and not worry, Brett decided he had to do something himself. He threw off his cloak, strode out to his car and started the engine.

He was almost twenty minutes behind them, but this whole Max Sargent investigation needed to end, this evening!

19

Max came off the 27 at Eastport and by the time they joined the 495 a few minutes later at Manorville, he could now see two vehicles trailing him about four cars back.

"What are we going to do Max?"

"We keep going until they make a move. They won't want to let us get into the city, so be ready, they're going to try something in the next forty-five minutes!" warned Max.

Jeremy gripped his rifle for reassurance but kept looking behind to check where the pickup and car were.

Brett was on the phone to Liam.

"I don't care what you do, just get them soon," he shouted, "but don't start blasting away with your guns in the middle of the highway, we can't have some other driver calling the police!"

Liam couldn't think of any other way than to try to force them off the road. He instructed the two guards in the pickup truck what he wanted them to do, but not to use their machine guns.

Jeremy heard the thundering engine of the truck behind them roaring and as he looked round, could see it closing in on them.

"One of them's getting closer Max!"

"I see!"

As the pickup drew closer to the back of Max's car, he started swerving gently, changing lanes between other cars, keeping the pursuers at bay.

The guard driver saw his chance and floored the pedal, forcing the growling truck to bear down on the smaller car in front. As he moved in, his front wing drew level with the back of Max's fear fender, and he twitched the wheel sideways.

The back of Max's car hung out to the side and as the truck decelerated, it sent the car into a snaking swerve from side to side. Max fought the steering wheel counteracting each time the rear kicked out, and managed to bring the car back under control.

He noticed there were no other cars too close on the highway.

"Jeremy! Use the rifle and take out the pickup!"

"How?"

"Unless you can single out one of the front tyres, put a couple of rounds into the front of the engine!"

Jeremy climbed into the back seat and lowered one of the side windows. He could see the two men in the truck looking at him anxiously, trying to figure out what he was doing. When he raised the rifle and poked it out of the window, they both looked horrified! The truck started to pull back, but was still an easy target for the long-range rifle.

Jeremy took a second to line up the centre of the radiator grill in his sights and fired.

The sound of the two crack's were instantly lost in the humdrum noise of the highway and cars on the opposite carriageway.

The first round passed through the grill and smashed into the alternator of the truck, splintering it into pieces and breaking the fan belt. The second shot did the real damage, passing into the casing and through the timing chain concealed within. Without this vital component controlling the management of the camshaft and pistons sequencing, the instant catastrophic failure blew the top of the engine up into the underside of the hood. Smoke, oil and water spewed out and the momentum alone, carried the truck along enough allowing them to pull off the highway, inflicting more damage inside the disorientated engine as they went.

"Yes!" celebrated Jeremy, "they're out of it!"

"Nice one!" agreed Max, still keeping a lookout for the car that was still following, ignoring their broken-down colleagues as they passed them.

Liam watched, exasperated! He called Brett back.

"The truck's out, Sargent's friend shot their engine! I've left them and am still in pursuit." Liam was out of ideas. "Not sure what we can do boss, while they have that high-powered rifle on them?"

Brett thought, sighing.

"Let me see if I can speak to them, bargain with them. Stay with them okay!"

"How can you do that?" asked Liam.

"I'm guessing Max Sargent came across Brandon Cuffney today and used his robe to get into the ritual. Aren't they in his car right now?"

Liam had been so busy following Max he hadn't given the car model a thought. Now it was obvious.

"Yup, it's Brandon's Ford!"

Brett explained to Liam what he was going to say, and more importantly what Liam was to do. He then rang off and called Brandon's mobile. It rang in front of Max who could see the caller was 'BB'!

"Yes?" he answered curtly.

"Mr Sargent, and sniper friend?"

"What?"

"I want to prevent the guys following you from simply shooting you both through the rear screen, or ramming into you causing a fatal pileup!" Brett waited for a reaction, but got nothing. "Can I suggest a trade? After all, you have something that belongs to me."

"A trade," repeated Max playing along for more time to get nearer the city.

"Yes. Let my colleagues have the book, and I will pay you each ten million, into accounts of your choice, or offshore which I can set up, and execute the transactions as you hand over the book, so you know my word's good and payments' have been completed?"

Jeremy gave a pretend look of interest at the mention of

the ten million.

"And then have your men shoot us anyway, take the book, cancel the payment, no thanks!" Max pushed back.

Smash!

The distraction of Brett's intriguing call had been just enough to allow Liam to pull alongside them, then turn hard into their car, accelerating. Max and Jeremy were violently shunted to the side, over the service lane and came to a halt on the grass verge. Jeremy dropped the rifle which lodged behind the front seats against the floor in the rear. Max's Glock flew from the centre consul through a front side window and was now lying on the service lane of the expressway! They were both momentarily disorientated.

The other car that had rammed them pulled over about sixty yards past them. As Max raised his head, he saw two men get out and slowly walk back towards them. Both were holding guns.

Max quickly weighed up the options.

He grabbed a small bundle, shoving it into his belt, then moved the old book to the back of the passenger footwell.

"Jeremy! Move! We need to get out into the bushes, now!" he ordered.

Keeping their heads down, they both exited the car and using the opened doors front and back as cover, they dived into the shrubbery just two metres away and frantically crawled deeper into the undergrowth to hide.

Liam and his guard saw the two figures leave the car, but weren't close enough to try firing at them. They now trotted to the empty car, but kept behind it so they wouldn't be shot at from within the treeline.

Liam then saw the Glock on the road, while the other man shouted out that the rifle was wedged in the back of the car. Liam came back over to the vehicle and started looking around the car himself. He spotted the old book on the floor and leant in, grasping it firmly.

"We've got what we need, I'll go back with it, you stay

here with their car. If you see them, shoot!" he told the other man.

He grabbed the keys out of the ignition and dropped them into his pocket. Then skirted around the front of the car and ran back to his own car up ahead and drove off.

Max and Jeremy had been watching them, hidden amongst the thick bushes and trees, about five metres apart. They were relieved to see one of the men go, but were now both watching the remaining man peering into the undergrowth, holding a handgun!

Jeremy had gone deeper into the shrubbery than Max, who was still wearing Brandon's black robe. He quietly pulled the hood over his head and with the darkness and dense foliage, was almost entirely concealed.

The guard came to the edge of the undergrowth and peered in, keen to impress his superiors by finding the runaways.

Jeremy could see that Max had crouched down and disappeared, between him and the gunman, off to one side. He hoped Max would be up for this and reached out grabbing a small branch to his right. He lay low and rustled it.

The stirring noise caught the attention of the man, who cautiously waded into the bushes towards the sound. He raised his gun as if about to fire, paused, then came forward further. Jeremy gave one more pull on the branch.

The gunman now had a bearing on where the noise was coming from and moved forward again, assuming neither of the men hiding had weapons, or they would have fired by now.

'Easy prey!', he thought, and readied himself to shoot towards where Jeremy was lying.

Max slowly rose behind the gunman like a ghostly apparition, in his black cloak and hood. Just as his robe caught on a twig and made a rasping sound, the man started to turn round.

Whack!

It was too late! Max brought his clasped fists down hard

on the back of the man's neck, crumpling him down to the ground. He remained motionless, out cold. Max checked he was still alive, he was.

"Nice diversion," he said to Jeremy who stood up and came over.

"Bloody hell Max, I thought he was going to start shooting before he got to you. Thanks!"

Liam had placed the familiar old, tattered book he knew so well, onto the dash of the car when he'd driven off, very pleased with himself. He pulled off the westbound carriageway at the next exit, junction 135, and looped round under the expressway and back on again heading eastbound.

He called Brett.

"I've got it boss! The book!"

"What happened? Are you guys okay?

"We're good," said Liam proudly. "We did what you said. Your call distracted them enough for us to shunt them off the road. They did a runner into the bushes and had gone by the time we got to the car, but they'd left the book behind in their rush to get away. I didn't want to chase them in case they had another gun with them, so left the other chap there with the car. I took their keys!"

"Brilliant Liam, well done!" said Brett, cheerier now. "Just look after that book!"

Liam leant over to get the book off the dash and stow it in the glove compartment. As he lifted the book up and brought it closer to put away, Liam got his first close look at the ancient bindings. Something didn't quite feel right to him. The outer cover of the book was definitely familiar to him. He'd held it many times and was unique with its tears, stain marks and ageing. But the pages of the book within the covers, now he could see them up close, weren't quite right. They looked just a little too good, not in keeping with the rest of the book's wear!

Now in his lap, he could see it was definitely the book, on the outside. He opened it up in the middle, expecting to see the records of one of the brothers.

His face dropped as he realised the book's bound pages weren't attached to the outer covers! He scanned the open pages. They were full of printed text. Picking up on some of the wording, he realised it was some psychological thriller, an old novel!

When Max had quickly detoured into the Manor House's library, he'd chosen the first book he could find with old looking pages inside, the same size as the book of souls. He'd ripped out the bound pages of both books and placed the pages of the novel inside the Hades ledger outer covers, just in case he was challenged at the gate before Jeremy had got there!

"What's going on?" demanded Brett, shouting at the phone.

Liam replied with some trepidation. "Sorry, but it seems Sargent has swapped the inside of your book with another! He's probably still got your book with him!"

The line was silent. Brett was containing his seething anger at the situation.

"Boss, you still there?"

"Go back to their car immediately and get my book!" Brett yelled down the phone. "I'll pull over when I see you, I'm ten minutes away."

Liam had to drive five miles back to come off again at the previous junction, then loop around and return westbound back to where they'd left Max's car and his guard.

In the meantime, Max had covered over the unconscious gunman with his black robe and with Jeremy, emerged from the shrubbery. The book of souls was still lodged in Max's belt. Their car was battered but still looked alright to drive.

"They've taken the keys," noticed Max.

"No problem," said Jeremy, "I'll jump-start this in no time," which he did, disabling the steering lock mechanism. The starter fired up the engine and they continued on their way back to New York, thirty minutes away.

Liam reached the spot where they'd left Max, and was

perturbed to find their car had gone and no sign of the guard he'd left there. A few minutes later Brett pulled over behind him and got out.

"So, where are they?" Brett suspected he already knew what the answer would be.

"The car's gone, it was right here, and our gunman's nowhere to be seen."

"Never mind about him."

"They must have got it going again," said Liam stating the obvious.

Brett hit the roof of their car. "Damn it!"

"Let's get after them again," suggested Liam keenly. "If that book's all the evidence they need to shut everything down, maybe we can catch up with them?"

"They're too far ahead now," said Brett shaking his head. "But hang on a sec, what you just said, about the book being all the evidence they need."

"What boss?"

"The reason Sargent went out to Nevis was because they also need proof of our payments and deals. They need actual evidence of money being transferred and received."

"But they didn't get that in Nevis did they?"

"I don't think so," speculated Brett, "otherwise they would have moved on us earlier."

"Then they can't get it from anywhere else then can they?" said Liam naively.

It struck Brett. "Oh my God! The only other place outside the offshore bank that has details of the payments, is on my desktop computer, at the Chrysler Building!" Brett started to return to his car, yelling, "That's where we need to go now Liam, in convoy, just in case they get the police to raid the office tonight or in the morning!"

Max and Jeremy were now fifteen minutes ahead of Liam and Brett on the 495. They passed through Queens, over the vast Calvary Cemetery, then at Long Island City, took the Queens Midtown Tunnel to Manhattan.

Although it was almost ten PM, the New York skyline and offices were still lit up, occupied by maintenance staff, cleaning and an army of late-night workers eager to get ahead of their workload or impress the boss.

They emerged from the tunnel and after three blocks, turned into Lexington Avenue and parked up across the road from the famous skyscraper, towering over a thousand feet above them in the moonlit sky.

Originally built for the Chrysler car company in 1930, most of the floors were occupied by companies including media, law firms, retail and technology.

"Wait here in the car," said Max, "I'll call you if I need help getting in, just keep a watch 'til I'm back."

"How are you going to get into the Headshell offices?"

Max turned back as he exited the car. "Confident bluffing, usually works!"

Max crossed the road and went into the building and was immediately transformed into its long since, art deco, post-war times. The light brown, amber marble and furnishings engulfed him in the lobby as he strode over to the row of lifts. On the wall was a long sign showing the various tenants throughout the building, and he quickly scanned it noting, '57th, 58th (Reception) Floors – Headshell Corporation'. He took the lift up to the fifty-eighth.

The lift doors opened up revealing a dimmed reception area where an empty, large polished wooden desk confronted him like a barrier. There was no sign of any reception staff, who'd gone home by six PM.

Max could see through the glass walls into the open office expanse behind the desk. Some areas were still lit up, while other parts of the floor lay darkened. He spotted just two young lads on the entire floor, in separate areas, both diligently working at their desks, typing away on their keyboards.

'Perfect', thought Max. He needed someone to let him in and preferably a couple of easily persuaded youngsters!

Max went over to the glass door and politely knocked on it. The nearest lad looked up but not directly at him, almost as if he'd heard the noise but didn't believe it. Max knocked again. This time he turned right around and saw Max at the door. He looked at his watch, then mildly irritated at being disturbed, pulled a face and got up to come over.

"Yes?" he inquired, screwing up his face in disbelief anyone would be visiting the office so late.

"Mr Brookshaw asked me to pick something up for him, can you let me in?" asked Max hurriedly, as if under time pressure.

"Brookshaw! Brett Brookshaw?" repeated the astonished staff member, none of whom had any idea about how business for their consulting operation was doing so well! "Yes, of course!" he said opening the door.

Max went through. "I need to hurry, he wants me to pick up some confidential papers from his office, lead the way, quickly!"

The lad got caught up in the rushed explanation of urgency and didn't want to do anything to get in the way of something his firm's boss had asked for. He started to lead the way to Brett's office.

"I'm sorry, can you just tell me who you are so I can explain this in the morning?" he asked timidly.

"Of course," agreed Max heartily, patting him on the shoulder. "I'm one of Mr Brookshaw's personal staff from the Manor House in the Hamptons!" Then to complete the bluff, he pretended to start looking for a card in his pockets. "If you really want to see my ID I've got it somewhere here…"

"No, that's okay," said the lad quickly, not wanting to cause any annoyance. "This way, do you need me to help you look for anything?"

"No, that's quite alright thanks, it's some confidential papers, he gave me an idea of where they were so I should be able to find them quickly. Can't keep him waiting can we!"

The staff member showed Max into Brett's large office

suite which unlike most of the other offices, had two solid walls to it, one at the side and the wall with the doorway. The third inner wall was a glass partition with another door, allowing Brett to have access to and see his personal assistant's small team alongside him. Max thanked him and closed the door after the young man left, who was still in a daze of being swept along by the hurried request.

Max surveyed the room, deciding how to best spend his time searching for something, anything, that might show the bribery and bonus transactions relating to the Hades members' deals for the firm. There were a handful of filing cabinets, some bookcases, a large unit with shelving and cupboard compartments and finally at one end of the meeting table, the main desk with a computer and screen.

Max noticed the samurai sword display and in the corner, the small, valuable painting depicting none other than the God of the underworld himself, Hades. This was Brett's office alright! He started with the filing cabinets, working his way quickly but carefully through each separator leaf and file label.

Outside, Jeremy had turned on the radio and was watching the entrance to the Chrysler building intently. So intently, that he was unaware of much else going on around him, ignoring passing cars and pedestrians, a handful of local residents coming and going, late-night office workers making their way home, or diners walking back to their apartments after dinner.

He was suddenly aware of his door opening violently and seeing someone lunging at him!

Liam's hard, single punch to the side of his head was enough to jar his brain into unconsciousness! He slumped across the passenger seat out cold. Liam got into the driver's side and propped him up in his seat, to make it look as though he was sleeping. Then he waited, as he watched Brett on the other side of the road, go into the main entrance.

When Brett and Liam had both arrived in their separate cars, they'd seen Brandon Cuffney's car, so parked up short of it. With only one person sitting in the car, it was now apparent to Brett, that Max Sargent was likely attempting to gain access to his offices! How he'd get in, Brett had no idea, but he needed to just get on up there and delete the incriminating file off his PC. Brett told Liam to deal with the 'sniper chap' in the car and wait for him, while he would go up to the office.

Max flicked through files, occasionally pulling out documents that might have any accounts on them. Nothing in the filing cabinet. He moved over to the shelving.

Brett got into one of the lifts and hit the button for the fifty-eighth floor! He braced himself to potentially confront Max in the reception area of his own company's offices! He then cursed to himself that he didn't have a gun with him, no matter he thought, just so long as he could delete that file.

Max was coming up with nothing, unsurprisingly. He looked around, the only place left was the most obvious location for the file he so desperately wanted. Brett's computer, which was of course turned off! He went over to it and half-heartedly switched it on, knowing it would be password protected.

The screen came up with the user login field, with its cursor blinking at him mockingly.

He thought about calling Alan the techie back in London for any suggestions, but before he did this, went over to the door. He opened it a crack to check the two office staff were still busy at their desks. The furthest one was there, but not the young man who'd let him in. Max searched for him. There he was, talking to someone in the reception.

It was Brett Brookshaw!

'Jesus', thought Max, 'what the hell's he doing here, why didn't Jeremy warn me?'. He realised what the answer to that would be and immediately felt the ferryman henchman was no doubt 'looking after' his colleague!

He quickly closed the office door and looked around again, frantically searching for somewhere to hide. But there was nowhere! Max knew Brett would now be walking through the open-plan office towards where he was!

Holding the book of souls still lodged into his belt, he dived across the room and hidden by the solid office wall between himself and the main office, went through the adjoining glass door to the secretary's area.

Brett burst into his office angrily, wanting to catch Max in the act, followed by the bewildered staff lad. Brett was ready for a fight!

Somewhat startled to find the office empty, he turned to the youngster.

"I thought you said you let in one of my staff, so where is he?"

"I did Mr Brookshaw," he insisted, "from your Hamptons home, he said you'd sent him to get some paperwork for you."

"Well, where is he?" he repeated angrily.

The lad looked around the empty room and shrugged. "I honestly don't know sir!"

"Is there any possibility he left again, via reception or the fire exit stairs?"

He looked back into the main offices. "I don't think so, but I guess he could have got out when I was busy working?"

Brett sighed. "Okay, look, thanks for telling me everything, you carry on with what you were doing, I'll take it from here," ushering him out of the door.

"Sorry sir," apologised the lad again.

Whilst Brett thought it was a possibility that Max had already gone, he was painfully aware that he might also still be somewhere in the offices outside. But right now, that wasn't his top priority.

He went over to his desk and sat down. The login screen was already waiting for him!

Brett went on high alert now. He always turned his PC off when he left the office, so Max had clearly tried to get into it, but with no success. The simple login password would have prevented any attempt to access his system.

Just outside the office, Max was crouching down behind one of the many cluttered desks, peering through at the back of Brett sitting at his desk. He could just see the screen to one side of Brett's arm. He got out his phone, just as Brett glanced around behind him!

Max ducked down, only just in time not to be seen.

Brett's home screen then appeared. He waited a few moments for the machine to boot up and perform all its preliminary tasks. 'Always annoying' he thought to himself. Then without pausing on any other applications such as emails or messages, he went straight to the file manager icon and brought up a screen full of navigation options.

After a few clicks, his mouse icon was hovering over the one electronic file he kept, which mirrored everything that was recorded in the book of souls. But this digital file also had details of the actual monetary transactions, payments and receipts of all of the bribes, or bonuses, that had been paid out to Hades brothers. It held the one file of proof that could bring him down.

He glanced around once more!

Max froze, hoping he hadn't been seen as he held his eye line to Brett. Any movement now would be seen.

Brett returned to the screen and as if wanting to check the file one last time before it got deleted, double-clicked on the icon.

A new password prompt opened up, this time to access the ledger file.

Brett punched in the password and the file opened up on the screen. He quickly scrolled through some of the many pages of detailed accounting, showing every transaction and payment made, with names, bank details, dates and proof of payment.

He then closed the file, sat back in his chair, and triumphantly pressed 'delete'! He then opened up the 'deleted files' menu, selected the same file and deleted it once more.

The incriminating file was gone!

Brett logged out of his computer and just as the screen returned to its black, empty, off status, he noticed a tiny movement in its reflection! Someone was behind him. Max Sargent!

Brett tingled with rage and excitement. He slowly rose from his seat, opened the glass adjoining door between himself and where Max was hiding, then strolled back across his office. He turned around.

"Max Sargent?" His voice was firm and commanding. Max froze again, cursing under his breath. "I know you're there, behind the desks! Aren't you a little too old for playing hide and seek?"

Max knew his cover was blown. There was no point in him continuing to crouch down anymore. He now needed to get out of here in one piece. He had what he needed. The pages of the book of souls were still lodged into his trouser belt.

"I'm waiting," said Brett impatiently. "We can at least talk about all this can't we?"

Max slowly stood up, looking Brett directly in the eyes.

Brett immediately saw the pages of the inside of his book of souls! He couldn't believe his luck. He'd deleted the soft file before Sargent had got into his computer. And now Sargent had arrived in his office, with his precious book! He had everything to play for, fate seemed to be favouring him.

"Ah! My book!" Brett said calmly. "You've decided to return it to me? How wise."

Max put a hand over the book protectively. "I don't think so! It's over Brett. Too many people have died for this book. You and your Hades sect, you're finished!"

"You're an intruder, trespassing in my office, a thief, dangerous. I have every right to defend myself against you. Even kill you!" he sneered.

Brett then leant across to the display stand next to him and lifted up the glass casing lid, exposing the priceless artefact underneath!

He lifted it from its stand and ceremoniously gripped the

Tsuka handle and Saya scabbard. He withdrew the samurai sword from its resting sheath as it glinted in the light, as if acknowledging its release from captivity in the display unit.

Max and Brett both gazed at its lethal splendour. Its Yakiba blade edge was amongst the sharpest of any cutting tools even of today's technology.

Brett now held the sword out in front of him and without any further discussion, made his way towards Max!

20

Max held up both hands in a pleading gesture.

"Now come on Brett, let's not be stupid, we can talk about this, like you said? You've got two witnesses over there," nodding to the staff at the other end of the office who hadn't yet seen what was happening.

Brett had nothing more to say, he wanted his book back and greedily eyed it on Max's waist.

Max edged back and desperately searched for something to use to defend himself. He knew he had to get that lethal sword off Brett immediately, as it would only take a handful of slashes at him before he was wounded or killed. As he backed up he realised he was allowing himself to be cornered down an aisle between two rows of desks!

Brett slowly and menacingly followed his path, then drew the sword back. Max easily saw the strike coming and sprung back.

The tip of the long blade just missed his chest and crashed into a computer screen on a desk, slicing effortlessly through the electronics and plastic outer casing! For a second, it got stuck in the device, before Brett twisted it free and swung it round at Max again.

With the end of the row of desks approaching, Max was already leaping across two back-to-back desks, regardless of what was on top of them. Screens, filing trays, pens and mugs were sent flying, as he slid across the tops into the next aisle. Behind him, he noticed a fire exit door, possibly his only chance of escaping as Brett was covering his path back to the office main entrance.

The two staff had been alerted by the crashing noises and were craning their heads over the other desks and partitions to see what on earth was going on. To their horror, it looked like their boss was attacking the staff member he'd sent in to get something for him. They both froze and stared on in astonishment.

Max grabbed a metal hole punch and hurled it at Brett, who rebuffed it away using the sword's blade. He then grabbed a pile of papers and feebly threw them at him. Brett ignored the flurry of documents and continued on, ignoring them. Max was running out of options, then he spotted a brightly painted rock on a desktop, being used as a paperweight, a child's gift to a parent from art class in school.

Brett was closing in again and readying himself for a decisive blow. But the look in his eyes telegraphed the moment he decided to bring the sword down.

Max grabbed a tray of paperclips and flung them up into Brett's face. This was just enough of a distraction, for him to narrowly dodge the arc of the deadly blade, which struck into the desktop and embedded itself.

Brett cursed as Max then grabbed the heavy rock from the desk and smashed it against the top of the blade with all his strength. The six-hundred-year-old blade made from layering Japanese tamahagane steel was incredibly hard, but now also very brittle. With one end embedded in the desk and the handle tightly gripped by Brett, the blade had no give, and broke cleanly three inches below the Tsuba hilt!

Brett looked at his broken, priceless samurai sword in utter disbelief, holding up what was left of it. They both looked down at the length stuck firmly in the desk, but Max was the first to take advantage of the surprise time-out. Without wanting to get too close to what was still a dangerous weapon, albeit a short one now, Max threw out a stamping kick down onto Brett's left knee. He crumpled to the floor crying out in pain, as the articular cartilage around the kneecap gave way with several small breaks.

Max moved back hoping that would suffice and Brett would give up. But rage and adrenalin serve as a powerful protagonist, and although painful, Brett fought through his injury and hauled himself back up onto his feet, with only a slight limp. He held up the handle of the sword with its three-inch blade, nodding to himself, satisfied that they both still knew… it remained a lethal weapon!

Max looked around and before trying to outrun Brett through the office and get to the reception door, he decided to try the easier option. Turning on his heels, he ran over to the fire escape door, pushing the safety lock bar, praying it would yield. It did and the door burst open as he flew into the stairwell.

He wanted to get to the lifts via one of the next floor's offices but wasn't keen on the idea of going down to the floor below, as this was also owned by Brett's Headshell firm, where there could be more staff, even security. Max went up the stairs, just as Brett came through the fire door, swearing at him.

Max bounded up the narrow stairs and quickly reached the back of the fire door on the fifty-ninth floor. But there was no opening bar, that was on the other side. He pushed against it to discover it was firmly shut! Brett was making his way slowly but surely up the stairs behind him, so he went up another two short flights of stairs to the sixtieth floor, but was greeted with another firmly closed and inaccessible fire door.

"Damn it!"

He could see Brett through the stair rail gaps still coming up at him. He'd try one more floor.

As Max cleared the top of the stairway once more, the fire door appeared to have a handle this time! He rushed over to it and tried to open the door, but again it was locked. Figuring this door only had a cheap door lock as opposed to the more sturdy fire door bar locking mechanism, he drew back a few paces and drop-kicked at the middle of the door.

It burst open, revealing a very different setting. Max was on the sixty-first floor, which was the observation deck of the Chrysler building!

Through the large windows of the atrium he stood in, he could see the beautiful lights of Manhattan twinkling from the surrounding buildings and skyscrapers.

Brett was coming up the stairs behind him, so Max ran over to the lifts and frantically pressed the call button. But as Brett emerged from the fire doorway, Max knew none of the lifts would get to this floor in time. He backed up as Brett wielded the stub end of the samurai sword blade. Its hilt provided him some protection and even though the sharp edge was only a few inches long, it could still slice through an arm effortlessly.

"Give me back my book Sargent!" snarled Brett, fighting back the pain of his damaged knee. "Last time I ask!"

Max looked around but had nowhere to go, except the nearest outer door to him. He went through and out onto the observation terrace!

The chill of the night air hit him as he came through the unlocked door and out onto the red-tinged paving. The area was eerily up lit by the floodlights nestled into the heads of the eight steel eagles protruding each side of the corners of the building. The terrace was surrounded by only a low-level wall with a waist-height metal rail above it, not much of a barrier between the safety of the patio and an eight hundred foot drop!

Max was running out of places to go or options to tackle Brett's weapon. After all the running around, it was only now that he remembered the small knife blade hidden in his belt buckle. He pulled it out hoping it would provide him with some way of defending himself, but looking down at the two-inch blade, his heart sank. It was no match for the robust short sword end Brett had.

Max was about to discard the small knife, when its uselessness prompted him to realise he had one other tiny item at his disposal. The miniature pepper spray!

He peeled apart the two leather sides of the belt near the buckle, to reveal the miniature aerosol sandwiched inside a small groove the guys at Thames House had made. He took out the tiny canister which was just an inch long and as he'd been advised, was 'only good for one spray discharge of concentrated pepper aerosol'!

Max replaced the little canister back into its slot within his belt, just as Brett confronted him on the terrace. He noticed the tiny knife Max held in one hand and laughed, cautiously approaching him.

"Without digital evidence of money transactions, you know the book proves nothing?" he sneered.

Max wouldn't be drawn in. "I'll hang onto it just the same!"

Brett lunged at him with the broken blade end, and as Max swiftly dodged the strike, Brett brought the end of its handle into the side of Max's arm with a painful hit.

Max staggered back a few steps towards the end of the terrace. Brett advanced, limping slightly but with a determined look on his face. As he came towards him Max could see that Brett was putting all his weight and momentum into this attack and committing himself to finish him.

Just as Brett came upon him, Max ducked down to the side of Brett's good leg, making it hard for him to react with his injury on the other side. The sword stub swished past Max who slashed out at Brett's hands, cutting a gash into one of them. Brett cried out, let go of the handle which clattered to the floor of the terrace's corner and with his forward momentum, staggered into the railing just by it.

Max quickly followed after him and pinned him against the metal bar, holding up his small knife, pressing it towards Brett's face. He pushed, with all his might, and Brett's upper body started to fold over the rail.

Brett was thrashing out at Max, when one of his hands found the precious book he was after. Instinctively he pulled it from Max's waist belt, but then losing his grip on it, the book flew past them both onto the top of the nearby steel eagle! It lodged into the recess of the floodlight located just behind the eagle's head, shining up at the building's crown spire.

They both looked at the prize, pages gently fluttering in the breeze.

Brett took the opportunity to stoop down, desperately grasping out with one arm for the sword's handle on the floor.

Max fumbled at his belt and grabbed the small tube. Aiming and pressing down the tiny button, the single puff of oleoresin capsicum derived from chilis, went into Brett's left eye and partially his right.

Brett cried out in pain from the spray and nursing his eyes, let go of Max, yelling obscenities at him.

Max was able to now heave Brett over the rail away from the sword handle, landing him on the top of the eagle just short of the floodlight, right next to the prize!

Brett felt the book, now at his elbow, as he lay over the shiny sculpture, realising how precarious his position was!

"My book!" yelled Brett, reaching for it in desperation.

Despite the excruciating sensation in his eyes, he instinctively grabbed the book with one hand, slightly unbalancing himself. One of his legs slid over the edge of the monument and started to draw him off. He grabbed out at the floodlight.

Turning triumphantly to Max, he shouted out, "I have it! You've got nothing now!" He slid another inch towards the edge.

Max held out his arm leaning over the rail. "Take my hand Brett, come back here, you're going to fall!"

Brett stared at him defiantly. He was resigning himself to the likelihood he was going to fall, as he was not willing to accept Max's help now. "I'm taking this book! The Hades sect will carry on with or without me. If you don't have the book of souls, you have no proof. The brethren will remain hidden," he gazed down quickly upon Manhattan, "amongst you all!"

"No Brett," shouted Max, trying to reach out further to grab his leg. "It's over! I have the evidence we need, and the names, and the proof of your payments!"

"What?" replied Brett in disbelief.

Max got his phone out and held it up. "It's all here! I downloaded the files from your computer when you sat at your desk. Once you logged in and opened that secret ledger file, with all the Hades accounts I suspect, I got a copy on this!"

"Brett looked indignant. "How can that be?" and slid another inch closer to the point of no return.

Max was about to shout out once more, to plead for Brett to take his hand, but as their eyes met, stopped himself. In that moment, there was a brief understanding by both men that this was indeed over now. Brett was responsible for bribery, insider dealing, gaining illegal advantage in business, fraud, money laundering, coercion and murder. He was only coming in off that eagle if he thought he could get away with it. That likelihood had disappeared with Max's revelation about the ledger file copy.

Max slowly withdrew his hand, knowing it was never going to be accepted. He felt sadness for this man, a gifted businessman and entrepreneur that had simply got ahead of himself, his ambitions and the law.

Brett gasped, as both of his legs slipped to the side of the majestic ornament and were now dangling down. He refused to let go of the book, using only one hand to grasp the edge of the light recess.

Max peered down past Brett's hanging legs and felt sick at the sight of the drop to the four roof tiers of the lower parts of the building, each side of the Chrysler tower.

Brett groaned and he felt his grip tire and start to slip. He looked at Max, his face filled with anger, which then turned to shock as his grip finally gave way. As his outstretched hand and torso slid down the side of the shiny eagle, he glanced helplessly at Max for the last time. His expression was that of sheer terror!

Brett descended. Away from the eagle and from Max. And was gone!

He clutched the book of souls to his chest as he fell through the air. After a few seconds, anticipating the fatal impact at about one hundred miles an hour, he screamed at the top of his voice.

Max listened to Brett's dying cry and as he looked up at the nearby Met Life building, he heard the faint thud seven hundred feet below him.

Brett had remained determined and resolute to the end, clutching his precious book.

The book!

Max's objective returned to him once more. He now had to get that damn book, again! He ran inside towards the lifts, googling which floor he'd need, to get out onto the third stepped roof.

On Lexington Avenue, Liam Welling had been minding the unconscious sniper man slumped in the seat next to him. His window was half down and upon hearing a man scream from above, sounding surprisingly like his boss, had looked up.

He just caught the last second of Brett's body dropping fast onto the building's third-tier roof!

"Jesus, Mary and Joseph! What the …!" he exclaimed out loud.

He had to go and see what had happened! He left the car, slamming the door behind him and ran across the road into the Chrysler Building!

Moments later, Jeremy started to come round in the car, with a large bruise on the side of his face and an almighty headache!

Max arrived on the twenty-seventh floor first. A financial services firm was due to move into the office space in three weeks, so the whole floor was undergoing a complete redecoration with new furniture.

There were ladders, heaters, paint pots, dust sheets and piles of flat-packed office furniture strewn around the whole of the floor. Max picked his way through everything towards the front of the building which would overlook the flat roof Brett had landed on. With no signs of any access doorway to get out, he picked a window with openers and lifted it just enough to climb through.

He could immediately see Brett's body lying nearby, crumpled and distorted in an unnatural disfigurement. Despite the high-velocity impact, the book lay at his side intact. Above him, one of the corner Chrysler winged hubcap gargoyles looked down on the scene dispassionately.

The roof was not used as an observation deck or terrace, so only had a small retaining lip around the edge. Max went over to Brett's lifeless body and bent down to collect up the book. As he did so he noticed the car he'd arrived in with Jeremy, still parked below on Lexington Avenue at the front of the building. He could see that the driver's seat was empty and wondered if Jeremy was on the passenger side. He thought he caught a glimpse of someone moving around in the rear of the car!

This seemed odd to Max, who was about to get his phone out and risk trying to call Jeremy to see if he was okay. But he was interrupted!

"Get your bloody hands up in the air!" ordered Liam, as he climbed through the open window out onto the flat roof.

Max was startled, but slowly turned around, hands up.

"Let me guess, the murderous ferryman?" he said with no emotion.

Liam laughed mockingly, still walking over. Max could see he was holding Brandon Cuffney's Glock, the same one he had once held against this man and all the brethren at their ritual earlier!

"You've got a nerve, calling me murderous! Look what you've done," he said, gazing down at his boss and saviour's tangled body. "What the hell happened up there?"

"I tried to save him," said Max, "but he wouldn't let go of that book to grab my hand!"

"Yeah right, you expect me to believe that? You've killed

him. The Grand Master! He was like my brother, he saved me, gave me purpose…"

"What, killing innocent people?" interjected Max sarcastically.

Liam held the gun up at Max, shaking it at him. "Throw the book over to me, now!"

Max continued. "I was there that night in Sussex. I watched you taser my colleague and throw him into the lake to drown! God knows who else you and your other British assassin have killed?"

Liam now stretched out his arm ready to pull the trigger on Max. "The book?"

At that moment, a tiny red dot appeared on the side of Liam!

Max saw it first but said nothing. He watched as the dot adjusted itself, rose up Liam's arm and settled on the side of his head, hovering near his temple!

Max let go of the book he was holding up high and as it dropped to the floor, he looked to his left, down towards the car, and gave a nod.

After Jeremy had come round, he'd figured whoever had knocked him out had gone into the building to help Brett Brookshaw. He'd clambered into the back of the car where the sniper rifle still lay wedged behind the front seats. Pulling it out and using the night scope, he'd started to look around the building to see if he could find out what was happening. As soon as Max, joined by Liam, had come out onto the lower roof's edge, he had a good view of them both in his sights!

Liam saw Max look down and momentarily distracted by the book falling to the ground, turned his head to where Max had glanced.

As he did so, the intense laser had flashed across his eyes. Then he saw the muzzle flare from the rifle's barrel in the back of the car below!

The bullet hit Liam in the cheek and with Jeremy's low firing point, passed upwards through his brain and out the top of his head!

He instantly fell to the floor dropping the gun.

Max breathed a sigh of relief and waved down at the car below. Jeremy waved back through the window, beckoning Max to hurry on back to the car. With all the commotion of Brett's fall from the sixty-first floor, his scream and impact, and now a muffled shot in the middle of Manhattan, the police would be on the scene in minutes!

Max picked up the book once more and leaving the fallen bodies of Liam Wellings and Brett Brookshaw on the roof, made his way back down to Jeremy.

Within a couple of minutes, they would be at the British Consulate General just four blocks away at 1 Dag Hammarskjold Plaza on Second Avenue, well before the New York police arrived at the Chrysler Building.

Max had an awful lot of explaining to do after the day's events and would be up all night talking to his people at MI5 in London.

But he had Brett's computer files downloaded onto his phone, and the book of souls in his possession!

The first thing he did was to send his superiors a scan of the entire book and the unlocked ledger file.

He knew that once MI5 got to see the evidence and the names of those involved with the Hades sect, all hell would break loose!

MI5's Deputy Director General stepped in, when it quickly became clear that they needed to extract Max and Jeremy from the US, before the CIA and FBI both insisted they remain for questioning. Once news broke of events, the deaths, foreign agents operating in New York and a CIA man in detention, the Americans would come down on this like a ton of bricks.

The UK needed their agents back in London, from where collaboration with their American counterparts could be better controlled and negotiated.

The DDG pulled a few strings with the Royal Air Force who had a Boeing Globemaster cargo plane leaving La Guardia airport first thing in the morning. Consulate staff collected Max and Jeremy's belongings and drove them to the airport in nearby Queens to catch the flight back to Northolt, West London.

They were both told to try to get some sleep on the eight-hour flight, during which time everyone back at Thames House would be working up a plan to coordinate the many arrests that would be actioned on both sides on the pond.

It was a huge operation, given the breadth and scale of the infiltration across businesses, locations and industries by the Hades members.

Having gone through the book of souls, it was found to have twenty-four members of the sect in the US, and a staggering thirty-eight in the UK. The so-called brothers ranged from chief executives of big firms, entrepreneurs, board members, non-executive directors, the military and most notably, the government. In particular, a member of the UK government's cabinet!

Talks continued throughout the day with numerous calls put into Max on the plane for clarification of things only he knew about, being the lead investigator. On both sides of the Atlantic, agencies were involved, police, military services, with a steady flow of status reports going to the White House and 10 Downing Street!

The Globemaster landed at nine PM where a car took Max and Jeremy back to Thames House for the debriefing to continue. The young New York based agent was taken off to be questioned separately, while Max was reunited with his boss Si Lawson up in the DDG's top floor office.

"You've certainly been through it these last few days, Max!" said the DDG. "We're glad to have you home in one piece."

"You've done an amazing job, Max," added Si. "To be able to get your hands on both the book and the payments soft file was incredible!"

"Could have all gone very wrong, many times," mused Max. "Was good to have Jeremy there, and I suspect lady luck had a few parts to play. What will happen to Jeremy by the way?"

The DDG looked to Si to respond.

"Given everything you both told us from the Consulate and the reports we've now gone through, young Jeremy's done a great job for us and you," said Si. "He really got thrown in the deep end, as you have, so once he's been fully cleared in a few days, we'll give him a choice for his next posting. He's got family here in the UK, but has always wanted overseas postings. I've heard him mention that he'd quite like to visit Australia!"

"I'm sure if that's what he wants, Max, we can accommodate his next role at the Embassy out there in Sydney. Don't worry, he'll be looked after," assured the DDG.

"So, are you able to tell me what the big plan is to bring these Hades people in? This Operation Trawler I've heard mentioned a few times?" asked Max.

The DDG chuckled at the codename chosen by the Met and somewhat apologetically explained, "Well, after all, we are dragging the bottom to catch a lot of different fish! Si?"

"Nine AM GMT tomorrow morning is when all the arrests will be made, at least of those we know about," said Si. "We're bound to find out more once people are interrogated, staff, employees, guards and the like, all implicit in the crimes even if they aren't in the book. It's a huge task to coordinate both here and in the US. Almost all of their Hades names are on the East coast, so they're moving in at four AM their time."

"Wouldn't we usually also go for early hours raids here as well?"

The DDG replied. "Normally yes. The PM got involved in choosing the time. Because of the enormity of this whole thing, with Hades' ability to infiltrate such a wide cross-section of influential figures, he wanted the busts to coincide with his cabinet meeting in the morning. That way his ministers will be the first to hear about it as it happens. He's also asked for a news embargo. We can't have any of this coming out, both us and the Yanks would look like a bunch of idiots!"

"And Gillian Brookshaw, my procurement bloke Joe Patterson, they'll both get the knock?"

"Absolutely," Si confirmed. "Gillian may have let her brother run it all but she knew what was going on. Yes, Joe Patterson our MOD procurement director will definitely be getting a visit in the morning, he's in the book of souls with 'MOD consulting deal pending' written under his name. Wonder how much he would have got for that contract? The whole process will of course be redone."

"The police and lawyers will handle the prosecution of the Brookshaw Consulting firm over time," added the DDG. "They'll never be able to trade with that name again. With the boss dead, I suspect when rumours do get out of insider dealing and bribery, staff will jump like rats off a sinking ship. I imagine the company's assets will be seized, used to repay fines and damages, and the firm will probably get dissolved?"

"I wonder what the freemasons will think about it all?" posed Max, remembering his visit to the Grand Lodge.

"Not much I shouldn't wonder," pondered Si out loud. "There was never any question of criminality in their organisation, so they should be proud their rules and traditions have held fast, not allowing anything untoward to take place within their ranks."

"They won't be at all happy though about the association they had with Brett Brookshaw," said the DDG.

"Indeed. Their masonic renegade! Along with his ancestor Appleby," said Max. "Speaking of renegade's, what's happening with Brandon Cuffney? It's hard to know if he was dodgy or the CIA were just letting him loose to see what they could gain out of Hades intel?"

"That'll all come out in the wash for sure," replied the DDG. "From what I've read in the reports, I think we may find out that our CIA friends thought they could get intel on us Brits through the Hades network. For now though, the Director of the CIA has told us Cuffney and his boss were acting alone without authorisation and unbeknown to anyone else there. Either way, deals will be done, embarrassment spared, points scored and favours given in return for bargaining chips on some other negotiation being done. That's the way it works in the Intelligence Services sometimes," he shrugged.

Si leant over to Max. "By the way, we finally got a make on your assassin chap, an Eduardo Davies, an employee of Gilliam Brookshaw no less, the guy that kept on trying to bump you off! Undoubtedly Durham's mysterious killer at the Chelsea football match and we believe he also killed another businessman in the book, a Rob Malony, in the pool at the Pall Mall Royal Automobile Club!"

"Busy chap wasn't he!" said Max, "him and the so-called ferryman I had the pleasure of seeing in action! Poor Graham, rest in peace."

"Yes, the ferryman to the underworld, a busy job. There'll never be a shortage of souls lured by the promise of wealth and riches!"

The UK government's top thirty politicians filed into the famous cabinet room in 10 Downing Street, past the two large white pillars on either side of the entrance. They each sat at their designated light brown leather cushioned chair, of which only the Prime Minister's had arms on it. There were twenty-six chairs around the boat-shaped long table, plus another four against the wall.

The unusual tabletop narrowed at the ends, so those furthest away could better participate in discussions and allow the PM who sat in the centre with his back to the marble fireplace, to look everyone in the eye!

On the mantle sat a carriage clock showing nine o'clock, above which a painting of the first Prime Minister of 1721, Sir Robert Walpole, looked down upon every meeting.

The PM waited for everyone to be seated and the hushed chatter to abate, before addressing them.

"Good morning. Before we start the meeting and refer to the cabinet agenda and minutes of the last meeting, I have a matter of grave concern regarding the security and integrity of this country, which I must now appraise you of."

Given the subject matter of the impending topic, the PM paused to glance down the table at the Defence Minister, and then across at the Business Minister. Both shifted in their seats uneasily.

"This information will carry a press embargo, so you are not to speak of it outside this room unless authorised to do so, but the repercussions will affect all of us, so my team is working with MI5 to coordinate what we'll each need to do."

Pausing once more, he surveyed his most trusted ministers. The silence in the room was deafening and many of these senior officials now looked uncomfortable and anxious. This was a most unusual opening to a cabinet meeting.

On cue, the door opened and one of the Cabinet Office secretaries came in, stopping short of the end of the meeting table. She waited for the PM to nod to her.

"I'm sorry to interrupt your meeting PM, but one of the ministers is required urgently outside the room?"

"Yes, of course," agreed the PM. "Who?"

The lady looked around the officials sat at the long table. The tension in the room was palpable.

"The Secretary of State for Environment, Food and Rural Affairs!"

The named minister looked shocked. Then glanced over to the PM hoping to be saved from having to leave the room, but to no avail.

"You'd better go," said the PM, with a hint of disdain in

his voice.

The minister felt sick, with guilt and shame. They knew exactly what this was about. They'd been persuaded to join Brett Brookshaw's Hades organisation many years ago when they were a key figure in the food sector, before even becoming a member of parliament. After being voted in as the local MP, a few years later they were offered the environment minister's job. Brett had recently seized upon the opportunity to entice them with large payments for interesting intel from government meetings. The environment role wasn't one of the top high profile ministerial posts, so often fell under the radar.

But it still had a seat at cabinet meetings, where all the big topics were covered!

All eyes were on them as they left the room. Once outside, the door closed and the waiting armed police and security escorted them away!

THE END

Max Sargent Corporate Espionage Mystery Thrillers
available in the series by the author BEN COLT
can be read in any order

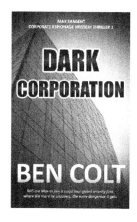

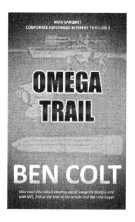

ABOUT THE AUTHOR

BEN COLT

He grew up in the house previously owned by notorious British-Soviet double-agent Kim Philby.

A senior executive of three decades in the corporate world, having been a management consultant and Chief Procurement Officer for many big brand companies in various industries.

Most of his roles had a global remit, which took him around the world on business to many different countries and cities.

His procurement teams had a privileged role in firms, with unquestioned business-wide access and control of large spends, suppliers and intellectual property.

His extensive procurement and management experience gives him first-hand insight of the potential for corporate corruption and espionage, to quickly become dangerous.

www.BenColt.com